THE IMPROBABLE WONDERS OF

Moojie Littleman

THE IMPROBABLE WONDERS OF

Moojie Littleman

ROBIN GREGORY

Mad Mystical Journey

THE IMPROBABLE WONDERS
of
MOOJIE LITTLEMAN

A Novel
by
Robin Gregory

FIRST EDITION, November, 2015

ISBN: 978-1-942545-00-2
Library of Congress Control Number: 2015904563

Cover art by Catrin Welz-Stein.
Typset in Minion and Caslon Antique.

Published in the United States of America

Published by Mad Mystical Journey,
An imprint of Wyatt-MacKenzie Publishing, Inc.

Visit us at www.MadMysticalJourney.com.

Publisher's Cataloging-in-Publication Data

Gregory, Robin S.
  The Improbable Wonders of Moojie Littleman : a Novel / by Robin Gregory.
  pages cm
  ISBN 978-1-942545-00-2
  Summary : Abandoned by not one but two sets of parents, a disabled boy seeks to
find a family of his own while staying at St. Isidore's Fainting Goat Dairy.

1. Orphans —Juvenile fiction. 2. People with disabilities —Juvenile fiction. 3. United
States —History —20th century —Juvenile fiction. 4. Spirituality —Juvenile fiction. 5.
Alternative histories (Fiction)—Juvenile fiction. 6. Bildungsromans. 7. Historical fiction.
I. Title.

PZ7.G86238 Imp 2015
[Fic] –dc23   2015904563

For my son

PROLOGUE

Once I dreamed of being crippled and lost in the woods.
Using umbrellas for crutches, I circled back to a giant oak
tree three times, fell to the ground, and burst into tears.
The leaves of the tree rustled, and I looked up and asked,
"Which way from here?"

"Depends on where you're going," said the tree.

"I want to go home."

"You are home."

"But I want to find my real home."

"You don't have to go anywhere," the tree said.

I cried all the more.

The tree continued, "All right, go on a journey, if you
must. Just get up and walk."

"But that would take a miracle."

"A miracle, you say?"

"I don't believe in miracles."

"Why, you're talking to a tree, aren't you?"

— M.L.

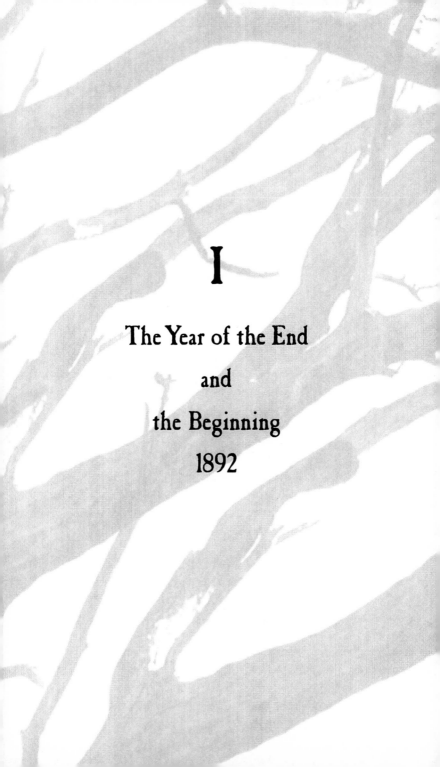

I

The Year of the End
and
the Beginning
1892

Chapter 1

Saint Moojie

He arrived on the heels of an earthquake. A minor hiccup as disasters go, the murmur rippling undersea, causing dories in the bay to bob and spider crabs to flood the beach like a ghostly pink tide. It was the sort of earthquake that hushes everything for an instant before nesting birds and sleeping butterflies burst out of trees. It makes your heart jump for joy because you realize the earth is flying through space at one thousand miles per hour and you have been spared the dreadful experience of the whole world falling apart and having to put it back together. It was the sort of earthquake that the nuns of San Miguel de las Gaviotas would call a mystical grumble. Really, there was nothing about it to suggest the terrible wonders looming on the horizon.

At a quarter past seven, the candelabras in the chapel stopped swaying. The nuns crossed themselves, went outside and found a wooden fishing bucket on the porch. Expecting the catch of the day, they were nothing short of horrified to see a baby boy bundled in fur and tucked inside it. He had bright black eyes, enormous ears, and his hair was the texture of caterpillar fuzz.

"He's a Hostile, if I ever saw one," said Mother Teagardin.

The word *Moojie* had been smudged across his forehead. And that was what they called him—a peculiar name for a peculiar boy, who wasn't particularly welcome. Against her better judgment, Mother Teagardin, who always said the natives were ill-suited for local society, hadn't the heart to surrender him to the local Bureau of Questionable Peoples. She appealed to the local families to adopt him. But the villagers were a superstitious lot. They believed the mysterious child to be, well, too mysterious.

It didn't help that before he cut his first teeth, Moojie amused himself by magically snuffing out candles with the blink of an eye, and by sending objects into flight with the power of his mind. When he didn't get his way, he caused the wind to rip off the nuns' veils and flash their knickers. Like Odysseus, he was quick to act and slow to regret. Meanwhile, the sisters clicked their clickers, and swatted his bottom, and continued looking for a family for him.

Except for one early chapter of his childhood, Moojie was a virtuosic flop when it came to the only thing he cared about: finding and keeping a family.

This golden parenthesis began just before he was one year old, when Henry and Kate Littleman, a childless couple who had moved from the East Coast to San Miguel—along with hundreds of recent immigrants from Europe and the Far East, since America had opened her doors to the world—took him home to raise as their own.

Mamma immediately left her post as a science and French teacher at the Charles Darwin Free School to look after him. Mornings, she tucked him into a knapsack suspended from a tripod, and went about her housekeeping. He grinned and giggled as she baked bread, smoked little cigars, knitted hats and booties, and arranged his wet flannel diapers on a drying rack near the fireplace. She wheeled him to the beach in a wicker pram, where they collected spider crabs and napped in the salty sand; she rocked him before a glowing wood stove; she bathed and coddled him. He watched Papa, a mapmaker, spin his curta and level his transit, slurp scalding tea, and leap out the door every morning in a pocketed vest. Sometimes, in the afternoon, Papa played piano for him or showed off his soccer moves in the backyard.

In those days, Moojie was a model child, the ambassador of lovability. He delighted at being the center of attention, always looking intently into people's eyes, always smiling, as if he were in on some cosmic joke. In those days—before San Miguel de las Gaviotas had gone the way of Atlantis, that is to say, before it fell out of favor with the gods—Moojie was passed around at church like a peace pipe. Warmed by his charm, suspicious villagers now lined up after the service to take turns holding him. Once Mrs. Littleman contrived a plot to put the smiling Moojie into the arms of a miserable scrooge, and everyone sighed with awe as the long-suffering soul wept and sang praises to God in heaven.

"Have you noticed, my cupcake?" Mamma said to Papa as she pushed the pram home from church. "This is no ordinary child."

"He'll make a fine field hand, lovey," Papa said.

At the time, San Miguel de las Gaviotas was a nick on the Pacific Coast of America, a clammy, cluttery mishmash of thatched rooftops, crumbling walls, and crooked towers surrounded by rugged mountains that rose out of fog like ancient pyramids. Moojie's new home, Number 11 Wimbley Wood, a mildewy cottage with a drip line and assorted mushrooms growing in the basement, appealed to otherworldly visitors. Only Moojie could see the celestial bodies spinning and whirling all about him. And he sometimes heard voices beyond the range of normal hearing—gifts, of course, that he did not yet understand. In the witching hours, lights floated down through the ceiling over his crib. He giggled and tried to grasp them as they bobbed playfully into and out of his hands. Mamma came in and held him in the rocker, while moths and flower flies haunted the spirit lamp—like all that is born, seeking to return to light.

Having landed in the nucleus of love, charming, handsome Moojie surpassed his parents' every expectation, blessing them with unmitigated joy.

But all of that was soon to change.

Moojie didn't talk or walk when he should have. As well, his left arm seemed only half-awake.

"I don't expect he'll ever teach school or fly air machines," said the doctor. "He'll be lucky if he can tie his own shoes."

"This is a disaster, Kate!" Papa said.

"Fiddlesticks, my darling!" Mamma said, as if something fierce and silvery had risen from the depths of her being, surely as a sword. "This boy will show you both just how wrong you are."

To his father, Moojie became a pair of legs to be trained, something to toil after. In a panic, Papa took him to the backyard often to entice him to play soccer. "Send it, son, send it!" he said, waiting for him to stand on his feet, which had grown quite large. Day after day, Moojie just sat there smiling, while Papa worked up a sweat.

As if it were her personal mission to prove Newton's

First Law, Mamma hired Orangie the circus clown to come every Wednesday to move Moojie through a vigorous exercise regimen. Outfitted with carnival knick-knacks and full of good cheer, Orangie trained the boy wonder to sit with a duck perched on his head, to ride a goat, and to crawl through a burning hoop. He applauded when Moojie lifted a ten-pound dumbbell over his head with his mighty righty, and he cursed when he ripped off his rubber nose and wig.

All the while, Mamma forbad Papa's use of the words "crippled" or "moron," and coined the term "diff-abled" to describe their son. She stretched and pulled and massaged Moojie's arms and legs. She baked him Graham Green Gem muffins; she sang to him and recited French nursery rhymes and made animal sounds to try to get him to talk. Even so, he never repeated so much as one *moo* or one *baa*. On the contrary, he seemed quite content to observe the world in silence, as if he were the watcher in the story of his own making.

Worried that Moojie might fall down or fall behind or fall into bad company, Mamma kept him home from school and became his private tutor. Other children his age were learning reading, writing, and arithmetic. Never mind that. He and his mother were experimenting with balloons and bottles, straws and bubbles, traveling nuts and plummeting potatoes. As well, Mamma, being a lover of stories—for what is science but stories?—often read aloud to him. In English and French. He preferred classic tales and fables over nursery rhymes, especially stories involving magic and great acts of courage. With rapt, wide-eyed attention, Moojie's days were filled with mad hatters and swirling atoms and genies, with falling apples and sea gods.

In light of the fact that Moojie wasn't improving, Mamma eventually forsook science rooted in the past and sought alternative means and methods to cure him—means and methods dubbed by Papa as "tomfoolery." She got hold of a book entitled *The Waltzing Lobster,* and could hardly tear herself away long enough to cook lunch. "Oh, the wonders that await discovery!" she chirped, marking pages with dried bay leaves and puffing on a cigar.

"Did you know there are ancient aliens living on Earth?

"Did you know there are monks who can sit naked on frozen lakes at the height of winter, and thaw, by their own body heat, icy, water-soaked sheets wrapped around their bodies?

"Did you know there are tribes who hold down their boys while loved ones slash off little pieces of their flesh?

"I tell you the high road is not plum pudding!"

She positioned Moojie on the living room sofa so he could look out the window. She wound up a little music box with a revolving nativity scene, placed it beside him, kissed the top of his head, and left him to daydream to a lullaby while she studied.

Plagued by loneliness, Moojie watched the neighbor boys, Royce and Bentley Markham, ride bicycles up and down Wimbley Wood, hair flying in the breeze, charging invisible enemies.

It was a mixed blessing when Moojie finally started walking. His oversized, pigeon-toed feet were buckled into knee-high braces, but his legs weren't weak by any means. Quite the opposite, they were tighter than fiddle strings and just as hard to move. Mamma strapped cushions to his front and backside, and he humped about the house on crutches, demolishing everything in his path—chairs, doorjambs, walls, piano legs, shins, and anklebones—making his father curl his fists and howl in frustration.

"He's no field hand; he's a wrecking ball! Look at this mess! And sardines for supper again! I can't take it anymore. I can't concentrate. I can't even keep my pencils sharpened."

Once Moojie tried to befriend the Markham boys. "What kind of name is *Moojie*?" they asked. "Sounds like a half-wit." They locked him inside their mother's potting shed, and he broke out by pulverizing the door with a shovel. Making his escape, he stumbled away on his crutches, toppling into the path of a runaway horse. By the grace of heaven, the horse performed a spectacular jump over him, and not one fuzzy hair on Moojie's head had been touched. His knees were skinned and trousers ripped, but it was his pride that was most injured.

In Moojie's lonely world, great warriors were born out of heads and auspicious children had their very own planets. Lying in bed at night, he stared out his window imagining stars to be bright insects captured in the web of a very clever spider. Occasionally, dark warriors galloped through his dreams lopping off people's heads. Such terrors inspired him to push *The Waltzing Lobster* across the kitchen floor to his mamma, wanting her to read him a certain passage, time and again:

> "It is said that they appeared on Earth many, many centuries ago, when great beasts, and barbarians, nomads and warring hunters, ruled the land. They came in silent, heavenly legions, walking in the shadows of trees, among few followers, speaking of their visions, enshrining the way of peace. For a long season, the people had been warring and brutal. They had been trapped in the endless midnight, worshipping beasts and heeding the forces of darkness. Suddenly, in

the twinkling of an eye, everything began to change.

The people heard these words in the depths of their souls:

'You have called and we have answered.'

They were the first wayshowers, sent to liberate the world from darkness, the Akil-Nuri—heavenly messengers, otherwise known as the Light-Eaters."

Moojie would have liked his parents to play with him and to hold him in their arms more often, like they had before the doctor's proclamations. But they were too busy trying to fix him. After a while, this made him nuts. Without the benefit of words, his only recourse was to stage a conniption fit. A surge of fire would run up his spine, he shuddered, he roared, and as if by magic, books, pots, plates, toys, and mops got swept into an indoor tornado, impelled by the dynamism of his rage.

"There, there, Moojie," his mother would say in French, slipping a gumdrop into his mouth. "Mamma loves you. Mamma will always love you. Now, stop behaving like a brat."

Moojie didn't notice the effect he had on his parents. In fact, he wasn't all that interested in the way other people felt. He cried like thunder if he was made to wait for a gumdrop or when his parents ignored him while talking to one another.

"You needn't be sad, Moojie, darling," Mamma said. "You're very special. Why, in fact, I believe you have an auspicious destiny. If life were all sunshine and chocolate, there wouldn't be any saints, and we'd never find our way back to heaven."

This gave Moojie an odd sense of hope.

Phineas, the chubby cat with a cantaloupe head, gold eyes, and great clumps of brown fur which no one was allowed to brush, was Moojie's only friend. And Phineas suffered for it. Deaf as a turnip, Phineas never heard the flying objects falling around him. Having gotten shaved on occasion, he hid under the furniture, tail twitching, even in his sleep. And yet, Moojie and Phineas had an understanding.

Gradually Papa's face weazened, as if the wide, bright world had leaked out of it.

Mamma tried to cheer him up by making his favorite meal: fried tomatoes, green corn, and Finnan Haddie. But he was so overwrought he didn't take a bite. In fact, he didn't speak a word. He just rose from the table and withdrew to his dim, tidy cubbyhole of maps and bevels upstairs in the attic.

"Stubborn fool," Mamma said, scraping the dinner dishes. *Crash,* went a plate, breaking on the floor. "Miserable fool!"

Moojie slammed a piece of broken plate against the cupboard.

"Moojie, darling, you're going to kill your father if you don't stop your shenanigans."

Around the age of six, Moojie finally started talking— a French word here, an English phrase there, a stutter, a stammer—but he talked nonetheless. "You had us all fooled," Papa said. "You're smarter than you look."

And then, the summer of his eighth year, Moojie's golden chapter came to a close, and all because of a seagull.

It happened one day, during a beach picnic, that Moojie and his mother discovered a badly injured seagull. Moojie put down his sandwich and studied the poor creature, whose wing was turned inside-out and hanging loosely from its mantle. Their eyes met in an eerie recognition and Moojie's heart welled up with a new feeling. A great pulse of warmth poured out of his chest, and when this light and heat surrounded the seabird, it suddenly and magnificently took to the air on two perfect wings. All at once, Moojie's world was filled with light and butterflies and soft white clouds. Too young to realize what had happened, he believed it was the most wondrous bird in all the world.

Astonished, Mamma told Papa what had happened, but he didn't believe her. They argued furiously, making the house throb with tension. Phineas threw himself against the window screen, hanging by his claws like an obese housefly. Feeling the first of many premonitions, Moojie hid in his room, covering his ears to try to stop the icy, tingling sensation.

Only minutes later, Mamma bolted out of the house in her nightdress and met with a terrible end. Heaven knows where she was heading. There didn't seem to be a cause for the accident other than carelessness; a moment of distraction, a lapse of reason, and too quickly it was over. In the village she had sometimes wandered in front of horses while stargazing, which always drove Papa crazy. "For the love of God, Kate," he would say, "watch out." A neighbor said later that he had come up the road, joyriding in his new auto buggy, when Mamma stepped directly in front of him. He tried to steer out of her path and when he did this, the vehicle flipped onto two wheels, tossed him into the Littleman's hedge, and killed Mamma on the fly. In a state of shock, Moojie tried to buck up when he heard the news. He turned to his father for comfort, but was met with a stiff, flat expression that he couldn't read.

Lying in bed that night, Moojie heard the sound of silk brushing against silk. Was it the wind against the curtains? No, it wasn't the wind; it was his mother's spirit—only he didn't know this at first. In her nightdress, she sat on the bed. Phineas leapt to his paws and hissed.

"Mamma!" Moojie said.

"I'm sorry, darling," she said. "But I can only go this far. It hurts me so much to leave you. Don't worry, you'll be fine. I'll be fine. Don't be sad. I love you, darling. I will always love you."

Moojie didn't know what to do. He had never said he loved anyone.

With a queasy feeling, he watched her get up and fade into the night. He looked out the window at the moonlit sea. He pictured a young mariner with the weeping and wailing dead grabbing at his ankles, a demon spirit breathing fire at his back. Behind the ship, a mad sea god swinging an oar. Moojie blinked and they were gone. Like his mother: he had blinked and she was gone.

The next morning, he got out of bed and peered into his parents' bedroom. She wasn't there. Nor was she in the living room. He found Papa in the kitchen curled over a whiskey crock, dressed in yesterday's clothes.

"Where's Mamma?" Moojie asked.

"What? For Chrissake, she's gone, son. Gone."

Who will look after me?

How will I get along without her?

Who will make me muffins?

All well and good for Mamma in the afterlife; but there Moojie was, left to manage his own befuddled self without her. He wished he had taken her hand the night before. He wished he had followed her spirit. Sadly, he knew this would have been impossible. That was how it was with spirits. He had not learned this from catechism or fables or missals; he just knew that it was true. Like the earth being round, he knew.

In the space of one day, eight-year-old Moojie had witnessed a miracle and lost a mother. And he was, for the first time in his life, afraid.

Chapter 2

The Prevaricating Light

When they arrived at the chapel, there were so many seagulls flying overhead that Moojie and his father had to cross the courtyard under an umbrella. The summer sky had been weeping for three days. Sea mist and crying gulls swirled over the gray cemetery, making a collage of rose petals and bird droppings. Wearing a tight wool blazer, short pants, and leg braces, Moojie hesitated at the entrance before the hand on his back prodded him to go in.

High in the chapel shone twelve stained glass windows. A saint in each one. Saint of the Month Club. Moojie's eyes turned toward the chancel, where the eye-teeth of Brother Juan, the canonized saint who had put to rights the savage nations, were kept in a tin reliquary the size of a tobacco box. Moojie had attended Sunday School with Mother Teagardin in the airless, vaulted, side chamber. Tall and thin as a black-winged insect, she instructed him and three other boys while the spirits of pirates and priests played chase with the saints overhead. Gifted with extrasensory perception, only Moojie could see them, and it delighted him to no end that Mother mistook the rattling candelabras for earthquakes. "Stand unmoved before the perverse and the crooked and you will know the power of love!" she once had said. In response, Moojie had clapped his hands and laughed and said, "The power of love!" three times, as if it were a magic incantation. When the acrid dust had settled, Mother, visibly shaken, lifted Moojie by the ear and said, "The first time I saw you, I knew you were trouble."

Villagers in starched clothing tilted into the aisle to eyeball Moojie, the way they had always done from the village windows and doorways. He wanted to grab them by their noses and show them something wrinkled. Pie-eyed and whispering, children pointed and hid behind their mothers. "Whathappened? What'swrongwithhim?"

No one would have looked at Moojie and thought, "Here is a wonder worker."

As he had been told to do, he sat in the front of the chapel next to his mother's father, Pappy Finnegan. At the opposite end of the pew, Pappy's estranged wife was hunched under a hat resembling a birdhouse, and her sister, Auntie Tilda Pettibone, was dressed in an African get-up, a brightly printed *bubu* gown and turban-like *kufi* hat. Her hands and feet came to points outside the dress, in the way of a starfish—not at all in keeping with the local fashion of plain woolen skirts, pinafores, and shawls. Behind her were rows of bereaved strangers.

The saddest of the congregation was the sad, sad Mitropolis family. The neighbors, Mr. and Mrs. and their children, Bruno and Sylvie. They were so terribly sad they couldn't sing. Mr. Mitropolis in particular. He had the most cause to be sad. He had been driving the auto buggy that killed Moojie's mother.

Red velvet curtains along either side of the altarpiece got stirred by something. Moojie saw that it was his mamma's spirit, clear and bright, drifting toward the crucifix behind the altar.

"She's here," he whispered.

His father rolled his eyes, as if seeing nothing.

Fog drifted in through the open doors, quieting the villagers' scuffling feet—storekeepers, bakers, stargazers.

Pappy Finnegan kept to himself at the end of the pew, stroking his mustache. Frowning and elegant in his tweed coat and herringbone cap, he planted his elbows on his knees and rested the bridge of his nose between his thumbs.

The dreary guitarist came in and strummed a dreary hymn. There was a great hoop of white roses, lilies, mums, and snapdragons propped on an easel. No coffin. Only the pretty blue and white jar on the white satin-draped table.

"What d-do the ashes look like, Papa?" Moojie asked.

"I don't know, crushed seashells."

Father Grabbe and two altar boys appeared from the sacristy. The father incensed the altar, pink smoke causing a flurry of sneezing in the pews. He crossed the congregation. "*In nomine Patris et Filii et Spiritus Sancti.*"

Moojie fidgeted with his bow tie. He couldn't follow the priest because of the horrifying image of boots crushing seashells and the seashells falling through the Father's ringed fingers and waves lapping them up salty and wet, the cold wild sea closing its mouth. The wild sea coming and going. In out in out.

Moojie felt everyone's attention shifting between the Pretty Jar and himself, between the creepy vessel of Mamma-sand and her misfit of a son. Papa didn't seem to know what to do with his hands. He cracked his knuckles. He rubbed his hands together, sat on them, and held them between his knees. Pappy remained still as a landmine, arms crossed, clear blue eyes fixed upon the floor. Nana Finnegan cried till her nose bled.

Since early life, dreams of undersea forests had haunted Moojie, twisted faces and open mouths tangled in kelp. Without Mamma, there was no one left to understand him, leaving in her absence a dark and terrifying sea.

He hooked a finger into his collar. Not yet sure himself what had happened the day they encountered the injured seabird, he still asked himself why Mamma had thought he had anything to do with its miraculous recovery, which had ignited the argument with Papa.

"Love comes in all stripes," the priest said. "There's family love; there's husband-and-wife love; there's parent-and-child love. And then there's the love of Our Lord who took the deceased home." He looked at Moojie and Papa. "Ours is not to question why."

During the closing hymn, the Mamma-spirit fell gently over Moojie, a veil of light that warmed him to tears. All at once, a raging squall snuffed out the candles. The music and singing halted.

"Cheese 'n' rice!" Auntie Tilda said.

Moojie's heart shattered like glass as his mother got taken up in the wind, up, up, and over his head, reaching for him while being pulled away, lengthening, fading quickly, too quickly, and then vanishing through the leaded window of St. Francis, a thin wisp of light. Gone.

"No!" Moojie cried.

Papa cupped a hand around his head and held it against his chest. "Shush now. Shush."

After the funeral, Moojie refused to get out of bed for three days. Auntie Tilda took him boiler broth and cornmeal porridge and wholemeal scones, but he wouldn't eat.

"I-I want everything like it was before," he said to his cat, Phineas. Mamma had been his tea and toast. Mamma had been his world. Without Mamma, Moojie had no appetite for life.

Papa and Auntie Tilda tried to look after him, but failed to live up to his mother's memory. She had trimmed his hair, manicured his nails, and cut his meals into bite-size pieces. She had cheered him through his daily exercises, cleared the way before his stumbling feet, calmed him when he got peevish. Now, all thumbs, Papa was the peevish one, trying to dress him.

"For cripe's sake, would you bend your legs? It's like dressing a crucifix!"

Auntie Tilda made clumsy attempts to help Moojie bathe, but twice he slid underwater, and once, while getting out of the tub, he slipped and cut his head.

It was a foggy afternoon when Moojie overheard the grownups talking in the back patio.

"Henry," Auntie Tilda said, "he's your child, adopted or not. Do you not give a tinker's cuss?" She sounded like Nana and her side of the family, tongue-rolling and whistling and rounding her "o"s. Like a leprechaun.

"When are you going to stop sticking your freckled snout into other people's business?" Papa said. "If you're so bloody virtuous, you take him."

"That's all I need, to raise a child at my age!"

"He's a nitwit, all fouled up. I just don't think … I'm a man, you know. I'm not a saint."

"Listen," she went on, "do you hear that? 'Tis his mother. She's rolling in her ashes. Mark my words, Henry

Littleman, she will haunt your flimsy bones if you fail that boy."

Hearing this, Moojie's head started pounding and his stomach cramped. *I don't give a tinker's cuss if Papa doesn't give a tinker's cuss; Papa and I belong together.* The fire went up his spine, as always before a fit. He staggered into the house and, shaking from head to toe, smashed Papa's piano bench with a wrought-iron fire poker.

Two days later, at the train station, Auntie Tilda lectured Papa. "Children make the grandest teachers, don't they? Talk to them and you learn to listen; listen and you learn to love." At this, she swallowed Moojie in a pentamorous hug, her body all tentacles and suction pressing in and taking out and spooky altogether. Normally, Moojie didn't like it when people hugged him. It made him feel trapped, suffocated with pity. "You're going to be fine, lad," she whispered. "Your father may be one sandwich short of a picnic, but he's still your daddy." She then looked at Papa. "I feel your loss, dear, I do—the awfulness of losing beloved Katie. Raising the boy won't be easy—"

"Tilda," Papa said, "you have my word on it, he'll be looked after. Now, go home."

"You're a saint, dear Henry, you are. But mark my words, if you should prevaricate … should that boy come to harm … why, I, I'll … a poisonous mushroom in your stew, strangulation in your sleep. A torch to your wagon. You won't see it coming."

From the platform, Moojie and his father waved politely as Auntie boarded the train.

The blue sky that was reflected on the train window disappeared when Auntie lowered it down from inside. "'We are worms, in need of comprehension, born to bring forth the angelic butterfly,'" she quoted Dante. The train crawled along the tracks, taking Auntie Tilda and her final words eastward through the hazy golden hills toward her distant home.

Moojie's hands were cold. Something was wrong. Were he and Papa going home now? *Must I ask?* Auntie's perfume faded, as if it were the end of a magic spell keeping Papa and him together. What it smelled like Moojie couldn't say. Sweet-sour. Soft-biting. Prevaricating.

Teeth chattering, Moojie took his father's hand. "Papa, I-I'm better now. You'll see. No more fits." He searched his father's tired face—the thin line of his mouth—for a response. "Don't be sad, Papa. I-If life was all sunshine and chocolate, we wouldn't have any saints a-and we'd never find our way back to heaven."

"What's your meaning?" Papa asked.

"Nothin'," said Moojie.

Papa remained motionless, staring at his feet. "I'll be gone for a spell, son," he said. "Just a spell."

Papa, Moojie, and Phineas arrived at St. Isidore's Fainting Goat Dairy in the Valley of Sorrows after nightfall. In the kitchen, the yellow, bob-tailed mutt named Millie-Mae barked and turned circles. The spirit lamp cast a cool green light upon Pappy's face as he greeted them. Moojie clumped into the guest room. Without removing his shoes or braces, he got under the covers fully dressed and lay with Phineas on the cot, straining to hear the conversation in the kitchen.

"How long?" Pappy asked Papa.

"I've got nothing more to teach him," Papa said. "He's a hard case. Sometimes he acts like an imbecile, other times you could say he's normal. But then, he's unteach-able …."

"Maybe he's got something to teach you."

"Oh, what might that be?"

"I don't know. Maybe you can't make a map and expect a river to bend to it."

Moojie stroked Phineas. "I-I ought to march in there and tell Papa I-I got some fine qualities," he whispered. "You like me, don't you, Phinny? Mamma said I-I'm a saint on training wheels."

"So," Pappy Finnegan said.

"So, there's a boy's home up north," Papa said. "The Steel Barn, it's a home for boys … like him. They have a nursemaid and chickens."

"Chickens. Really," Pappy said.

Moojie's ears got hot. "I-I know a thing or two about atoms. I-I could blow a moon-sized hole in this farm."

The screen door snapped shut, and for a time, every-thing was quiet inside the cabin. Then buggy wheels skidded and the hooves of Papa's burro clopped out of the yard.

Soon a glass slammed down on the kitchen table.

"You awake, boy?" Pappy asked from the hallway outside Moojie's bedroom. Moojie could see the slit of light below the door. He squeezed his eyes shut, pretending to be asleep.

Pappy crept back down the hall. Mattress springs groaned under his weight. He blew out his lamp.

Curling into a tight ball, Moojie pretended to be an egg. The Steel Barn. He knew all about places like that from *Oliver Twist*. They were workhouses where orphans got ear-boxed by Sikes and Crackit if they didn't pick pockets and build coffins. He shivered under the covers and whispered to his mother in French. "Mamma, are you there?" A cold sea welled up inside him, an invisible ocean, with fish and kelp and rocks in it. Home. Family. That was all Moojie had ever wanted. To belong. For the second time in his brief life, he had neither. The cold, the water, the fish, the rocks—they had stolen his island.

Chapter 3

Which has set Moojie at liberty,
much against his will, to begin a new adventure
not at all to his liking

Six years later, Moojie was still living at St. Isidore's Fainting Goat Dairy, in the tin-roofed, board-and-bat cabin with deer antlers mounted over the front door, surrounded by stables and sheds, rattlesnake grass, thistles, and squirrel-spitting trees. He had gone from foundling to left-behind. After ditching Moojie at St. Isidore's, his father had left word at Tilly's Tavern in the village that he was going on a mapping expedition in the West Indies. He had not been heard from since. A reunion seemed so unlikely that Moojie preferred to think of his father as dead. That made it easier. Somehow.

Moojie and his grandfather had not yet worked through the difficulties of their forced kinship. When he arrived at St. Isidore's, Moojie, who was accustomed to

Mamma's doting, had never bathed himself. Right away, Pappy Finnegan expected him to wash up in a horse trough, which set the stage for a battle of wills. "No soldier on my watch will go stinking," Pappy had said every evening. And to this day, he had to insist that Moojie bathe himself, by steering him toward the bathroom. "Into the bog you go. You don't wash, you stink. You stink, and the bears come looking for you. Every twelve-year-old knows that."

"I'm fourteen."

"What's that?" Pappy asked, turning on the shower faucet, and pointing to Moojie's right hand.

"A hand, sir."

"How many hands does it take to do this?" Pappy wet a sponge, slapped it over his own face, splattering his shirt and trousers. He turned and tripped on Moojie's crutch. "Cutty sark!" he howled.

As if bathing hadn't been enough, Moojie also had to dress himself, which he had not previously been required to do because of difficulties with his left hand. Even as a young man, his trousers and shirts bore the damage of the overzealous right hand, "Droitie," and the underachieving left hand nicknamed "Gauchie." Moojie's brilliant solution was to forgo socks altogether and cram his braced feet into shoes lacking laces. "It's the end of green beans," he said in French to Phineas. Something his mother used to muttter when she was at wit's end.

Fourteen years old, clumsy, homesick, and most cruelly exiled to the wilderness where there was little hope for friendship or the semblance of a family life, Moojie grew to resent the rub of his grandfather's voice, the scrape of the rooster's crow, and the grunge of every square inch of the cramped kitchen that opened into the living room and reeked of fish oil and coffee grounds. He knew every wrought iron detail of the wood-burning stove, and the exact order of knives on the wall rack. Mason jars lined the open shelves, dried kelp and pickled kelp, canned sardines and more canned sardines. Unwittingly, the covered piano, the rifle cabinet, the gramophone, and the grandfather clock missing an hour hand had entered his dreams.

Tension mounted, and one morning when Pappy threw a cold, wet rag upon Moojie's sleeping head to wake him at dawn, Moojie hurled it back at him. Pappy seized him by the pajamas and threw him up against the wall. "Do that again, boy, and I'll fry your flanks and pack you off to the Steel Barn faster than a minnow swims a dipper." The boy's home rattled around in the atmosphere for the day, and at suppertime, Pappy stabbed his fork into his fried tomatoes and said, "I am your church. Like nature, I demand respect. And you and I both know nature can be grim as it is holy."

"Grim and holy, Sir."

Phineas plopped down on the braided rug and rolled onto his back, letting his legs fall open.

"That's one fat cat," Pappy said.

Phineas blinked at them upside down, a golden soul peering through two horned moons. Moojie held out his hand, palm down, and scratched the air with his fingers, his signal for Phineas to come. The cat rolled upright and jumped onto his lap. "It's a good thing h-he can't hear," he said.

"What's that you said?" Pappy asked.

"Nothing."

"Your cat may be deaf, but his nose ain't broken," Pappy said, holding out a piece of bacon. Phineas turned toward the bacon, eyes dilated. Pappy stuffed it into his own mouth and snorted.

"H-he senses things," Moojie said.

"Listen boy, I could use a little help around here,"

Pappy said. "My cow thinks she's a politician: she'll eat from anybody's hand, and she's so blind she can't see a train comin'. The goats need groomin' and the fences need repairin'. And you're goin' to do it or so help me God I'm shippin' you out."

Looking out the window, Moojie caught sight of a barefoot girl slipping out from behind the barn, cupping what looked like eggs to her chest. She went tree to tree, making her way toward the field—ragtag, dark-skinned, with a white smudge on her forehead, in every detail fitting the villagers' descriptions of a Hostile. Be still my heart! A year or so before, Moojie had seen the girl at a distance, crossing the field. He had sneaked outside and tried to find her. Not expecting to meet anyone new at the farm, much less a girl, this time, at closer distance, he saw her fine, dark features, and his heart flew into this throat.

"What?" Moojie asked distractedly. Was she a Hostile? McTavish, the neighboring rancher, wild game poacher, and retired field medic, often argued with Pappy over whether or not the Hostiles—any or all of the Native American tribes—were truly done away with. Moojie let his mind linger there a minute, recalling how Mamma used to field the doomsayers as she picked through the green grocer's produce, how the villagers were so worried that the natives' dead ancestors were coming back as ghost cannibals to take revenge upon the land grabbers, and she would laugh and say, "Blessed are the crow counters."

"And don't get me started on the cost of livestock feed," Pappy said. "Have you seen—"

"I-I haven't seen anybody," Moojie said.

Pappy looked at him suspiciously.

Moojie excused himself and went out to the porch. The girl was gone. And standing in her place was a great, empty twilight, the hollow cold of six lonely years. In his younger days, when the Markham boys would jeer at him or turn their backs as they saw him coming, or when his father growled with resentment, Moojie had always gravitated to his mother for reassurance; but those days were far gone. If there was during his time at St. Isidore's any one occasion that marked a turning point it was this day. Moojie could no longer tolerate Pappy's threats of sending him away. He ached for friendship, to be a valued member of something. That girl couldn't have been alone. There had to be more like her. And whether they were Hostiles or cannibals or the ghosts of dead dinosaurs, Moojie was going to find them.

But Captain Finnegan had other notions.

The next day, Pappy, who farmed goat's milk, eggs and produce, insisted that Moojie accompany McTavish and him on the morning deliveries. After listening to the usual litany of McTavish and Pappy's bickering, Moojie mentioned that he would like to ride horseback to the Cave of Fire, which was high on El Serrat, the southern mountain bordering the ranch. McTavish straightened and said: "Cave of Fire? Cave of Fire! You're dafter than the old man! Enter that cave, boy, and prepare to meet Lucifer, for he will summon you into his snare, and if you don't go he'll take you by your scrawny neck, strip you naked, and tear out your heart just for jings."

Moojie pictured a snickering cauldron of devil's minions—sour-smelling and scratching through his flesh in search of a loaf of heart. He could feel the claws spreading wide his ribcage, and shuddered at the thought of them sifting through his innards.

"No, man. The Hostiles are either smokin' with their ancestors or livin' on the reservations," Pappy said.

"Au contraire, there are stragglers up on El Serrat. I'll stake money on it," McTavish said.

"You're wrong," said Pappy.

"So why's everyone afraid o-of them?" Moojie asked.

"A while back a hunting party went up El Serrat and never returned," McTavish said. "Ended up a pile of bones picked clean at the Circle of Trees."

"Circle of Trees?" Moojie asked.

"Above the cave," McTavish said. "Five trees, five points, you know, like the devil's pentagram."

"Could've been a mountain lion," Moojie said.

"Yeah," Pappy said. "And I reckon it was a mountain lion that torched San Miguel twice before you were born, killing fourteen men, women, and children. But that was a long time ago. They're far gone, I tell you, far gone."

"There he goes again, bumpin' his gums," McTavish said.

At first light, Moojie got up before Pappy, planning to ride out to the woods to look for the elusive girl. Hocus Pocus, Pappy's retired, arthritic, circus horse, took great pains to get down on one knee to let Moojie flop onto her back, hindsite first, then he'd flatten out, spin around, and sit up facing front. Before Moojie crossed the yard, Pappy bungled down the ramp and stopped him.

"I can smell it ... you're up to no good," he said. A bear sizing up a warthog.

"Just going to the creek, Sir," Moojie feigned innocence. As soon as the men left, he rode out to the woods, toward El Serrat.

Pappy and McTavish returned late that afternoon after drinking themselves loopy. They bickered like two old hens, drank more whiskey, then broke into singing:

War to the hilt, theirs be the guilt,
Who fetter the free man to ransom the slave.

Up then, and undismay'd,
sheathe not the battle blade,
Till the last foe is laid low in the grave!
Till the last foe is laid low in the grave!

They argued politics. They argued union strikes, and livestock feed, and the metaphysical effects of ale versus Guinness. They argued until they were hoarse. They harped and chortled and slapped their fingers. Having spent most of the day looking for the girl and failing to find her, Moojie stayed in his room, dangling a shoelace playfully for Phineas. Pappy came in and just stared at him, rolling a wooden match between his yellow teeth.

That night, Moojie dreamed of two young boys leading him into a deep, spacious cave where they drew graffiti on his arms and chest, and then presented him to the girl he had seen. She was wearing a sheer green veil and had an exotic bird perched on her finger. She smiled as if she knew him, then offered him the bird. When Moojie awakened, his ears were icy, and he knew it was a prophecy. He belonged with the girl and her kind. He didn't know how or when, but he was going to find a way to connect with them.

Sardines, sardines, sardines. Moojie had never eaten so many sardines. Fresh sardines for breakfast. Dried sardines for dinner. Pickled sardines for lunch. Having not acquired a taste for the fishy fish, he had learned to spit his bites politely into his napkin, and feed them to Millie-Mae and Phineas on the sly.

After serving cucumber and pickled sardine sandwiches one afternoon, Pappy announced: "So boy, the honeymoon's over. You're fixin' fences today." Slurping coffee through chapped lips, he seemed to be waiting for an answer. Moojie expected another speech on the glories of ranching, and he was prepared to respond, as usual, with a long, empty stare. The prince of light had by then developed an art for avoiding work. He waved his crutch in the air. He didn't know why he did it. It was just that he had some inner demon determined to test the limits of his welcome.

"You know," Pappy said, "I got a mind to march you right back to the chapel, where you will live out your days under Mother Teagardin's reign of misery."

Just then, they appeared outside the window, the two boys from Moojie's dream, sneaking across the west field in the direction of the creek, moving as swift and playfully as rabbits. Moojie choked on his sandwich. Evidently, Pappy didn't see them because he rapped Moojie on the back, then sat in his winged throne and plunked his dusty boots down upon the coffee table. "Eh, you know, I think it's time for you to go, boy," he said. "I'm a simple man. I like my rifles and my goats and my cow and my birds. The chickens are good. They give me eggs, they make good compost, and when I get a hankering, I eat them." He blew three smoke rings that rose and thinned to nothing.

"Yessir," Moojie said, eyes darting. What was he going to do? Well, what had Odysseus done when he was trapped by the goatherd? He got the villain drunk. Moojie took the whiskey crock off the shelf and poured a shot. Pappy took a noisy swig.

"Out here, you can feel the ghosts," Pappy said. "You can feel them hanging in the trees. They're the kind that can take your soul." His eyelids closed. Two breaths and he was snoring.

Moojie emitted a little sardine belch and reached for his crutches. Legs trembling, heart thrumming, he sneaked ever so quietly out the screen door.

Chapter 4

*First sign of purple: Moojie pursues the
white-dotted boys and a very tall lady*

Moojie had grown used to falling, getting up, and brushing himself off. It no longer surprised him that he could do this. Pappy had built a ramp off the porch and established early on that he wouldn't run after Moojie every time he stumbled.

This time, Millie-Mae was there to lick Moojie's face as he got up.

Convinced that he would fare better with the strange, white-dotted tribe, Moojie was willing to risk everything—being sent to the boy's farm, or worse yet, being sent back to Mother Teagardin—just for the opportunity to meet them and follow this premonition. Barely able to contain his excitement, he passed the loft where his grandfather's pigeons fretted like nuns, pumping their gray heads and crowding into the back. "Yep," Moojie said, "you're locked in, and I'm locked out," and then he moved on because he didn't want to stop and think about what he had just said. He had always felt that if he kept separate from the activities of the dairy, that if he stayed indifferent to Pappy and the critters, it would be easier to leave. The sign above the barn door read GOAT LOCKER. Two goats in the stable sized him up through fence boards—bulging white-blue eyes and coin-slot pupils, jaws working like nut grinders.

"You should see the other guy," Moojie said, limping past with a forced look of insolence and pride he had always affected for busybodies.

A surround of fruit trees grew outside the vegetable patch, trees that bore fruit the size of dreams—black figs, plums, and apricots the size of apples, apples and oranges the size of grapefruit. And beyond the trees, the rolling, golden fields, and haze from a distant fire. Overhead, a flying turkey vulture dropped a dead snake onto the yard. It was hot to Moojie's touch.

He followed the path to the creek and came upon the two scrawny, white-spotted boys he had seen in his dream. At first, they didn't seem to notice him. They were busy catapulting over long bamboo poles, from one point in the sand to another, saying, "Prometheus the firelighter!" One didn't seem to have a knack for acrobatics and went soaring over the other, landing in the lilac, graceful as a sack of flour.

Millie-Mae went barking after him.

"Millie-Mae!" Moojie said. The boys stopped and looked him over.

They were identical: dun-brown faces framed by ragged, sun-streaked hair, their eyes unblinking, black and glittery, and young enough to be in elementary school. Dressed in flour sacks, the only way to tell them apart was a headband that one of them wore. Moojie picked a wild iris and held it out to them. "It's okay," he said. "The dog's just looking after me."

The head-banded boy took the flower, and held it as if it might catch fire in his hand.

"Purple," Moojie said.

The twins made a happy, buzzing sound, all gleaming and white with their teeth and white spots. They petted Millie-Mae. Moojie thought maybe he had some new friends.

"My lord," the boys giggled and bowed to him, their voices like squeaks out of a balloon.

"I am Manish," the one with the headband said. "He is Shar."

Moojie appreciated their nice manners. "W-where'd you come from?" he asked.

Manish hesitated. He opened his mouth and moved his lips. He looked upward as if into his own skull, cleared his throat and opened his mouth again. His pink tongue danced about, but no sound came out. A strong gust of wind did, though, whipping up sand, and causing buck-eyes and acorns to pop off the trees. Moojie heard a window shatter nearby. But no audible words.

"I-I guess you're not from around here," he said.

"From away come we far," Manish's voice rang clear as a bell.

"You c-come from far away?" Moojie said, trying to decipher his meaning.

"Farandaway!" both boys said. It was like they shared the same brain.

"Where is your house?" Moojie asked.

The boys looked around, shrugged, and then tugged on Moojie's crutches.

"Hey!" Moojie said.

The twins stood to either side of him. "What purpose do they serve?" Manish asked.

"They're for earthquakes and whatnot," Moojie said. "Something t-to hang onto." Best not to tell them he was crippled; who knew what might happen if they knew he couldn't outrun them.

"*Melammu*," Shar said.

"What does that mean?"

"I greet your halo."

The boys started humming together, then performed a whirling dervish dance while reciting this verse:

"Water is fickle,
Earth is more.
Turn a somersault,
and open the door."

A warm kind of calm crept over Moojie. The twins skipped in a circle, kicking up sand, flavoring the morning mist with giddiness. Manish reeled over to him, grinned and put his hand out flat. Moojie figured he wanted a handout, and while he was racking his brain for what to offer, a coin magically appeared in the boy's palm—right out of his palm!

"Whoa! How'd you do that?" Moojie asked.

Millie-Mae barked, startling everyone.

"Y-you best get out of here before the old man finds you," Moojie said to the boys.

Without ceremony, Manish and Shar took each other's hands and skipped around the nearby granite out-cropping, singing, "Purple, purple, purple!"

"Hey, where are you going?" Moojie called after them. He glanced in the direction of the cabin and, despite bells clanging out a warning inside his head, staggered after them, puffing air, feet gashing the sand, crutches sinking. But they were gone, completely gone. He decided to put off running away. Anyway, it was nearly time for supper.

Chapter 5

The miracle of Elsie the cow and other notable incidents worthy of scientific scrutiny

Moojie dared not breathe a word to Pappy about the boys. It was enough for Moojie to know there was someone he could reach out to—at least two *someones*—who knew how many more like them were hiding in the mountains?

But he couldn't sit back and expect time to put things in their rightful place. He knew this as he jiggled side-to-side on the wagon seat next to his grandfather as they rode along the pitted trail that ran the length of the property. An odor of menace rose from the buckboard's ungreased axels, mixed with tobacco smoke and summer and fresh-sawn wood. Loaded shotgun at his feet, Pappy manhandled the burros, Aggie and Baggie, veering and overcorrecting and veering again. "Dagnabbed mules." He handed Moojie a pair of field glasses. "Keep your eyes peeled, boy. Scour the fields, mind the fields. McTavish lost another buck to the cougar."

Hot dust kicked up as they rode along the split-rail fence, past great clotted trees and cactus, past a headless scarecrow dressed in red plaid.

Pappy didn't seem to notice when the wagon ran over a sunbathing snake. "The dairy's looking pretty doggone pitiful these days," he said. "Pitiful fences. Pitiful road. Pitiful fields. Thanks to my pitiful back. I blame the war, you know."

Across the pitiful countryside, Moojie peered through the field glasses. There, grazing in the high grass, stood an immense black cow with a white stripe around her girth.

"That's Elsie," Pappy said. "She's close to calving. You know about girls and boys, don't you?"

"Yep," Moojie said, clearing his throat, and feeling a fraction unsure of where he was leading. "Girls … girls are kind of, kind of tricky, these days. Believe me, I-I've been through it." He was thinking back to one girl in particular, Sylvie Mitropolis of Wimbley Wood, the one who could count backward in Spanish and who didn't wear skivvies under her skirt, and he asked again what was the cow's name.

Pappy tipped back his sombrero. "Elsie's the name. She's a Dutch cow."

"Sounds more l-like a Greek name."

Through the white-hot dust they rode. Flies and dust blew into Moojie's face. Unsinging birds hid in the trees, and idle rabbits lolled in the shrubs alongside the road.

"What about the Hostiles?" Moojie asked, anxious to see the twins again. "Did you ever meet one?"

"Eh, long time ago, during the Removal days, two of 'em came to the cabin forecastin' doom and gloom, smellin' like mushrooms. They got no claim to this land."

To the south, Moojie saw what looked like a cougar slip behind a thicket of shrubs. His throat went dry and he coughed. He didn't want to say anything about it—he didn't know why, he just didn't. "What kind of m-mushrooms?" he asked Pappy, trying to divert his attention. "D-do you mean the orange kind, the big poisonous ones w-with the white dots, and maybe gills, o-or do you mean the little brown ones that grow, you know, in the basement?"

"I mean mushrooms like ... oh for cripe's sake, it don't matter what kind of mushrooms! We ain't talkin' mushrooms here, we're talkin' history." He jerked back the reins, set the brake, stepped off the buckboard, picked a buckeye off a tree, and sank it in his trousers pocket. "For rheumatism," he said.

They continued, took a fork in the trail, then kept on until they reached a pile of stones at the wayside. Pappy pointed south past El Serrat Mountain.

"Boy, this farm is big, very big," he said. "If there was a rope to round that mountain, you'd throw it south an hour before it landed. I know every inch of this land. If there was any Hostiles left, I'd be the first to know. It's just an old wives' tale."

On the way back to the cabin, they found Elsie lying in the grass. Pappy stopped the wagon, jumped down, ran a hand over her monumental belly, then looked under her tail. "You'd think things could go right once in a while, but no," he said. "Even cows are botched up these days."

A hot breeze blew across the field, stirring up insects and seeds and dry grass.

Pappy signaled for Moojie to get down and come over. "Listen, the calf's comin' out bottom first. It'll kill 'em both. Keep an eye on her. I'm going for McTavish."

The old buckboard squeaked away on a cloud of curses.

Elsie struggled to stand and collapsed back onto the

ground beside Moojie with a dusty *flumpf!* What a pickle. *Keep an eye on her? What in the blue skies was his meaning?* Elsie's mouth fell open as she panted and gasped and panted some more. Moojie lowered onto his folded legs and stroked her ears—great, soft cones that reminded him of gramophone horns. Blue sky glistened like the sea in the giant black marble of her eye.

"Easy, girl," Moojie said.

Elsie moaned and convulsed.

"Come on, sir," Moojie said. "Get a wiggle on!" He had never seen such a thing, and he wished his mother were there. Her explanation and steady hand were needed, her knowing of birth. With Elsie's every sigh and whimper, he tried to soothe her. He breathed with her. In out. In out. His legs prickled with numbness. Not knowing what else to do, he did the only thing he could think of, and it appeared to be the right thing, for as he did it, Elsie's great soft ears swiveled toward him: he fetched his mother's music box from his pocket, wound it up, and sang the French lullaby his mother used to sing to him.

And that was when it happened, the ringing in Moojie's ears, and the sudden sensation of a pressure above him pressing down, of warmth pulsating all through his body and out his fingertips, mysteriously, unexpectedly. It felt like he was merging with something invisible—a vague remembrance of childhood, the same sensation he had experienced when he encountered the miraculous seabird—a presence all about him, a powerful, unseen something, and the air smelling of roses.

Elsie lay perfectly still but for her wide, roving eyes and the slowing rise and fall of her ribcage. It wasn't long before a silver leg poked out of her, and then another, and then there came two white stripes, the middle, the head, and two front legs, shiny and bluish—a newborn calf.

It was the first time in a long while that Moojie's sense of torment dissolved, and his melancholy succumbed to a terrible joy and bright sense of wonder. Elsie licked her calf clean as he wobbled onto his ungainly legs.

Two figures approached Moojie from the field, one tall, one not so tall, appearing so quietly he imagined they fell from the sky like pigeon feathers. He shaded his eyes from the sun, but couldn't quite make them out. At the moment, he didn't think he could handle another mystery.

But not all mysteries come as screaming riddles. Some appear more in the manner of mirages wavering above a plane of grass, like question marks rising out of the earth, dressed in hand-me-downs and rope sandals, a chalky white blot on their foreheads—a lady and a girl. The cougar Moojie had spotted in the field earlier was plodding alongside them—magnificent, serene—sniffing in Moojie's direction.

Heart thumping, Moojie watched the figures draw nearer. He watched closely, not unkindly, but with a curious eye, eerily suspicious of what they might want. Thin as a plucked bird, the lady approached him, scrutinizing the scene, while the girl stayed back a ways with the wild cat. The lady had a triangular face, brown eyes, gigantic and orange-flecked, like a reptile. And yet she had two arms and two legs and appeared to be a warm-blooded, breathing white-dotted human. Moojie's belly fluttered.

"He could be useful," the reptile lady said over her shoulder to the girl.

"I somehow doubt it," the girl said.

Moojie recognized her. The beautiful egg thief. His eyes were filled with a new kind of curiosity that made him tremble. Elsie the cow, still lying in the grass, sniffed in the lady's direction, trumpeted a loud moo, and then rocked herself to standing. Anxiously, Moojie searched for any signs of Pappy's buckboard on the county road.

"Would you care to pull up a chair?" the lady asked him.

"Chair," he said. "What chair?"

Her laughter rose like beating wings above the field.

Moojie got up on his crutches. *What was that, a cannibal joke?*

The lady smiled and said, "I find it amusing that you tread upon our land without an invitation," as if reading his mind.

"Your land!" he said.

She looked at him for longer than was polite, a long, liquidy, deep-lake stare, a sizing up stare. "He does possess brightness," she said to the girl.

Moojie's face burned.

"You have done well," the lady said to him. She held out a gourd that was hanging from her shoulder by a braided cord. "Give the poor cow to drink," she said.

Moojie took the gourd and held it sideways to let the water trickle sideways into Elsie's mouth. Her gigantic tongue reminded him of a fish. Pink. Scaled. Side-swimming.

"Tell me, my lord, who are you?" asked the lady.

"I-I could ask you the same question."

She inhaled and pulled her hair back from her face. "I am the sun and the moon, the river and the clouds."

"Pappy says you're a lazy bum."

"See? He is of little use to us," the girl said.

Moojie felt the air bristling between them. "Are you ghosts?" he asked. "I mean—"

"Would that I were invisible!" the lady said. "It is infinitely safer to be a ghost in your world."

"So you're not a-a ghost," he said.

The lady introduced herself as Ninti, and the maiden

as Babylonia. She explained that they came to America long before when there was much darkness, much weeping, and gnashing of teeth, and nations warring against nations.

"Where did you come from?" Moojie asked.

"We came to teach the way of peace … and what are we offered in return? Worldlings hunt us like common thieves. Worldlings do not want happiness. They want land. They want gold. They want what they cannot have. There is no gratitude, no praise for what is given." Her eyes, like daggers.

Was she talking about him?

"A certain dread besets my days," she sighed, "the fruit of our labors rotting, year upon year, century upon century. What a stubborn lot your kind is!"

Recalling Pappy's cannibal theory, and the story of the mauled hunters at the Circle of Trees, Moojie wondered if she was hungry. Maybe these white-spotted types weren't a good bet for friends after all.

"Gotta go," he said.

"My lord"—she cocked her head—"do you have troubling visions? Do you sometimes dream of great warriors striking terror into the hearts of many?"

My lord. He felt a warm rush of delight when she called him this. He felt important.

"Ah, well, I am told that in your previous life, you knew much tribulation," she said.

"Couldn't've been worse than this one."

"You, dear fellow, in a past life, might have been one of the nastiest barbarians on Earth."

"What?"

"Does the name Lugalzagesi mean anything to you—large-scale assaults, shock attacks upon reeling troops and terrified civilians?"

"Swell."

"Ah, yes. I quite agree. You and all the others! This world-dream is rather vexing, is it not? Before our kind came here, we were living as happy children."

"You shouldn't've come." He kept a leery eye on the pair of fangs in the shade, and the pink tongue hanging out.

"Her name is Anahita. You needn't be afraid."

"Anahita," he repeated. He was still afraid.

"What is it that you want, my lord?" she asked.

It was a simple enough question. He had been disappointed by life so far, and didn't think to hope for much. "I-I want to find a family," he said. "I want to go home."

"As we all do," she said, plucking a burr from her rope sandal. She stood and scanned the distant road, and then scraped the air with her fingers, bidding him to follow. It was a small thing, but this familiar gesture put Moojie at ease. He knew what it meant because it was the signal he used to call Phineas. Funny to be summoned like a deaf cat. He followed Ninti into the purple shade of an acacia tree, where she sat cross-legged on the ground and motioned for him to sit with her, which he did, fleetly landing against her leg like a tumbling side of beef. Sorry. Oops. Well. He backed himself into an odd half-sitting pose bolstered on one arm.

In the field, Babylonia combed her fingers through her hair, the great cat panting beside her. Unperturbed, the nursing cow and calf didn't seem to half mind.

Ninti tugged at her earlobe. "You must not tell a soul …" she said. "The business with the cow …."

"I need to get away," he blurted out.

"Sorry, I cannot help with such matters."

Moojie stared at her with a feverish intensity and said, "I-I don't want to go to the boy's farm, but I don't belong here, either. You know what that's like, don't you— t-to not belong somewhere, but there's nowhere else to go?" It seemed to strike a chord of compassion in her since she sighed and shook her head.

"Who are you?" she asked again.

"Nobody. Orphan. Mother dead. Father gone."

"I fear you misunderstand," she continued. "Tell me who *you* are."

Too much sun, too many questions. "Are you kidding?" Moojie asked. This tall white-haired *someone* was magical and annoying and frightening all at once. Was she a Hostile? He imagined the look on Pappy's face should he find them socializing in the field. And then there was Babylonia, standing in the sunlight with the big cat. Gaw.

"Footdragger," he said to Ninti. "I'm a footdragger."

"And?"

"Lamptosser. Bull in a China shop."

"From where came all those names?"

"From my father."

"For the sake of heaven, could he not make up his mind? And your mother?"

Moojie felt again the dull ache in his chest and flashed upon the night after the accident when his mother came to him in her spiritual form. Yes, she had loved him. He knew that. If only he could go back in time.

"You see, I do not trust worldlings any more than I would trust a serpent underfoot," Ninti said. "Nonetheless. Inasmuch as you have demonstrated kindness with the cows, I will lend you a bit of advice."

Moojie straightened and leaned in closer.

"If you do not wish to be sent away," she said.

"Yes, yes."

"Make yourself useful."

"But—" he started to defend himself.

"Feed the goats. Water the cows. At least it will give you time to find a new family."

"Wait a minute, I-I can't do chores. Can't you see? I'm the one who needs help! Me doing chores, that's j-just plain stupid. Aren't I crippled? Crippled kids don't work on farms. Hard enough to operate these crutches. How would you like to do chores o-on crutches? I don't need that kind of advice."

"My lord," she said, "if you want to survive, you must know where your shovel is."

Ninti and Babylonia seemed to sense that Pappy's buckboard was coming from far off. How they knew was a mystery. They just knew. An instant before the burro-drawn wagon turned off the country road and onto the dusty driveway leading to St. Isidore's, the visitors vanished. He got back to the cows just as the buckboard pulled into the field. Pappy and his friend McTavish looked at Elsie grazing sleepily with the fresh calf slurping at her udders.

"If that don't beat the Dutch!" Pappy said. His eyes filled with puzzling colors and swiveled back and forth—calf to Moojie to Elsie, Elsie to Moojie to calf.

The men got down.

Moojie searched his mind for what to say. He could have said it was a miracle, but grownups never believe in miracles. "I-I was scouring the fields, sir," he said. "Minding the fields." Those words always grabbed Pappy's attention. Scouring the fields. Minding the fields. Holding one's own. Moojie could feel them now quaking up his spine.

A hot wind snatched Pappy's sombrero away, causing his gray hair to stand out from his head like dry twigs. Moojie shielded his eyes from grass particles bearing through the air.

Pappy scrutinized the countryside, reached for his canteen, tipped back his head, and drank, pinky finger pointing up, while watching Moojie sideways. McTavish cut through the grass toward Elsie with his leather bag, rolling back his sleeves. The red tattoo on his forearm—two snakes on a winged staff—matched his red shirt and red face that was so splotchy it looked like it had caught fire and someone put it out with a shovel. He lowered onto one knee and listened to Elsie's rib cage. Then, he rose and brushed off his pants. "Like a clock," he said. "Nice work, lad." He offered Moojie an arthritic handshake.

Pappy's narrow blue eyes turned narrower and bluer. Unmoving, Moojie withered in the heat, feeling more like a cooked blue belly than a boy.

"What the dickens did you do?" Pappy asked.

"I-I was singing, sir. A song Mamma used to sing."

The men glanced at each other.

"He misses his mother," McTavish said.

"I reckon since it's your bull, you'll be wanting to name the calf," Pappy said to McTavish.

"Oh, let the lad give it a name," McTavish said.

They turned to Moojie.

Moojie considered the way the calf came out, its legs and nose and ears and stripes coming out every which way, and he said, "Odds and Ends!"

The men nodded approvingly.

Thrilled by Elsie's miracle and the meeting of new friends, Moojie grinned from ear to ear. He petted the newborn calf and then, like a sail filled with a headwind, climbed onto the buckboard in silent celebration of his newfound talent for bamboozling grownups.

Chapter 6

*An account of Moojie's quarrel with Pappy;
and the succeeding hazard, which leads to
a change of heart*

Pappy never talked to his own children anymore. Neither did he have any contact with his estranged wife, Nana Finnegan. St. Isidore's Fainting Goat Dairy was no center of social activity, but delinquents and streetwise discards at the boy center were a far cry from the kind of company Moojie wanted to keep. In order to avoid any such possibility, he followed Ninti's advice and started helping with the chores. He fed the critters and mucked the stalls. He washed the dishes and greased the wagon axles. It seemed to work for a while. To say that Moojie and his grandfather had struck a friendship would be an exaggeration, but at least they bore each other's company with no malice. Moojie went about the dairy feeling not just a little more hopeful, but as if he might, after all was said and done, have a bright future. As if he could do anything he wanted—anything he put his mind to. Why, if he got the notion, he might just stand up and walk to the village!

As he lay in his cot one night, he looked out the window and deep into space. The stars seemed to be talking, beaming out a bright message to him. He opened the window and sniffed the cool, dry grass, listened to the laughing creek and trilling crickets. He looked and watched, and suddenly what had once seemed ordinary now struck him as extraordinary—the quivering light, the summer air, the rippling water—the stars, the creek, the moon, it all felt holy to him, there, alone in the night with his cat. It was like he wasn't the only one *seeing* something; the universe was, actually, somehow, strangely, mysteriously, *seeing* him. He lifted the sleepy Phineas to the window to look outside. "Look, Phinny. That's love."

At breakfast, Moojie was in his own mind-world, day-dreaming about meeting up with Ninti and the twins, plotting to ride Hocus Pocus up the mountain as soon as his grandfather left to make deliveries.

After being unusually quiet, Pappy said, "Well, boy, inasmuch as I ain't runnin' a flophouse, and seein' as your father's got some burr up his kazoo, you're gonna need some proper lookin' after. I reckon it's time for you to go to the Steel Barn."

Moojie always knew it was a possibility, but it was a shock to hear it. He froze, like he had just been hit on the head, like he had a concussion.

Pappy tossed an open letter onto the table.

Moojie just stared at it.

"It's from your aunt," Pappy said. "She says you're better off at the boy's home because you'll get schoolin'."

"What's she, the Pope?"

"She's right, you know."

"Well, I'm not going."

"What's that?" Pappy bristled visibly, eyes blazing, jaw flinching.

Heat shot up Moojie's spine. "Y-you can't make me go. I'll decide where to live. Not you, not anyone else!" He stood to his feet and made a move to throw over the chair.

Pappy lunged right up close and jabbed a finger at him. "Kill it," he cracked. His face was a leather cover polished by time, a book with stories churning in it. Stories of burning villages and rumbling cannons, held in and spinning.

Jumpy as a cricket in a henhouse, Moojie went out to the porch to try to calm down, to sit and rock and think. *People think they can hand me off like a day-old sandwich.* In the field, yellow jackets swarmed on fallen, rotting plums. The inland sun was different from the village sun: its rays cut across the outer buildings of St. Isidore's, sharp and slanted like an axe to a log. Blinded, Moojie couldn't see the horizon. He couldn't see ahead at all.

He stormed into his room, slammed the door, and collapsed onto the cot. He growled and smashed his fist into the pillow. He rolled over and there was Phineas on the chair, looking alarmed.

"Gaw, Phinny, even rats have families, you know. Even monkeys and fish. Aren't I as good as a fish?"

In a panic, he thumbed through his mother's diary, making out a word here and there, hoping to find some indication of hope or guidance. His mother's handwriting was lacey with fancy capitals and he still couldn't read well because of his messed-up brain. He wound his little music box and listened to the lullaby. It pained him in every part of his body, a physical sensation that hurt more when he breathed, an icy air trapped inside his chest.

Chapter 7

*Of which is recounted Moojie's plan of action;
with other truly diverting incidents*

If anyone understood the risk, the possibility of his being roasted on a spit by a tribe of ravenous Hostiles—if that was what they were—Moojie did. But what other choice did he have? It was either take a chance and reach out to the cave clan or be exiled to a work farm to live out his days as a first class derelict. Despite the stories he had heard about the Hostiles, he was determined to find their cave and to see for himself what could be done to avoid such a miserable plight.

Meanwhile, redoubling his efforts to prolong his stay at the dairy, Moojie worked as hard as a galley slave, rising at dawn, lighting the fire, emptying the ice tray and slop bucket, mucking the stalls. As it turned out, he was able to do more than he had thought he could. He even cooked dinner when Pappy and McTavish came home late. Eggs, toast, and sardines. Often in the morning he helped them nurse away their sottedness with Pappy's recipe of bay laurel and ginger root tea sweetened with honey. He milked the goats, fed the critters, and collected the chickens' eggs. He flew the pigeons, letting them out before feeding time, then calling them back to the loft with the kazoo. He groomed Hocus Pocus and the burros, finding new ways to stabilize himself as he worked, holding onto one crutch, either leaning upon hay bales or the sides of the barn. He would never admit it, but he actually *liked* having chores. He liked being useful and getting dirty. And at the end of the day, when the goats came in from the fields, he went inside, showered, and Pappy sang, "Alleluia!"

But passing the time of day wasn't enough to keep Moojie happy. Tormented by loneliness, he yearned to meet up with Ninti and the twins again. Daily he scanned the hills through field glasses, but there had been nary a trace of them for weeks. He thought about packing his satchel, riding up the mountain, and telling Ninti he had been forced to run away from a lunatic, drunken grandfather and had nowhere else to turn. But would they accept him? What could he do to make that happen?

It started with the chickens.

One morning he stopped short at the bottom of the ramp, sensing something strange. It was an inborn sensitivity, extrasensory perception. He didn't see anyone in the yard, and yet he *felt* someone, maybe several *someones.* He got a crazy, fluttery feeling in his belly. Was it the pickled sardines from the night before? Or was a person hiding inside the barn? As he was collecting the morning's eggs, the twins shot out from behind the hutch, raced across the yard and out to the field.

"Hey!" he whispered loudly, so as not to alert Pappy.

Inside the barn, Babylonia, the egg thief, was waiting

for him with a pitchfork.

"Whoa!" he said.

She backed against the hay bales.

"I-I won't hurt you," Moojie said. He offered her a bucket of eggs. "Take these."

"They are not blue." She threw down the pitchfork and sped out the door.

"Wait! Come back," Moojie said, trying to keep his voice down.

Babylonia raced into the tall grass, long braid whipping at her back.

The cabin door flew open, and Pappy burst onto the porch, brandishing a rifle. He took aim and fired at her as she fled into the woods. "Freeloader!" he shouted. He took another shot. "This is a citizen's arrest. Stop in the name of the law!"

Millie-Mae chased after Babylonia, but she had already made it to the woods.

"Blistering sea biscuits," Pappy said. "Did you see that? The dagnabbed Hostiles are back!"

"It was just a-a girl," Moojie said.

Pappy took hold of his rifle as if it were a bayonet and thrust it forward as he lunged along the porch. "Miserable soaplocks. I'll show them no mercy. Off with you, scalawags. Off with your heads. These are my hills. My hills!" He knocked over a potted geranium.

Moojie was far from dissuaded in his desire to befriend the mysterious interlopers.

"Here's the ticket," he told Millie-Mae later. "Th-they want blue eggs? Well, they're gonna get blue eggs."

Most of Pappy's hens laid white or brown eggs. Only three laid blues. And not often. So starting that day, Moojie marked the blues with a red heart, tucked them into a corner of the hutch, and covered them with straw. He continued doing the chores and scouring and minding the fields, but it wasn't for his grandfather anymore.

And one day, it finally paid off.

After Pappy left to do deliveries, Moojie flew the pigeons and mucked the stables. A sound came from the creek, a rhythmic, tapping sound. He followed it. What he came upon astounded him: over a dozen people, young and old, dressed in all manner of sackcloth and denim, hitched-up, patched trousers, and blousey shirts. They were busy working at the water's edge. When he trudged cautiously onto the sandy bank, all eyes turned upon him. No one spoke. Only the rippling creek and birdsong could be heard. The fragrance of moss and lilac filled the air.

Ninti and a few older adults stood together, their rope sandals looking old enough to be in a museum. Babylonia, crowned with a chaplet of wildflowers, was rinsing her hands in the water. Beside her the brown-skinned twins were now dressed in overalls, and two insolent teenage boys in loincloths were poised as if ready to pounce on Moojie.

"My lord," Ninti said, approaching him. She put her hands together, prayer-like, bowed her head, and uttered some indecipherable greeting.

Moojie tucked his crutches under his arms, held his hands together and bowed his head.

Ninti said something in their language and everyone started back to work, taking strips of fig bark from shallow soaking pools, beating them flat with scrap wood against the rocks, then laying them out in the sun to dry.

"What are you making?" Moojie asked.

"Paper," Ninti said.

The twins reached into Moojie's pockets.

"What're you after?" he laughed.

"*Sukulutu*," Manish said. "Choco-choco."

"Chocolate?" Moojie said. "Sorry, fresh out."

That day, Moojie met most of the clan, including the muscular, loin-clothed Sarru'kan, a kid with the face of a dark Greek god and hair the color of raven feathers. His body was covered with decorative scars, waist up, his skin a hacking of hieroglyphs and ciphers and geometric shapes that looked unholy as disease, something dark and pocked, an ancient text that had been warped. Notches and ticks ran down his arms. A scar the shape of a scorpion crawled across his navel. There was a triangle in the middle of his forehead, and of course, a white spot inside it. Odysseus lost on the wide sea, Moojie felt his face flush, embarrassed and uneasy, mostly uneasy, for he had yet to prove whether the natives were violent and lawless or hospitable to strangers.

Another boy, about Moojie's age, approached him and introduced himself. He was festooned with acorn strands, dried peas, seeds, and animal teeth the color of berry juice. "I am Zagros," he said, "Lord of the Bees." Moojie bowed his head, thinking that was what you do with the natives. At first Zagros seemed hesitant, but then he returned the greeting.

"Zounds! What kind of name is *Moojie*?" he asked.

Sarru'kan stepped between them.

"It would please me to crush him," he spat.

Ninti took Sarru'kan aside, gave him a few chosen words, then sent him off.

As the clan members worked they switched back and forth between English and a throaty, clopping language that sounded of distant thunder, wind through trees, and falling walnuts. Their English sounded old-fashioned and formal, as if Charles Dickens had been their teacher. Numbering twenty-one in all, they called themselves the Akil-Nuri.

"Akil-*what*?" Moojie asked Ninti.

"Light-Eaters. In English we are Light-Eaters."

Zagros explained that the clan was divided into three groups: *olders*, who were wise beyond the ways of the world; *youngers*, including the twins, who had not been exposed to the ways of the world; and *handsome ones*, like himself, Babylonia, and Sarru'kan, who fell somewhere in between. He said they had come long ago from the Far East, sent by the Council of Uta, the seven enlightened ones.

"Never heard of Uta," Moojie said skeptically.

"We came to teach the way of peace, you see," Zagros said. "It is basic to The Cosmic Code."

"Th-the Code? Never heard of that either."

"Nay. And yet, it is written upon your soul," Ninti said, "and upon the soul of every living being. You see, if worldlings were to honor it, heaven would exist on Earth. But alas, you have forgotten."

"Right," Moojie said, a little bewildered.

"My lord," Ninti said, "there are two rules of action for all sentient beings, for all galaxies, and for all time. Where these rules are honored, above and beyond the manufactured laws of government, there is always peace, freedom, and abundance. The first rule of action is: *Feed the poor.*"

"Feed th-the poor," Moojie said. "Well, I-I haven't seen you passing out any vittles."

"Things are not always as they appear."

"Well—"

"Who do you think has been tending the growing patch all these years? Why do you think your grandfather has had bumper crops without lifting a finger?"

"You mean it wasn't an underground spring?" Moojie asked.

"There have been many others like us, some working behind the curtain, so to speak—Sanat Kumara, Lord

Babaji, Eashoa, some seen, some unseen—all working to lift the earth out of darkness. Unfortunately, your kind rather likes to kill us."

"B-but I'm different," Moojie said, surprised to think of this as a virtue. He forgot to ask about the second rule of The Cosmic Code because, as the workers soaked and pounded the fig bark at the water's edge, Ninti counted off the world's methods of eliminating their predecessors: hanging, arrows, poison, bullets, and cannons. As well, many had died in prison: without sunlight, their kind couldn't survive for long. Others had succumbed to the lure of materiality; they had abandoned the original mission for wealth, power, and the pleasures of the body. What strange, tragic people Moojie had stumbled upon.

"So you are the leader," he said to Ninti.

"In a sense. However, our guidance comes from the ancients, from prayer and visions." She looked up at the sky. "And the stars. They are our maps to the future. We attempted to explain this to your grandfather, long before the forced removal of the native peoples."

Moojie squinted at the sun.

"Your grandfather would not heed our warnings. Neither would any other worldlings. Alas, the prophecy of pandemonium has fallen upon deaf ears."

"Pandemonium," Moojie repeated.

"Mars will be highly visible, you see, and the moon near one-quarter waxing. It was written by the ancients … our visions correlate … the precise astronomical configuration of the next vernal equinox will mark a violent upheaval of this region. There will be signs: the earth will sweat and the moon will redden. Without preparation, there will be grave losses, chaos, lawlessness."

"We have guns," Moojie said.

Ninti sighed and shook her head. "Come, come," she said, heading toward the creek, "we haven't all day."

Moojie followed her to the water's edge where she took up a strip of bark and laid it over a granite boulder. With the flat side of a wooden scrap, she beat the bark, causing it to flatten. Then she handed the scrap to him.

"What's the paper for?" he asked, while pounding.

"For now, we will write on it. Later, it will have another use. Tell me, do you still want to run away?"

"Yep."

"Where are you going?"

"Well—"

"You would be wise to avoid the village," she said.

"Why?"

"The pandemonium!"

"Earthquakes happen a-all the time around here. They don't scare me."

"Ah, but the coming earthquake will have power such as few have never known."

"Gotta go," Moojie said, feeling anxious.

"You, my lord, have visited many houses, have you not?" she asked. "And you have yet to find your true home."

"But, how'd you know that?" Moojie asked.

She looked at him quizzically. "My lord, we came for one reason and one alone: to bless humanity. To deliver the light of heaven, to teach the way of peace." She spoke with an accent similar to the green grocer's—prolonged "a"s and curled "r"s—a Sinbad the Sailor accent.

"Light of heaven. You mean God."

"You could say that."

"W-why not just say God?"

"It is not our word."

"What's your word, then?"

"All right," she said. She drew a breath and began to shape the sound with her lips, the same way the twins had done when they caused a whirlwind and shattered the barn window with their word for *home*.

"Never mind!" Moojie said, holding up his hand. "No more broken windows."

"You worldlings are a pigheaded lot," she said.

Moojie was offended by the term "pigheaded."

"I bid you to sit," Ninti said. She brushed off a boulder and sat beside a scrub of wild lilac. Her dark eyes were shimmering like mountain lakes with underwater worlds in them, old worlds and other worlds, battlefields and great migrations, burning pyres and crumbling pantheons. Moojie imagined that if he looked into them for too long, he might fall into a strange universe. He scanned the surrounding trees and shrubs, fearing his grandfather could show up with a cannon. Half-reluctant, he took a seat next to Ninti, leaving a safe distance between them.

"Now," she said, "what about your quest?"

He had to think a minute.

"Certainly you have a quest," she said.

He was wary of telling her too much, but decided that if she tried to do anything *cannibalish*, he would just have to deal with it. "I-I told you, I want to find a family," he said.

She looked down her nose at him. "Perchance I can help you," she said.

"But you're a ... you're a ... what are you?" he asked.

A blue dragonfly zipped onto the scene, hovering directly in front of them. Ninti laughed a throaty laugh and said something to it in her language. Moojie could see its reflection in her eyes. Then all at once, off it spun toward the creek, a glimmer over the water.

"Did you see him?" Ninti asked.

"Yep."

"Tell me, what is *his* quest?"

"I don't know."

"I see. Well, at the moment, he flies for the sake of

flying. But soon, he will fly for the sake of love."

Love? Moojie recalled being loved, once. But his mother was gone. He brushed his hands on his trousers. "What's a bug know about love?"

"Why, he can know anything he wants to know," she said. "Even dragonflies have imagination."

"Maybe h-he's afraid. Maybe he's not used to being alone."

"Ah, he thinks he is still a worm."

"Nobody likes a worm."

"Perhaps, my lord, the discovery of love has all been laid out for him, the momentum, the light, the building of energy. Perhaps he *is* love itself."

Moojie stared at his dirty, stable-mucking hands.

"There is an old proverb," Ninti said. "That which brought you here will take you home."

For some reason, Moojie was irritated by her words. He stood quickly.

"I see," she said. She rose, laid her hand gently alongside his cheek, looked deeply, gently, sadly into his eyes. This caught him off guard. And then with a *whoosh*, she and the others picked up their materials and left.

"Wait!" Moojie called after them. "What do y-you mean by calling me *lord*? What about my quest?" But she and the others had already vanished beyond the wild lilac, so quickly and quietly that he wondered if he had dreamed them up.

Chapter 8

In which Moojie makes a new friend and a new enemy, and during that time learns of the perils of fraternizing

It was the first of many secret meetings to take place between Moojie and his new friends. In hindsight, it marked the beginning of an extraordinary season. Moojie would always cherish the idle afternoons spent in nature, in kinship, learning their ways. He went along with their way of doing things, through his curiosity, and through his own belief that—save for Sarru'kan—no one tree would bear any more fruit than another in the loamy orchard of their friendship. Papa's abandonment may have been sudden and cruel, but it gave Moojie an opportunity to experience freedom he had never known.

Sometimes before leaving the dairy, Pappy Finnegan stationed Moojie on the porch rocker with a pair of field glasses. "You're my eyes and ears," he'd say. "Chin up, soldier! Shoulders back! Yonder in those hills lies the enemy. You will report any and all sightings." And the minute Pappy left, Moojie rushed out to find the clan. If they weren't at the creek making paper or weaving baskets or bathing, he could find them in the woods collecting berries and mushrooms, clucking like hens, or meditating in the shade.

When Moojie warned them about his grandfather, they seemed unconcerned. Zagros laughed and winked. "Aye, we know, my lord, we know. The cave is invisible when it needs to be. Unless your grandfather can ride a magic carpet up the mountain at sunrise, he will never see it open."

Okay, I'll pretend I understand that.

As time passed, it seemed to Moojie that the clan was more interested in practicalities, such as paper-making and dentistry, than death by hanging. It came as a surprise the day he saw Sarru'kan squatting at the creek brushing his teeth with a frayed piece of young bamboo, and then flossing with a strip of straw. It was silly, of course, to think cave dwellers didn't have to do that sort of thing.

"Aye, ground eggshells," Zagros said to Moojie.

"What?" Moojie asked. He hadn't said anything. Was Zagros reading his mind? It seemed as if he were.

"The toothpaste. It is made of ground eggshells." Zagros smiled and winked.

Moojie showed the clan how to work a yo-yo and how to make giant bubbles out of pine-twig wands that were dipped in soapy water, and the twins zoomed up and down the porch ramp, waving their wands, all joyous and giddy, making terrific sky-filled planets.

"Let there be light! Let there be light!" they pealed. "Where there is light, there is no darkness!"

For the first time in a long while, Moojie laughed.

"What is it like, out there?" Zagros asked Moojie.

"The village, is it nice?"

"Um, I don't know. Yeah. I guess."

When Zagros pressed him for details of the outside world, Moojie told him of the new flying machines and icehouses, of motion pictures and electric sweepers, of the great northern city of San Francisco, and its saloons and opera houses and parades and ice cream parlors.

Eyes dilated, Zagros devoured every word as if it were a magic grape. Moojie couldn't understand why he dressed like an exotic parrot, but could tell by his curiosity—by the mad rising and falling of his eyebrows—that he was something of a kindred spirit, a fellow freak, a brother apart. Finally, someone who was interested in his worldly wisdom—a friend.

"And the city dwellers, what do they wear?" Zagros asked.

"Men wear wool coats a-and felt hats," said Moojie, a detail taken from Pappy's newspapers. "Ladies wear skirts like pipes and hats with feathers."

Ninti had been listening, and she shook her head derisively. "Flying machines! Skirts like pipes!"

From that day on, Moojie couldn't seem to get rid of Zagros. Sometimes Zagros hid in the trees tossing olives at Moojie while he raked the yard. Sometimes he stood outside Moojie's bedroom at night flinging acorns at the window and making owl noises. One early morning in the barn he popped out from a pile of straw to ambush Moojie. They wrestled like cubs until Moojie flipped him onto his back and managed to grip him in an iron lock with his stiff legs. "Quiet!" he hissed, covering Zagros' mouth to stifle his laughter. "You'll wake the old man!"

When Moojie accepted Zagros' invitation to join him at the creek for the youngers' weekly writing lessons,

Babylonia, the co-teacher, took one look at Moojie and said, "You should not have come."

"Well, I did," he said.

Zagros said something to Babylonia in their language that seemed to quell her hostility.

It was Monday, and so beastly hot that the trout were hiding in the shade of the bulrushes.

Babylonia began the lesson by scratching cuneiform symbols in the sand with a twig. Then Zagros wrote the English translations under them: *sky, cloud, tree.* The twins giggled and buzzed and came up with more words they wanted translated. *Horsefly. Cow pie. Wart.*

"Mind if I-I follow along?" Moojie asked Babylonia.

She said nothing. She just continued to scribble peculiar wedges, arrows, zigzags, and lines, beautiful lines. Cuss words would be beautiful coming out of her hands.

Moojie tried to keep out of her way. He didn't want her to look closely at him—and yet, he did. He didn't like the way he looked—his stiff body was changing and he felt stupid and clumsy and in-between. He wanted to be invisible. If only he could watch her without being seen. He liked the way she tossed her loose braid over one shoulder. And when she looked at him, he felt something new and unsettling. Ordinarily, there had been one of three reactions when Moojie made new acquaintances: pity, mocking, or not-so-mild curiosity. He expected people to laugh at him, like the school children had in the past. His mother once took him to visit San Miguel's one-room schoolhouse. As he stood in the doorway on his crutches, the children stopped immediately and gaped at him as if he had just stepped out of a flying saucer. "Y-you can call me kind sir," he had said. Everyone broke into laughter, including the teacher. Moojie laughed, too, and then he realized no one else was walking with crutches. His mother took him home, and they never went back. At the creek that day, he chuckled to himself, imagining what that teacher might say if she knew the so-called Hostiles were not only reminding him to brush his teeth, but teaching him how to read and write—and make paper!

More and more the clan allowed Moojie to partake of their days. His initiative was spurred on by the irresistible allure of Babylonia. One day, kneeling next to her at the creek, Moojie drew a heart in the sand and wrote *love* under it. He knew he shouldn't have done it, but she was next to him and he had lost all sense of reason. She looked mildly annoyed. He expected her to laugh at him. *Stupid. I'm so stupid.* But something passed between them, an unmistakable something. Moojie wondered if she felt it, too. "Girls are like cats," his mother had once told him. "When you rush after them, they run off. Someday you'll have manly stirrings. You mustn't trust them. Your body will lie to you, but your heart will not."

What a dreadful thing—to hope for.

"Peculiar," Babylonia grinned. Moojie expected as much. "Your language," she said, "it is very peculiar. You have noses that run, feet that smell, and you keep an eye out." She chuckled. Her laughter was like jingle bells. Like flower petals and a sock in the eye.

"Roses are red," Moojie said, wanting to hear her laugh again. "Violets are blue, sugar is sweet and so are you ...."

"See?" she said.

"Wait, wait ... roses are blue, violets are red, sugar is lumpy, and so is your head!"

She sort of smirked. Maybe it was a giggle. Maybe.

"You must write a lot," Moojie said to Babylonia, in regard to the dried fig paper Zagros was collecting.

"Yes, we write, and we do other things." There was a tone in her voice that Moojie couldn't define. Something grave. Ominous. For some reason, it made him yearn for the village, for home. For his father.

"I-it'll be a miracle if my father ever comes back," he said.

"I believe in miracles," Babylonia said.

Moojie wanted to take her hand. But he didn't dare. She was far too pretty and far too smart to go for the likes of him. He was wishing things would go along forever like this, meeting the clan at the creek, or in the woods, learning about their language and their odd ways. But that afternoon, there arose a clamor of trills and chirps from upstream, and he was reminded of the risk he was taking.

"The signal!" Babylonia cried.

Without hesitation, she, Zagros, and the children snapped to their feet, gathered the fig paper, and headed into the shrubbery, dragging sprays of lilac over their footsteps.

Pappy came beating down the path. Having not seen or heard the wagon crossing the bridge, Moojie was petrified. Pappy took a long, down-the-nose look at Moojie, who had rushed to the water, trying to look busy by pounding a strap of bark.

"Boy, what in the name of cuttlefish are you doing?" Pappy asked.

The summer heat pressed down upon Moojie's head. "Well," he said, as if in all earnestness, "you've heard of Atlantis, right? Sir?" He kept his voice to an even keel so as not to betray another bamboozling.

"What in the—?" Pappy asked.

"Fig bark, Sir. It makes paper. Y-you strip it off the tree, you soak it, and then you beat it to a pulp, l-like so." He demonstrated, splashing water into Pappy's face. "It dries, Sir. In the sun."

"What in Sam Hill you need paper for, boy?"

"Mother Teagardin said t-to prepare for the end times. Paper will be in short supply."

"That's why they don't allow guns in the village," Pappy said looking around. "Hm. Since you're so smart, I don't imagine I need to remind you what mountain lions like to eat: soft, ripe teenagers."

This comment, of course, was meant to frighten Moojie.

But it was too late. He was bound by the governance of his heart to promise his loyalty to the clan. Cougars or not.

That night, in the dark, dusty bedroom, only Phineas was sleeping. Moojie gazed out the window at the bough of stars. *Love.* It was still a mystery to him. In a way, he felt that he was just starting to live.

A dark shadow appeared outside his window, eclipsing the moon. Zagros? There was tapping on the glass pane. Moojie opened the window. All he could see was a vague, long-haired ghost. The smell was unmistakable though. Onions. "Salam," said a voice, hissing and serpent-like.

Moojie was startled. He tried to close the window, but the thing stopped him.

"Tut, tut. I am a friend of the cave dwellers. I am here to help you," said the somewhat familiar male voice.

"What?" Moojie asked.

"That is, of course, if you could explain to me as to why you would settle for a measly little tribe when you can have your own kingdom?"

"Um, what?" Moojie asked.

"I know about you, your past lives. Hail, Lord Sacker!"

"Who are you?" Moojie asked, unable to identify the voice.

"We of the ruling class no longer need resort to such means. To rule your own kingdom comes easier these days."

"What do you want?"

"Hark ye! Every great man must learn to control his destiny. Ladyship says you are gifted. She favors you. I say, why settle for being her little pet when you could have all the land and gold and servants you want? All of these things I can help you get, for you see, I am favored as well."

"I-I don't want gold or servants."

The shadow's head twisted in an unusual manner and seemed to swell in size. "You are lying," he hissed.

"We're done now," Moojie said, reaching for the window. Again, the visitor stopped him from closing it.

"Do not cross me. Stay away from the Akil-Nuri."

Moojie jerked on the window, but the ghostly presence pulled it open wide, reached inside the room with a telescoping, chewing-gum arm, stretching in and down, and grabbed Phineas off the cot by the scruff of his neck. Phineas let out a spine-tingling yowl. Moojie took a swipe at the arm and missed as his cat was hoisted right out the window.

"I do so like cats," said the presence, dangling Phineas like an old purse. "You, on the contrary, I do not like. I do not trust you." He had a glowing orange aura that increased in brightness until it burst and the stranger disappeared into thin air. Phineas came flying back through the window, knocking Moojie backward off the cot and onto the floor with a resounding *thump!*

Pappy came like gunfire into the bedroom, lamp held high, Millie-Mae barking behind him. "Holy claptrap, what are you up to?"

In the dim light, it looked like Pappy was wearing a shirt, but he wasn't. His face and hands were suntanned, but he was pale from the neck down, pale as chalk rock, as if the sun had painted him brown then scraped off a shirt. Kind of like the walls of Moojie's room. New brown. Old white.

Moojie groped the cot, lifting himself up. "I'm no sacker," he said.

Pappy looked outside, took a sniff, and closed the window. "Cougar. I smell cougar. Best keep the window shut." He opened his big hand on top of Moojie's head, tilting his face upward. "I realize you're a bit slow," he said. "Don't worry about it. You got potentiality. I've got plans for you."

The midnight marauder's act of dissuasion didn't put off Moojie. He was just as eager to spend time with Babylonia and the clan as ever. As usual, he returned the next day to the creek for language lessons. With the youngers, he repeated and copied the ciphers of their language, finding it ever so much easier to put a twig to sand than pencil to paper. He copied the English translations as well, pretending that he already knew them.

"W-what's your word for *coin trick*?" he asked Babylonia.

"Show off," she hissed.

Moojie's spirit of curiosity had bloomed in a short time, pushing him forward at a feverish pace. He didn't know yet what to make of the clan's mentions of a distant homeland, or references to "the loved ones" and "the ancient ways." But he asked questions whenever he could.

"A-and the white spots," Moojie asked Babylonia, "what are they made of? What are they for?"

"Ground chalk rock and honey," she said. "For the opening of the mind and the seeing of wonders."

"And they help us to see each other in the dark,"

Manish said. He rubbed his spot and put some paste on Moojie's forehead. Moojie looked at his reflection in the creek. It was a small thing, but it gave him hope.

Suddenly, Sarru'kan appeared, jumping behind Moojie and knocking him off balance.

"Harken! A new word for you," Sarru'kan said. "*Atlak.* Translation: leave." His hands were tight fists, his eyes sparking.

"I'm not here t-to make trouble," Moojie said. He recognized the voice. It was Sarru'kan who had paid him a ghoulish visit in the night, outside his window.

"My lord," Zagros said to Moojie, "why not come back tomorrow and we will fish in the creek."

"You are out of your league, Claw Hand," Sarru'kan said to Moojie. "You see, worldlings fall into three groups: those who come down the ages, bearing gifts and superior blood strands, such as yours truly; those bearing gifts and lacking magic strands; and then there are those pitiful fools who lack magic strands and esoteric gifts altogether. Which one are you? Easy to tell by your looks. Oriental eyes, European hair—a mongrel …."

"Right," Moojie said, not really listening.

"Alas, some are born with magic, and some are not," Sarru'kan said. He opened his hand, extended it palm up, half-closed his eyes, and fell into sort of a trance. The youngers crowded around him excitedly, expectantly. He closed his hand and reopened it, and an ancient-looking coin came right out of his palm. He tossed it into the air and the children scrambled after it gleefully.

Ninti and an older man named Imi'tittu marched across the sand directly to Sarru'kan.

"Need I remind you this sort of display is strictly against The Code?" Ninti said.

"He is a pest," Sarru'kan said, looking at Moojie.

"A bitter grudge grows bitter fruit," a chubby-cheeked

woman named Kisha said.

"He is interfering with the lessons," Sarru'kan said.

"Interfering?" Ninti looked surprised.

"He wants to steal our language," Sarru'kan said.

"Indeed?" Ninti looked at Moojie. "Very well, then he is welcome to attend the lessons anytime he chooses."

Zagros and Babylonia exchanged glances.

Zagros put an arm around Moojie and escorted him away from the group, toward the cabin. "We love Ladyship the way one loves and fears a strict parent, however …."

"The coin," Moojie said. "How'd he do that?"

"As a rule," Zagros said, "we do not practice sorcery."

Moojie started up the trail alone, but turned back to eavesdrop from behind a shrub.

"Sarru is only being protective," Ninti said to Kisha. "It is a great burden. I find this admirable."

"Have you not seen how he treats Lord Littleman, who also bears a great burden?" Kisha asked.

"Sarru'kan knows to be cautious with worldlings," Ninti said.

"Forgive me, Ladyship. But if you ask me, Sarru'kan appears more like a worldling every day. Perhaps he has trodden too long upon the earth. Perhaps you ought to consider teaching Lord L—"

"I am a prophet," she said, "not a ringmaster."

"There are worse things than being untrained."

"Such as?"

"Have you not noticed something about Lord Littleman?"

"I am confident you will tell me."

"Clearly, he cares about us. And you know as well as I do that he is gifted. Would he not make a good wayshower?"

"He is no warrior."

"Sarru'kan is no prophet."

"Lord Littleman has yet to prove himself."

"Forgive my impertinence, Ladyship. I dare say at times I suspect Sarru'kan's motives for rejoining us were not entirely pure; that is to say, I fear his soul has not yet surpassed the rotten fruits of his former self who bore a religious fascination with his own navel. What I mean to say is, with the humblest of hearts, your star pupil has the sensitivity of a dung beetle."

Ladyship left in a huff.

Kisha seemed to know Moojie was eavesdropping since she parted the shrub and looked directly at him. "To whit, my dear lord, pride has no better cure than a mirror. Whosoever shall swear by our friendship, swears by The Code, and by all things therein. Betrayal could prove fatal."

The twins ran up the trail past Moojie, pointing twigs at objects as if they were magic wands. "Praise the light!" Manish chimed. Shar zapped the wild lilac, saying, "You are light!" in French, the language Moojie's mother spoke.

"Praise the light that makes wind," Manish said, pointing the stick at his belly. The twins buckled over with laughter. They ran back down to the creek and doused the olders, the handsome ones, the sky, the creek, a ladybug. "Praise the spirit of love! I see your light! All is light!" They said it in many languages, and after a while they were quiet.

Not so strange to see boys playing with sticks, thought Moojie, and yet the twins were acting as though they had read *The Waltzing Lobster*. "*The universe is light,*" his mother had read aloud to him, time and again. But Manish and Shar couldn't have learned this from a book because they didn't have any books. As far as Moojie knew, they had never studied atoms or electrons. How did they know this?

They crept up from behind, doused him with light,

and then buzzed off like punch-drunk honeybees. Surprised, Moojie stepped back. A bright spot appeared in his field of vision, a most annoying spot that he tried to blink away. He was nearly blind and could hardly see his way up the trail. Soon enough the light faded from white to gold to pink and then, like an eclipsed sun, disappeared altogether; just when he could see again, the twins sneaked up and zapped him once more. "*C'est tout la lumière!*" Everything is light!

And Moojie believed they were saints.

Chapter 9

Of mending fences and holding one's own

At the crack of dawn, Pappy and McTavish were busy in the kitchen, whisking eggs and slicing green tomatoes. Keeping his bedroom door ajar, Moojie eavesdropped on their conversation.

"They're a nuisance, I tell you," Pappy said.

"Jeez, one of the breeding does disappeared last week," McTavish said. "A sure sign."

"By my honor, which is bright and unsullied," Pappy said, "I'll see an end to that cat."

After the men left to make the milk and egg deliveries, Moojie set out to warn the clan. He rode Hocus Pocus to the creek, to the woods, and partway up the trail to El Serrat. They were nowhere to be found.

Pappy and McTavish came back early that afternoon and went straight to the rifle cabinet. Millie-Mae was wound up, whining, tail flashing, scratching at the door to get out.

"Not this time," Pappy said to her.

"Are you meaning t-to kill the cougar?" Moojie asked.

"Boy, I've been after that cat since before you were born."

"This is her land, too," Moojie said.

Pappy looked at him like he was speaking Chinese. He took the shotgun and gave McTavish the .38. Pappy mounted Hocus Pocus, tipped his sombrero at Moojie on the porch and the men rode across the field toward El Serrat. McTavish followed suit on his burro, his over-long, hanging legs giving the impression of a bestraddled orb weaver.

As soon as they reached the foothills, Moojie let Millie-Mae out of the cabin and she raced to catch up with Pappy, barking out a warning. Moojie blew the kazoo, loud and long. He banged the garbage can with a trowel. He turned the shiny lid into the sun to flash a light signal to the clan. He went to get Aggie the burro, hoping to ride up behind the men and create some kind of emergency story, but he couldn't even mount the old boy. When he tapped Aggie's legs, and told him to lower down like Hocus did, the burro only stood there, stiff-legged and dull-eyed.

Crazy with worry that Pappy would catch the clan unawares, Moojie couldn't think of what else to do but pray.

Pappy and McTavish came back before sundown, frazzled and hot and frothing at the mouth.

"Dagnabbit!" Pappy said to Moojie who was waiting on the porch. "I been up to that cave more than a dozen times. It's always been right there, at the third bench, behind the wall of bamboo, and I tell you, it's just up and disappeared. Ain't nothin' left but a lump o' granite to stop a train. Vanished! Poof!"

"No cougar, sir?" Moojie asked, concealing his delight.

"Gone," Pappy said, dismounting.

"He's right," McTavish said. "The bloody cave's gone. Caved in or something."

Pappy clunked up the stairs and along the porch, tripped on Moojie's crutch, and dropped to the platform with a terrible, bony *Clunk!* "Geez, boy!" he howled. "Outta my way!"

After supper, Moojie excused himself and went to bed, quietly triumphant. Pappy and McTavish carried on for hours drinking and arguing as usual, consuming enough bug juice to pickle a cow. The rooster was crowing when Moojie got out of bed grumbling about grownups who steal people's dreams and, unable to find his crutches in the dark, he crawled into the kitchen.

"Isn't there something y-you can agree on?" he asked, exasperated.

Eyes heavy-lidded and pink-rimmed, the men looked up to the ceiling, paused a minute, then simultaneously raised their shot glasses. "Women!" they said, flapping and cawing like a pair of crows.

Pappy wound up the gramophone and played his one and only record: Caruso.

"See, boy," he said, "real women are a thing of the past. None to be found. I thought your grandma was real, but she's just like all the modern dames: bossy and stubborn as hammered iron. You go after love thinkin' you'll get hitched. And to keep hitched, a man and a woman must love each other. But then you start bein' miserable. Therefore, to stay in love you must be miserable. But being alone makes you miserable, too. Therefore, you ain't gonna know a thing about love till you're alone." He looked at McTavish. "You may write that down."

"Where I'm from," McTavish said, "a good woman

knows the front from the back end of a rifle. She eats her share of haggis and knows how to make a decent *coup of tay*."

Pappy said, "Women today have only two faults: what they say and what they do." Oh, that was funny. The men laughed like whistling teakettles. Moojie crawled back into his cot and made like a hedgehog curling up and playing dead.

After McTavish left, Pappy took up his ukulele and brayed along with Caruso. There was a knife's edge in his voice that gave Moojie the creeps. He threw his crutches out the window and climbed outside, he and Phineas. They went to the barn, lay together on a fresh pile of straw that smelled like sunlight, and waited—quietly, invisibly, while Pappy crashed around inside the cabin.

"I miss Mamma," Moojie said to Phineas, who was kneading Moojie's chest with his paws. "I-I miss her garden and her kitchen. I wish I could tell her about Ninti and the others." He sighed, knowing the purring Phineas couldn't hear a word he had said.

Around midday, Pappy loaded the buckboard with tools and wooden planks and drove Moojie out to the west field. Madness drew his face taut across his skull as he trod back and forth, wagon to fence, fence to wagon, hauling tools, boards, and a posthole digger.

"Stand aside, boy!" he said. "Mind your toes."

A few sections down, nailed to the fence, a hand-painted sign read: TRESSPASSERS WILL BE NEUTERED.

While Moojie stood watching his grandfather, he noticed something move just a ways off in the grass, heading east. It was the cougar, Ninti's cougar, Anahita!

Going at the posthole with a vengeance, Pappy didn't seem to see a thing.

Millie-Mae looked in the big cat's direction and growled.

"What is it, girl?" Pappy asked. He dropped the post digger, spun about, and set a hand on his sheathed hunting knife.

Moojie pointed to Elsie the cow and Odds and Ends in the west field. "Just the cows, Sir."

Upon seeing the cows, Pappy volleyed the knife into the fence post. "Good grief."

"Yep," Moojie said, eyes scouring, hands wringing. He had a sickly premonition.

"You see, a man's got to defend his own," Pappy said. "It's the privilege of freedom. And freedom ain't gonna be doled out by no President Tom, Dick, or Harry. Freedom means holdin' your own, boy." He paused to take a gulp from the canteen and then lowered it slowly while looking eastward. Then he straightened bolt upright, plucked the knife out of the post, and said, "Get the gun."

Anahita moved southeast, somewhat concealed behind a shallow berm.

Moojie's heart thumped hard as a fist against a door. On the buckboard, the rifle's brass hardware glinted in the sunlight. As Moojie struggled to lift a foot onto the running board, Pappy blew past him, seized the rifle, snapped it open, loaded it, clacked it shut, and took aim. Moojie reached out for the weapon as it fired. A shot cracked through the valley and Millie-Mae took off toward the berm.

"Blast you, boy!" shouted Pappy. "What the devil—?" He took Moojie by the waist of his trousers and the back of his collar, and tossed him onto the buckboard, jumped onto the seat, whistled, snapped the reins, and turned Aggie in the direction of the berm.

When they arrived, Millie-Mae was growling and whining, cautiously circling the fallen cougar, Anahita.

"There, boy," Pappy said to Moojie, "is the price of freedom."

From the buckboard, Moojie could see the gunshot wound above Anahita's half-open eye. Hunched over, clutching his thighs, he trembled uncontrollably, the terrible ringing of gunshot in his ears. He was a mess of emotions. He wanted to run, to flee into the mountains and never turn back, but his legs were rigid as wooden bats. Wooden bats belonged to trees, and trees didn't run.

Pappy threw the cougar into the buckboard and drove to the creek. He dragged the body to the water, Millie-Mae whining and yelping as it floated downstream toward the Pacific Ocean.

Moojie wanted his mother. He wanted his father. Where was Ninti? He wanted to pick up the rifle, reload it, and shoot something.

That warm night of olden days, as cricket songs scraped at his bedroom window, Moojie dreamed of warriors fighting with deer antlers, of berry brambles strangling rabbits, of moldy grapes floating in lemonade, and squash blossom butterflies gorging themselves on the blood of a dead cougar. He awoke several times and prayed to the angels, to the saints, to the stars—to anything and everything in the seen and unseen worlds—to help him escape the fraying edges of the man he called *Sir*.

Chapter 10

More things related to the price of freedom,
which one who scours and minds fields
will attentively learn

Besieged with worry about what Pappy might do in retaliation for his trying to stop him from shooting the cougar, Moojie got up the next morning, lit the wood stove, made coffee, and emptied the icebox tray. He polished Pappy's boots and left them outside his bedroom door. He went out and fed the critters, flew the pigeons, mended a fence, repaired the chicken hutch, and tallowed the buckboard axles. He worked harder than ever, mucking the stalls, raking the yard, cleaning the pigeon loft—spic and span.

There was no time to consider his auspicious destiny, his quest, or his gift, about which he knew little. But at night his nose itched and his feet twitched, and he hoped with all his heart that Ninti was right: that if he made himself useful, Pappy would keep him at St. Isidore's and not send him away, just long enough so that he could get the clan to welcome him as one of their own.

St. Isidore's Fainting Goat Dairy had twenty-nine goats, pygmies, all variations of black and brown and white. "Small as dogs and tough as jerky," Pappy always said.

Pearl and Rainbow, the breeding does, were fainters. Rufus, the alpha goat, strutted around the yard, a wiry sultan mating with his woozy harem as he saw fit. He wasn't a fainter, but he had his own problems: knees like rusty hinges.

Something about Rufus aggravated Moojie.

Pappy had been an egg man long before St. Isidore's got its name, but when McTavish showed up with Rufus, everything changed. Rufus' front legs were deformed because of overgrown hooves, and he was forced to bungle about on bent knees with callouses like soccer pads. Pappy felt such pity for the goat that he nursed him back to standing. Other ranchers started giving him their oddball goats, mostly fainters, who had a strange condition that caused them to roll over and freeze up stiff-legged when afraid or excited.

"They even faint at the sight of supper," Pappy told Moojie. "Now that's what I call gratitude."

Moojie would have told Ninti about the cougar, but he was afraid she might hold him complicit somehow. He kept to the chores, hoping and praying to avoid her. Things were getting out of hand. He withdrew to the growing patch. Surrounded by a saggy fence, this square of earth made a decent sanctuary. He often lay there amid the carrots, kale, rocket, squash and berry brambles, while fruit flies and butterflies floated up through the vines and blinked in the sunlight. While the air smelled bittersweet with tomatoes and squash blossoms and berries. If the clan ever crossed the field on their way to the creek, he ducked down to avoid them. Once Pappy came home and found him asleep in the corn rows.

"It's a mystery to me how the stuff keeps growin'," Pappy said. "Could be an underground spring, I don't know. I tell you, I know diddly about it, but the food keeps comin'. Anyhow, it keeps the green grocer happy."

A week passed, and Moojie's lonely, chore-filled days passed like a ship through sand. In the growing patch, crows pecked at dry cornhusks. Blackberries oozed purple juice and crazed horseflies swooped over squash zombies. In the wretched heat, the fields had dried to salt, all of life seeming to come to a halt. No more swaying grass. No gladsome trees. No musical birds.

It felt like an eternity since Papa's hand had guided Moojie into the realm of Pappy's blue blazing eyes, into the land of poisonous shrubs and prickly plants and suffocating nights. Had his father simply forgotten him? As far as Moojie was concerned, Pappy hardly knew anything about family, or anything about anything. He plunged into a sullen, lethargic state. He refused to eat. Pappy failed to stir up the slightest bit of enthusiasm in him and complained bitterly when trays of food delivered to Moojie's bedroom went untouched. Tension between them mounted with every meal, and following a culmination of several days, Pappy realized the magnitude of the problem.

"Reckon you got worms, boy."

Being an expert in animal husbandry, Pappy knew what to do.

He put a bowl of curdled goat milk before Moojie.

"I'm not eating that," Moojie said.

"Hold your taters, boy. You don't even know what it

is."

"It's goat barf."

Pappy frapped Moojie on the head with a spoon and hovered over him until he ate every sour, curdled drop, which took nearly three hours.

Meanwhile, at night Pappy often crept through the cabin in socked feet, rolling and lighting cigarettes, sipping a peculiar tea. It wasn't English or Irish tea, but a concoction of unholy ingredients that polluted the cabin with a witch's haze, smelling of bats and beetles and dead snakes. Pappy soaked his hands in hot water, and rubbed them with King of Pain Relief Liniment. He never complained about his back, but Moojie knew it bothered him by the way he listed forward, and pumped his lower back with his fist. When Moojie offered to say a prayer, Pappy said not to waste his breath. Moojie decided that it wouldn't kill him to help out a little longer before running away. Following a cold, restless night, Pappy entered Moojie's bedroom with a spirit lamp that the groggy Moojie mistook for an otherworldly visitation.

"Up and at 'em, boy! Up and at 'em!" Pappy rung out.

In the kitchen, Moojie found Pappy flitting about, lighting the cast iron stove, filling the kettle, moving as if wound too tight. "Honeymoon's over," Pappy said. Moojie fixated on the match rolling between his grandfather's yellow teeth. "Listen, boy. Except for your mamma, I've been deprived of my own children. When Nana Finnegan took off, she took them with her—all eleven of 'em, seven girls, four boys. Your mamma sought me out when you were pretty young. She wanted you to have a grandfather. I know a thing or two about boys needing a firm hand. I'd like to keep you around. Now I can be soft as an apricot or I can bite like a snake. I don't like that about myself, but it's the way I am. I'll say this only once: STAY AWAY FROM THE HOSTILES. Should you disobey me, I will hog-tie you and pack you off faster than green grass through a goose."

Despite his grandfather's threats, Moojie took a peculiar comfort in hearing this. Now that Pappy had issued a willingness to let him stay, his worries were reduced by half. He watched from the bathroom doorway as his grandfather combed his mustache.

"This will be my finest hour," Pappy said to the face in the mirror.

He poured his whiskey down the kitchen sink, tidied the cabin and picked a bouquet of wildflowers for the kitchen table, at which Millie-Mae growled.

"Now, let's get you workin' proper," Pappy said to Moojie.

What?

After fried eggs and hominy, Pappy met McTavish in the yard, and they went to work measuring and sawing wooden boards, as always, to a symphony of bickering.

"It's a hare-brained idea," McTavish said to Pappy, shaking his head. "And it's dangerous."

While the men were occupied, Moojie planned to sneak out and look for his friends. He slipped behind the barn and waved a carrot at Hocus Pocus. He got on and rode her behind the cabin, hoping to get into the woods before the men noticed, but then from the other side of the cabin, his grandfather whistled and shouted, "Where you headin', boy?" It was like he had eyes everywhere.

"I'm bored," Moojie said, riding into the yard. "Thought I'd take a ride."

Pappy swabbed his forehead with a bandana and grimaced. "You get back here, or I'll fry your flanks for supper."

Red was gathering at the horizon before the men were done. At long last: a sawhorse with chopped-down legs and metal brackets holding a rusty old bicycle off the ground, an exercise bike.

"I don't like it," McTavish said. "Don't like it at all." The sunset threw pink on the whites of his eyes and teeth.

"A boy becomes a man when he can ride a bike," Pappy said.

"And all this time I thought a boy became a man when he started wearing skivvies under his kilt," said McTavish.

Moojie was supposed to get onto the bicycle, McTavish to one side, telling him to take hold of the handlebars, Pappy on the other, telling him to swing a leg over the frame.

"Are you blind?" McTavish said to Pappy. "Can't you see the lad can't lift his leg?"

While Moojie clung half-on and half-off the bike, a fresh round of bickering started.

"And who are you, Don Quixote, telling a horseman of my caliber what to do!" McTavish said.

"Up and over, boy. Up and over," Pappy said. Moojie gave a hop, planted his rear sideways on the saddle and, clinging to the handlebars, tried to bend and lift a leg to the opposite side. He slipped and McTavish caught him in a fall.

"Jeez, you'll kill the lad!" McTavish said.

"Eh, shut your trap you bleedin' beetroot," Pappy said. "Up up up."

"Anyone's got the right to be a lackwit, but you abuse the privilege," said McTavish.

"Dazzling wisdom. What's that, straight from Scotland yard? Come on, boy. Take the handlebars, and I'll give you a lift. On three."

At last, Moojie was on the saddle. Pappy and McTavish

tied his feet to the pedals with their bandanas and helped get his legs pumping. Soon Moojie got the hang of it and started pedaling on his own, a bit jerky on the up and down, but on his own, nonetheless.

Pappy and McTavish stood watching, arms crossed.

"You see? He can handle a bike as well as the next man," Pappy said proudly. "There may be hope for him yet."

"Even so, your mother shoved your face in the dough to make gorilla biscuits," McTavish said.

"Hillbilly."

"Leprechaun."

"Gaw," Moojie said, feeling like a circus monkey. "Get me off this thing!"

"Think of your mother. Do it for your mother," Pappy said.

So every day Moojie pedaled. Pappy started him off with a three-minute hourglass, and switched to longer times as they went. Under the old olive tree, amid the weeds and leaves and manure, facing the sprawling empty fields, Moojie pedaled and pedaled. His bottom sliding partway off the saddle, he pedaled some more. Like dry pistons, his legs rose and fell without grace. He pedaled until he shook with fatigue, until his legs could hardly carry him to the cabin. "One day, father of mine," he said aloud, "I'm gonna find you and kick your butt." Zagros, hiding in a nearby tree, chucked olives at him, and the pigeons shrieked with merriment.

Driven to the point of madness to rehabilitate Moojie, Pappy made out a *Daily Log* and pinned it to the cupboard, checking off the days and noting his times. He cracked Moojie's joints and stretched his legs and hounded him without cease. "Pick up your feet! Apes drag their feet! Enunciate! Purse those lips! Use that south paw!"

Moojie secretly tried standing on his own. But he couldn't. He stretched and kicked and pushed and pedaled, fueled in part by the fantasy of cycling away from this loony place where cowboy coffee and gunpowder separated the men from the boys, where one ate from jars, and the bathroom was a "bog," and eggs were "bum nuts." Where a wake-up call was a wooden match to a boot.

Chapter 11

Brotherhood of the barstool, socked feet, and the end of the world

Except for the prevailing earthquakes, which had over time buried the cultural ambitions of early explorers, gold hunters, and escaped convicts; and except for the Hostiles torching the village three decades before, San Miguel de las Gaviotas was quite orderly. One church. One religion. Every year opened with a potluck celebration of the Circumcision of Our Lord, and closed with an elaborate Christmas pageant, which involved fiddles, penny whistles, a staged nativity program, and a lot of hard cider.

And then there was Tilly's Tavern.

The day Moojie rode into the village with Pappy and McTavish, it was foggy as usual. Autumn had arrived, but it could have been spring or winter. With hardly a glimmer of sun, the long, flat light cancelled out the seasons. Early memories poured through Moojie's mind: his mother strolling him in the pram, merchants popping outdoors to sweep doormats like cuckoo clock figurines, picnics in the park. His heart puckered with yearning for the past.

Along Flum Street the wagon rolled, past old store-fronts and faded awnings. Past wood battens and high gables. Past hidden courtyards, and blind arches, and the tall, thin minaret at San Miguel Park whose origins remain a mystery to this day. High above the Town Hall, the astronomical clock chimed "Irish Eyes," and its black moon and *fleur-de-lys* hands pointed to four o'clock.

"No, he ain't back yet," Pappy said when Moojie asked about his father.

Tilly's, a dank, old alehouse, was a manly place, famous for local gossip, homemade ginger beer, and scorpion pepper chicken wings. The ceiling was carved, the floor black-and-white-checkered. Green velvet curtains. The pair of great, shiny, brown eyeballs of a stuffed moose-head over the bar followed Moojie as he clopped in behind McTavish and Pappy. Brimming with immigrants, it was a place where fisherman could wet their whistles, talk politics, nets, abalone knives, and form alliances against Oriental immigrants undercutting the labor unions at the canneries.

Moojie flumped past the tables, searching for a familiar face in the crowd, searching for any flimsy connection to the past.

"*Che peccato,* he's the one they found in the bucket," said one man.

"Bad stars, the boy's got bad stars," said another.

Moojie sat in a corner booth with sarsaparilla. Pappy and McTavish hopped to the crowded bar to see the barkeep's new Firefoam fire extinguisher, then joined Mayor Bingo and Father Grabbe in a private conversation, keeping Moojie out of the circle of knowing.

The man at the next table said to Moojie, "I knew

your mother. Fine woman. Your father run off, didn't he? Pity."

The mail courier drove his newfangled motorbike straight into the tavern, mustache swept back, cape flapping in the wind, handed Pappy a letter, threw back a swig of liquor, then turned around and zipped out.

Moojie sat upright, heart pattering. Could it be a letter from his father?

Pappy opened it and belched. "That old gasbag," he said. "*Are you prevaricating?* she asks. Ha! I bet she don't even know the meanin' of the word."

Mindful now in the green booth, Moojie was keenly aware that he didn't fit in. If anyone asked him, he would say he came from the land of Not Belonging. Where had all the angels gone? He couldn't see them anymore. It was too dark. He couldn't hear them. It was too noisy amid the grownup laughter and scuffling feet. Pappy and McTavish whispered and nodded, and made jokes easily, and the villagers laughed and cursed the fog, cursed their empty glasses, and laughed some more.

Pappy came to the table with another soda, and he, McTavish, and the mayor slid into the booth on either side of Moojie.

"Well, sonny," said Mayor Bingo, "how do you like living at the dairy?"

"I'm not living there, ma'am. I-I'm just visiting."

McTavish and Pappy looked sidelong at each other.

"I hear old gramps fries a mean egg," the mayor said, and winked.

"Well," Moojie said, "he could use a woman in the house."

Pappy was clearly taken aback and the mayor lost the wind in her lungs. "Why you're a plucky one, a chip off the old gramps!" she said.

"The letter, Sir," Moojie said to Pappy, "who's it from?"

"Eh," Pappy heaved a great sigh. "Ain't nothin' gets past you, does it? It's that blasted aunt of yours." He paused to drink his whiskey, but before the glass reached his lips, the floor jerked under the table, the walls creaked, and Moojie's soda toppled to the floor. A few villagers dropped under tables for cover, some covered their heads. Most just sat tight and held onto their drinks, while the barkeep made frantic swoops to capture glasses shimmying off the shelves.

"Eeeha! Third quake this month!" Pappy crowed.

When the quake stopped everyone went on with their merrymaking except Father Grabbe, who approached the green booth. "Dear moppets, don't you see? Lucifer *is* awakening the dead. It's the curse of the Hostiles."

"Bless Mrs. McClarty, good father," McTavish laughed. "It was just a wee tremblor. You'd think we ran out of milk."

"The seas are going to rise," the priest went on. "And the Day of Tribulation will follow."

With rapt attention, everyone gathered round to listen to the priest's theory, which was based upon an evil curse that followed the sainted Brother Juan's campaign to help the native peoples escape the ignorance of their religion and language, and his saintly sacrifices to help them better themselves by building the chapel and learning the rosary while enjoying the hospitality of the jailhouse.

McTavish sniggled.

"Go ahead and laugh," said the priest. "It's in the Bible. All are called, but few have boats."

"Ahem," Moojie said, recalling what Ninti had told him about the foreordained pandemonium. "It's in th- the stars. The big one *is* coming, just like it did a long time ago, only this time the village is doomed." His face felt hot.

"Here we go again," Pappy said. "He don't know how

to add two and two, but he's Galileo. Sit up, boy. You're slouchin'."

Mayor Bingo's lips through her glass looked like a red fish. "Tell me," she said to Moojie, "what you mean by 'the village is doomed.'"

It delighted Moojie to make this important announcement. "Yep. It's going t-to cool off around here. Mars will shine in the sky, and the moon will wax red, a-and roughly, the village is going to be knocked t-to hell and gone."

The grownups went silent.

"I-if you want to save yourselves," Moojie went on, "you must know where your shovel is." After all, that's what Ninti had said.

The grownups whipped into a fracas of laughter and the mayor gave Moojie a sympathetic pat on the head. "You mustn't read fairy tales, sonny. They cause nightmares."

Dismayed by the reactions, Moojie withdrew into himself, trying to imagine what Odysseus would do if he were present. As the night wore on, the villagers grew more and more boisterous, belching and snorting and stacking glasses. Pappy stood and held up his glass. "A hundred-dollar reward for every Hostile you can round up from my hills!" This got everyone's attention. It was no secret that times had been hard and labor cheap. The offer nearly caused a riot as people fell over each other to sign on.

That night, following a wild season of earthquakes, and guided by starlight, Moojie drove the wagon back to St. Isidore's, plugging his ears as Pappy and McTavish sang, "*Gory, gory, what a hell of a way to die. Gory, gory, what a hell of a way to die.*" Exhausted, he rested his head upon McTavish's shoulder, fighting the urge to sleep.

"Poor lad," McTavish said. "Is there nothing to be done? He needs a woman's touch."

"What the boy needs is discipline. Two days and a wake up. He can learn to run the dairy. I'm proof that it don't take any brains. If not, there's a place up north that'll take him."

That night Moojie was restless with worry that he wouldn't have time to prove himself worthy to the Light-Eaters. Unable to sleep, he crawled out to the living room. McTavish was snoring on the sofa with Millie-Mae's head on his chest, Pappy was in his winged chair mumbling to himself.

"Can't sleep, sir," Moojie said.

"Eh, go back to bed and count backwards. You can count backwards, can't you?"

"What about the posse?"

"Don't talk back."

"What if you get hurt? And the earthquake—"

"Nothin's gonna happen out here," Pappy said. "No earthquakes, no hurricanes, no end of the world. Out here pigeons fly, goats maa, cows moo, grass grows." He started to nod off with a cigarette burning between his fingers. Moojie took it and put it out.

"The Hostiles—" Moojie began.

"Best prepare to meet their doom," Pappy finished.

"Well, what i-if the Hostiles aren't even hostile? I mean, what if they're something else?"

Pappy's eyes popped open. "Listen, boy. I was at Pea Ridge. I seen evil you cannot imagine. I seen Hostiles whackin' off body parts and takin' them home for souvenirs. You see, them and the Negroes have no fear. They got some kind of mojo. Been known to summon the Earth to wreak death and destruction upon the whites. They're without souls. Indians and Negroes. No loyalty." His tone of voice had risen three octaves.

"But the Indians a-and the Negroes are free now, Sir," Moojie said.

"What the dickens do you know about it?"

"President Lincoln. H-his own father got killed by Indians. A-and he said they were free, free as anybody. President Lincoln said so."

Pappy sniffed and closed his eyes again. Soon he was snoring.

Moojie sat thinking about the Civil War, thinking about fear and hatred and what it can do to people. The native tribes and the Negroes had been driven off their homeland like a pestilence. Whether or not the ones in the hills were Hostiles, or Akil-Nuri, or cannibals, no one had so much as waved a fork in his direction. It was a clear night, starry and moonlit, and Moojie sat awake in his chair, worrying until dawn, feeling the pangs of injustice and the voice inside him kicking up, stirring, getting ready to thunder forth.

Chapter 12

The God of love and mischief visits St. Isidore's

With the wild-eyed, bounty-hungry posse of internationals looming on the horizon, Moojie decided to take matters into his hands, to rise above his limitations, and set about the enterprise of riding Hocus Pocus up the El Serrat trail. It was just past sunrise when he reached the third bench and the blind of bamboo. Unlike his grandfather, he found the cave open, like a great, gaping mouth.

The twins came down the path carrying dried gourds full of huckleberries.

"I-I came to warn you," Moojie said. "My grandfather's bringing a posse."

Manish just smiled and threw a berry at Moojie. The boys didn't seem at all concerned. In fact, they never did. They often asked him silly questions he couldn't understand.

"Can you tell me how butter flies?"

About Moojie's crutches: "Do they make music?"

"Tell Ninti," Moojie said. "Tell her to get ready. Tell her he's coming unhinged."

That night, Pappy and McTavish were digging in the east field with miner's lamps fastened to their heads. From the bedroom window, Moojie watched them work at a ferocious pace, like gravediggers in a hurry. The next morning, he bungled anxiously back and forth in the yard, waiting for Pappy to rise so he could go into the village to find out what he could. But it wasn't until after lunch that they set out, and Pappy and McTavish were uncommonly quiet as they rode in the wagon on either side of Moojie. By the time the men finished making deliveries, picking up feed, and banking, it was near sundown and they were talking "teatime at Tilly's."

The tavern was hopping busy, fishermen and farmers filing in, thirsty as bull ants. Everyone was there: the mayor, the priest, the courier, the jeweler, the professor. Pappy was in a festive mood, greeting the crowd just as if he'd just won an election. Moojie sipped on sarsaparilla and ate spicy wings, while watching the grownups drink and complain about everything from the cost of bananas to the Curse of the Hostiles.

"What are you going on about?" the professor asked Pappy. "Those savages are gone."

"That's where you're wrong, my friend," Pappy said. "They're makin' families in the hills as we speak. Next thing you know, their children will be havin' children and the hills'll be crawlin' with 'em."

"Aw, they're just a bunch of Italians with big eyes," said the mail courier. A couple of Italian fishermen stood up and started toward him. McTavish stepped in and offered them a beer.

Moojie strained to hear what Pappy was saying across

the room, and then Pappy raised his shot glass and said "MORE BUG JUICE!" and someone started playing the fiddle.

It was well past midnight before they left Tilly's, and Moojie had yet to find anything out. McTavish decided to sleep in the chapel, and Pappy slept in the buckboard, while Moojie drove home in the moonlight. When they arrived, Pappy congratulated Moojie, shook his hand, and promptly fell off the wagon. Loopy Pappy. What was he planning? Moojie was going to get it out of him.

In the kitchen, Pappy swayed on his feet, an unlit cigarette between his lips, as if erecting an imaginary fence around his troubles.

"Matches," he said.

"Next to the stove, Sir."

Pappy lit a smoke, piled into his winged chair, and lobbed his leather boots onto the coffee table. "Take them off."

Moojie worked his way around the tight space, got down on the floor, and pulled off the boots. "So, about th-the hole in the field—" he ventured to ask.

"I got another letter from your aunt," Pappy said. "The old cow aims to take you away from here."

"What?"

"Dagnabbit," Pappy moaned, "why did my Katie have to die?" he said as he slouched in his chair, his head cocked, acres of sorrow spreading out from him like rattlesnake grass through the valley. "Everyone dying." In the near darkness, Pappy waved an invisible flag. "Everyone dead."

Moojie ignored the news about his aunt and persevered with the interrogation. "Is that what the hole is for? Dead people?"

Millie-Mae, sleeping on the floor, whimpered, broke wind, and then turned onto her other side.

"What's it all mean?" Pappy went on, as if oblivious to the sudden fragrance. "I'm a sinner, that's what. I'm a rotten, lowdown, pig and poke, sinner." There was a grimy ring to his voice, a held-back ring. He stood and pounded his lower back with the top of his fist.

"I reckon not, Sir."

"So, your mamma—my Katie—is gone," Pappy had said when Moojie first arrived at the dairy. "It'll take a fair piece to work that one through. And, the old man's gone, too … a run of bad luck. Now, I know you ain't got the wherewithal of other boys: you got your perimeters. But that ain't no excuse for lack of discipline. There comes a time in every boy's life, a time when he knows his childhood is over, the cut is made complete. He leaves his dreams and walks straight into the future knowin' that every blessin' has a dark side, and every curse comes with a blessin'."

Moojie searched Pappy's expression in the dim light. Once again, he felt sorry for his grandfather. He realized how much it must have pained Pappy to lose his daughter Katie, Moojie's mother. For the first time he questioned his right to and reasons for fraternizing with the Light-Eaters.

Once Moojie would have liked to kill his grandfather. Once he believed coming to St. Isidore's was a terrible mistake, and having been forgotten by his father, he might remain a prisoner there for life. And now, Moojie wondered if he and Pappy could become friends. But then his grandfather said something that made his blood run cold:

"It's you and me, boy, you and me against those Hostiles."

Moojie instantly forgot the nice feelings he had just had. Pappy was just like his father, a gritty, old, small-minded codger. He didn't know who he hated more. Neither Pappy nor his father cared about him or his friends. And now Moojie didn't care anymore. He had done enough caring. He reflected on what Pappy had said about leaving childhood behind and walking into the future. Moojie didn't want to leave his dreams behind. He didn't believe that every blessing had a dark side, every curse a blessing. But then, the very next day, when he overheard Pappy telling McTavish he had hurt his back working in the field and wouldn't be able to organize the posse for a while, he wondered if it might be half-true.

The reprieve helped put things in a better light for a while. The next time he got the opportunity, Moojie headed straight out to the fields in search of Ninti. She wasn't there, but he found Babylonia and the twins at the creek making paper. He ducked behind some shrubbery to spy on them as they soaked and splashed and pounded the bark. They stopped and gathered on the bank to eat berries, chortling with blue-stained teeth. Unexpectedly, Babylonia loosened her braided hair, stripped down to nothing, and waded into the water. Naked as a bird.

Moojie couldn't move, couldn't breathe. The bones of his legs turned to pudding. Should his presence be discovered, he would die of embarrassment. As Babylonia waded into the water, he noticed something red on her back, between her shoulders, but couldn't make it out. The twins ripped off their flour sacks and charged into the water after her. Unable to contain himself, Moojie edged closer to them and fell through the shrub, onto the sand, with a piggish grunt.

Babylonia and the twins dunked underwater for what seemed an eternity. Manish was the first to surface, a pair of eyes and a headband. A head-banded toad. Then he and Shar burst out of the water and rushed toward Moojie.

"Prometheus! You stink, my lord!" Manish said, pulling at him. "You need a bath."

"No no no," Moojie said, pushing them away. "I can't swim!" Papa had once tried to teach him to swim in the creek, but he sunk to the bottom like a stone, legs jerking haphazardly, left arm frozen, right arm flapping in desperation. Papa dove under to rescue him, and later threatened him with a belt if he told his mother what had happened.

Laughter bubbled off the twins as they ripped off Moojie's shirt and trousers.

"Not the skivvies!" Moojie said.

It took a bit of doing, but it was finally Babylonia who drew Moojie into the water. She coaxed him to lie back and float while keeping one of her arms underneath his back. The twins scooped water onto his head and smoothed back his shoulder-length hair. Then they took turns holding him afloat while Babylonia wiped his face with the soft, wet ends of her hair.

Swimming, terrifying *and* beautiful.

Moojie peeked into the water to see Babylonia's body. She splashed him. He held his breath as if to stop time, as if to float on the forever feeling of happiness.

"Hail," Manish said, pointing at Moojie's arm. "Lord Goose Bump!"

Jolly, musical laughter.

Grinning and bubbling with joy, Moojie rose arm-and-arm out of the creek with Babylonia. The twins helped Moojie with his trousers, and then charged naked back into the creek. Dressed now, Babylonia lay back on the warm sand. Moojie listened as a thousand chickadees chirped and clicked and rustled in the brush. Shirtless, he lay back in the blazing sun, perfectly and mindlessly transported out of his worries, lost; lost to a new and reckless and wonderful feeling. The twins frolicking in the water, the trees rustling in the hot breeze, and next to him Babylonia, a bewitching, kind, wild, egg thief with a bounty upon her head.

"I miss my parents," she said. "My father and I used to swim and recite poetry as we floated on our backs in the Oman Sea. Sometimes we climbed the mangroves for heron eggs."

"My mamma was pretty as an April morning," he said, eyes closed. "She had her own scent, kind of like roses and tobacco. I remember weird things about her, like the way h-her hands touched a book's pages. She gave me the world, you know. She gave me Odysseus and Cyclops. Who dares to enter my home?" he growled.

She laughed softly. "And your father?"

"H-he never wanted a son. Not me, anyway. Can you blame him?"

"Are you looking for praise?" she asked.

A monarch butterfly landed on his nose. They broke into laughter. Then the butterfly flitted onto Babylonia's big toe and they laughed some more.

"When I first came to this world," she said, "I liked the feeling of my physical body. It was fascinating and complex, the muscles, the skin, the eyeballs."

"I hate my body."

"Oh?"

"It's just that sometimes it makes me think I-I don't belong here."

"I, too, have hated my body."

"Why?" Moojie looked at her.

She turned away.

"That's okay," he said. "I-If you don't, you know, want to talk about it."

She sat up and the butterfly flew away.

"Your smile was making the butterfly jealous," Moojie said.

She tossed him a plum and lay back again. "What do you call your true home?"

"Wimbley Road. And yours?"

"Always and Forever."

Moojie knew by now that she wasn't a Hostile, and Always and Forever wasn't just a different neighborhood. "What's it like?" he asked, tasting the plum.

"It is hard to describe our homeland in your language. It has a kind of geography. Valleys and mountains. But everything is lighter there."

"I like that," Moojie said, juice trickling down his cheek.

Three vultures circled and rasped overhead, seeming to enjoy a ride on the great wheel of life.

"And the seasons," she went on, "we can conjure whatever weather or climate we wish. Whatever we envision clearly—as long as it is for the good of all—will appear. It is unlike Earth, where you have dense layers of thought to slow the speed of manifestation. But I will miss the objects of procreation—things that hatch and bloom and calve."

"Did you say … *unlike Earth*?" Moojie reflected an instant on Pappy's claims against the tribe, on his accusations of devilment and sorcery and cannibalism.

"Never mind that!" she said. "What do *you* cherish most about this world?"

"I like things with four legs, especially a cat and a horse," he said, thinking of Phineas and Hocus Pocus. "People are complicated. People notice you on account of you're pretty, b-but they only notice me because I'm a freak." Moojie still wasn't sure why Babylonia was being friendly to him. This uncertainty, however, didn't persist; caution, like his heart, had gone up in flames.

Later that day, a strange cat arrived at St. Isidore's, plump and white and cross-eyed. Moojie lowered the field glasses and watched her from the porch rocker as she crossed the yard, long-haired and gray-tipped, fanning her rump. Behind him, inside the window, Phineas twitched his tail and pawed the glass. The wild cat looked back at his pancake face, her eyes crossed, one blue, one green, the south end of a live blue belly poking out of her mouth. She entered the high grassy field, swishing her rump, side to side.

A sharp pain radiated out of Moojie's chest. It was an unpleasant sensation, like a bird clawing at his heart. He knew what Phineas was feeling, and he pitied him. Moojie considered letting him go outside, but Pappy had warned him of the dangers in the wilderness, of wolves and vultures and rattlesnakes, of the Hostiles and their questionable diet. And Moojie had his answer: he would never let Phineas go outside, not even for love.

He, on the other hand, was going to take the risk.

Chapter 13

*Blood, teeth, and chicken feathers; Moojie learns
from Pappy what it means to be a man*

The next morning, Moojie took an unusual interest in
preening, then waited for Pappy to leave for the village
before riding out to find Babylonia. There was something
in him that would not accept the distinctions that the
villagers had made between the Europeans and everyone
else, between natives and immigrants, colored and white.
He didn't know exactly what he was going to say to her,
but his heart was filled with nervous expectation.

And then Pappy called him outside.

In the yard, Pappy was tying on an apron, the sleeves
of his shirt rolled back and gray under the pale olive trees.
The fields beyond the yard had faded to the color of
snakeskin, mottled with oak trees, thistles, and cactus.
The heat was rising, lifting the sun into a cloudless sky.
Down the ramp and across the yard past the full, glassy

water trough Moojie strolled, a pillar of blue moving through the warming shade of expansive trees toward Pappy.

His grandfather slipped his hunting knife out of its sheath and checked the blade with his thumb.

"Boy, today you will become a man," he said. "You're not goin' to gain freedom and self-sufficiency on good looks alone. Now, I got the mind to teach you a thing or two. School isn't everything. Not all of life's lessons come out of a textbook."

He motioned for Moojie to come closer and lifted open the nesting bin. The chickens shrieked and ran to the back corners.

"Go on then," he said. "Pick out a hen, a pullet that ain't layin' anymore. One with feet like old teeth."

With his mighty righty, Moojie reached in and pinned a hen against the side of the hutch. Sideburns like mut- tonchops. Tooth-colored feet. "No more yolks in this one, Sir."

Pappy took the hen, sat on a tree stump, and braced the fitful bird face-down between his legs. A cloud of fruit flies made a halo above his head.

"Watch and learn," Pappy said. "You'll be doin' this soon."

Moojie was relieved that Pappy's bottom was on the stump and not the chicken's neck. Leaning in closer, he expected his grandfather to check the chicken for mites or something.

Pappy stroked the hen's back. "Atta girl," he said in a soft, weary voice. She stopped kicking and slowly yielded to his massive freckled hands. And then, good heavens, Pappy pulled her head upward and with the knife slit her throat; he tipped her body downward, her old white feet scratching his hands, blood pumping out of her neck, blue-red cream puddling on the ground, and then he wound her head backward and snapped it off like the end of a dry twig.

Wet-eyed and feeling seasick, Moojie waved away the fruit flies. There were so many now, he could scarcely breathe.

When the blood stopped draining and the hen's feet went still, Pappy marched the plump bird into the cabin and dropped her into a pot of boiling water. After a minute, he returned to the porch and tied the feet of the headless body to an overhead beam. With blood-splattered hands, he plucked out her feathers, and spoke of life's cycles, and came to the conclusion that chickens must have souls, but not like dogs since dogs were smarter than humans. "Killing," he said, "always makes a man philosophical."

In the low morning light of that Finnegan autumn, Moojie expected any minute for his breakfast to come up. *Be brave*, he told himself. *Braver than brave.* The fragrance of blood and the sight of the flaccid, headless neck, sent his head reeling, and the minute Pappy plucked out a tail feather with his teeth, Moojie fainted dead away.

He awoke with a jolt, with Pappy waving the vile-smelling Spirit of Hartshorn under his nose. "Okay, boy. You're gonna live."

Moojie came to with a new, fiery spirit. Despairing over the threat of posses, and pandemoniums, and fruit fly battalions, he privately denounced Pappy's philosophical lesson and became more than ever determined to join the Light-Eaters.

II

The Subsequent Trials and
Misguided Adventures,
which the Venerable Moojie
and his Trusty Cat
Undergo at St. Isidore's

Chapter 1

Of Ninti's revelation to Moojie;
and how he is further challenged in his plans
to join the reviled clan

When Moojie presented Ninti with his plan to "migrate" into the mountains, her response was less than enthusiastic. He had approached her while she was picking wild onions in the woods with the twins. "I can't stand it anymore. H-He wants me to kill chickens. I don't want to kill chickens."

Ninti lowered her gaze and picked a foxtail out of her sandal.

"Let us speak of your quest," she said. "Have you begun to feed the poor?" With dirty fingernails, she fondled her necklace, a tarnished bronze medallion that hung from a leather thong. Moojie liked that. He had spent time with his mother in the garden—not actually working—but watching her dig and prune and plant flowers. Seeing the dirty fingernails gave him a weird feeling of hope.

"You are capable of doing much more than you think," she said.

"You mean Elsie a-and her calf? Aw, that was just a fluke. I didn't really do anything to the cows."

Anyway, he didn't *want* to believe it. It just did not fit with what he knew of himself.

Walking alongside Hocus Pocus, Ninti elevated her voice. "Let me tell you a story ... fifteen summers ago," she began, "a gypsy came to St. Isidore's, a young man, to be precise, with a gunshot wound to his leg. He was short, pale of complexion and muscular, quite comely but for his small feet. Dressed top to bottom in green garments, he called himself Adolf the Green. We took him in— against our better judgment—and we healed him. At the time, there was a maiden with us named Afsoun. Despite Adolf's contempt for the color of our skin, despite his barbarous manner, Afsoun was charmed by the man and ran off with him. Come spring there was a baby, my lord, a boy, which we learned had been left at the village chapel. What I mean to say, well, for all intents and purposes, I suspect the maiden Afsoun and the bandit were, in point of fact, your first parents."

Moojie pulled back on the reins to stop Hocus.

"The ancestors told me in a vision that Afsoun made her crossing just after your birth," Ninti said.

"You mean, she died?" Moojie asked.

"I am afraid so."

Moojie knew he'd been adopted, but he had always thought of Mamma and Papa as his parents. It was like another mother and father had just dropped down from the clouds and been whisked away from him. The realization was indeed enough to make his blood turn cold. "You can't be sure she was my mother," he said. There was long silence as he struggled to collect himself. "What was she like? This Afsoun, what was she like?"

"Why, she was most comely. She liked birds, especially seabirds. They approached her without fear. They ate out of her hand. At times, she would stand in the field as if she were a tree, with seabirds perched on her head, arms, and shoulders. She fed them wild berries."

Moojie, quietly pensive, bit his lip. It was wrong to have two mothers.

"You have her eyes, my lord," Ninti said. "Dark as tea leaves, bright as glass."

He sighed.

"What sort of student are you?" Ninti asked, tugging her earlobe.

He looked at the ground. *Embarrassing.* His strength—such as it was—had not been in studies. His mamma had tried to teach him to read and write, but she might as well have been teaching a monkey Latin. "Actually, I-I'm not much for schooling."

Ninti's dark, flecked eyes seemed to scan his bones for secrets. "What I have to teach has nothing to do with books," she said, "and everything to do with hidden treasures."

Moojie's thoughts veered off to Aladdin, a good-for-nothing who, after being freed from his father's oversight, was taken to a treasury replete with gold and silver, and then he was given a signet ring and a magic lamp and thereafter trees bloomed with gemstones.

"So you're going t-to teach me how to make magic coins," he said, offhand.

"Well—"

"And rain, to make rain?"

"When is your father coming back?"

"Never."

"Perhaps he will."

"Forget it. He's gone. That's the way it is."

"So you are free as an eagle. You are lucky, in a way."

Moojie was struck with a feeling he couldn't put into words: an ache, really. The twins came around to pet Hocus on the nose.

"So you see it would please me to take you in," Ninti said. "But it would put us at terrible risk."

"But y-you said it yourself," he protested. "You said I'm free, free as a bird … it'll be great! I'll move into the cave and Pappy won't be so quick to attack if I'm with you." He was nearly shouting as he fumbled to stand with his crutches.

"My lord, they will come after us to take you back."

"But I-I would be so happy…."

"You can find happiness where you are."

He whacked the tree with his crutch.

"Pray, forgive me for speaking plainly my lord, but you have yet to prove that you are even willing to honor our Code."

"What?"

"Have you made an effort to feed the poor?"

"Y-you can have all the eggs you want. W-what else do you want? Apples? Milk?"

"We do not need your help, the world does."

Manish and Shar talked back and forth with Ninti in their language, she shaking her head, they frowning and buzzing.

"How can I make you understand?" Moojie said, tearing up. "I need … if I can't be a part of … I need to be a part of something good, you know. Family, we could be like family."

She gazed at him. "We take The Code very seriously."

Chapter 2

An account of the memorable visit from
Babylonia and the twins

Overcome with despair, Moojie went back to the dairy
and took refuge in his chores. Why wouldn't the Light-
Eaters accept him? They weren't Hostiles. They had no
quarrel with him. They were more alike than not; they
were all misfits, square pegs in a big, round world, with
hopes and dreams and regrets.

One day, just when he had reached the bottom of a
deep emotional well, Babylonia came across the field
dressed in white, a crown of jasmine about her head.
Dark and shiny, her hair looked wet in the sun, like
molasses, like warm bread and hot cakes. Watching from
the growing patch, Moojie imagined that if he touched
it, he might not be able to let go. "Too beautiful," he
whispered dreamily.

The twins were with Babylonia, hands together, heads

bowing.

"Ladyship asked me to give you this," Babylonia said. She handed Moojie a little pigskin pouch. "Inside you will find a number of seeds—"

"Not just any seeds!" Manish broke in. "Certified Ali Baba watermelon seeds, ancient strains of Persia!"

"Ancient strains of Persia!" Shar echoed.

The seed pouch vibrated in Moojie's hand, and his heart jumped.

"May we visit the goats?" Babylonia asked.

Moojie put the pouch in his pocket and forgot about it for the time being. He let the goats out of the stall. Babylonia and the twins played with them as if they were puppies, chasing them and talking to them in their language, whistling and rattling their tongues. They referred to Rufus, the alpha goat, by another name, *Suhurmas*, or something like that.

Moojie tried to keep gardening, but it was no use. They wanted to pick fruit. He got onto Hocus and pulled Babylonia up behind him, facing backward, and together they passed under the trees, picking plums and apricots and figs, and tossing them down to the twins. At one point, Moojie dropped a plum onto Manish's head, and Manish hurled an apricot back at him, which started a monumental fruit fight that left all four of them spattered and crazy with laughter.

Before the three visitors left, Moojie opened the chicken hutch and offered them all the eggs they wanted. He would have given Babylonia the moon if she had asked for it.

"Only the blue ones," she said. "They have the right frequency."

"Uh, right," Moojie said, pretending to know what she meant. "Okay. Well, from now on," he said, "I'll leave the blue ones under straw in the corner. I-If Pappy finds them, I'll say they're keepers, for hatching."

He gave the twins each a sweet Ambrosia (*sukulutu*), and they left for El Serrat with scuttles of fruit and chocolate smiles.

"*Qarradu* is coming," Babylonia said. Her white clothes were splotched with fruit. Her dark eyelashes and eyebrows were lovely as butterfly wings, with ten thousand miles behind them. Butterflies. Moojie had them in his stomach. He wished the day would never end.

"*Qarradu*, what does it mean?" he asked, astonished again at how the Light-Eaters were able to predict Pappy's comings and goings.

"It means, Warrior."

"Yep, that about says it," Moojie said. He got on his crutches and scanned the county road for Pappy's buckboard.

"Not to worry," she said. "We have lookouts. They will alert us."

They walked toward the woods, squinting at the sun, he and Babylonia walking. Close up she was taller than he had thought, and her feet were longer than his. *She moves like a cat, taking her time, like being beautiful is her job.* He considered confessing what had happened to Anahita, the cougar, but didn't dare break the spell of enchantment.

"You know," she said, "long ago, I was a slave. The women of the palace were kind. They put makeup on my face. They dressed me in jewels and veils of fine silk. The emperor said my body was a gift from God." She undid the top buttons of her blouse and carefully lowered the collar down her back to reveal the tattoo of a red eagle between her shoulder blades. "The emperor thought I was pretty, but he wanted to make me beautiful."

Palace? Emperor? "Wait a minute. How old are you?" Moojie laughed, thinking it was a joke.

She hesitated before answering. "Pray pardon, I do not know! We came when worldlings still ate flesh from spears, before the land bridge appeared in the north."

"Gaw, y-you mean the Ice Age! Okay. This is getting interesting."

Babylonia bit her lip. "I have already said too much."

Moojie stopped to adjust the grip on his crutches.

"Is it difficult to walk with them?" she asked.

"Uh, I don't know, I'm used to it."

"What happened to your legs?"

"Born this way."

"How do they feel?"

"I don't know."

"Can you feel this?" She reached down and tickled his knee.

He giggled and jerked his leg away. "What about you?" He tickled her ribcage. "Can you feel that?"

Babylonia squealed. A covey of quail burst from the field. She went after his knee again, and the two spilled over one another, rippling, heaping laughter in the grass, wrestling, tickling, crazy squirrels, all light and joy.

"Truce?" Moojie finally said, sucking air.

For a while, they lay side by side, looking at the sky.

"You wrestle like a boy," he said. She narrowed her eyes at him. "No," he said. "It's a good thing."

"Ordinarily, I am not like this."

"Ordinarily, I'm not l-like this, either."

"So, you think that you are extraordinary?"

"No. I-I'm ordinary."

"You certainly are not ordinary, my lord. I think I like you."

A weight lifted from his heart. She smiled at him, and something lifted again. His head, full of bubbles. He picked a lupine blossom and gave it to her. "A piece of sky."

"When the pandemonium comes to pass," she said, "a light will shine, there, above the mountain." She pointed. "A light that worldlings have rarely seen."

"I-I want to be with you when it happens," he said, taking a foxtail from her hair.

"It will be dangerous."

"I'll take care of you."

"It will be dangerous *for you*."

"How did you get here?"

"Not the same way you did."

"What, you got a-a flying saucer or something in that cave?"

"Nothing so old-fashioned."

"So whatever Ninti says goes."

"It would be foolish to question her. She is enlightened."

"What does that mean?"

"She *remembers*. In the manner of true north, she remembers our true purpose."

"Purpose. You mean *quest?*"

"*Qarradu*, your grandfather, is he your only kin?"

"It's complicated."

"I must go," she said, as if suddenly wary.

Sarru'kan and two other boys were coming across the field toward them.

"Forgive me for saying it, my lord, but it can never be," Babylonia said. "You and I can never be ...."

He should have been surprised, but by now he was used to having his mind read.

"Sarru'kan—" she started to say.

"I don't care a holey mitten about Sarru'kan."

"My lord," she said, "you do not want to make him jealous."

"There's no one else for me." A jealous boyfriend? Moojie never stopped to consider the fact that when

Sarru'kan had said he would like to crush him, he wasn't talking about a nice, friendly hug.

He should have forgotten all about her.

But it was no use.

His heart had already begun to open. For as long as Moojie lived, he knew he would never forget the sound of Babylonia's laughter.

Sarru'kan and the boys looked as though they had stepped off a prehistoric cave wall (which they kind of had), long-haired and fierce, marching through the high grass with spears.

Babylonia greeted them and she and Sarru'kan exchanged some harsh words in their language. Once she backed away from him as if afraid. But soon enough all four of them trotted off to the west field to throw spears at the scarecrow. Babylonia could throw as well as any of the boys. She yanked her spear out of the scarecrow and threw again and again, her arms brown-shining and sun-gleaming, hitting the center of the scarecrow's chest several times.

Sarru'kan was everything Moojie was not: athletic, strong, close to Babylonia. When the scarred boy wrapped himself around Babylonia to correct her throwing position, Moojie thought about going for Hocus Pocus and galloping out to the field to close the gulf between the lovely maiden and himself. To consider something like this … was it love? It wasn't what he had expected. His knowledge of love had come from his mother's science lessons. He knew zilch about romance. Courtship. What was it exactly? The word should conjure princes and court maidens and fabulous carriage rides along the river. His introduction to such matters had been limited to bird rituals involving feather-fanning, crowing, strutting, and flapping of wings followed by the act of mating, which took roughly five seconds, and then off you go to look for worms.

Moojie dug up a carrot and held it out to the grazing Hocus Pocus. She raised her head and turned her great, glassy eyes toward him, traipsed over, and lowered down. On approach, Moojie overshot her back and ended up hanging on to her tail to keep from sailing headfirst to the ground. He thought he heard the pigeons laughing, and the trees, too, they were laughing. He hung like a winkle to a rock, as the merciful, longsuffering Hocus Pocus clopped into the yard and delivered him to a pile of straw.

Overcome with frustration, Moojie crawled to the pigeon loft, took hold of the kazoo and blew. Out came a coarse, rattling *frrrp*. Hocus shook her head and flapped her lips. Once more and with gusto, Moojie blew, this time sounding a terrific piratey *flurrrp* that made the pigeons go into a tizzy, flapping wings and overturning their feeding troughs, and sent the chickens spraying across the yard like a bad sneeze.

Babylonia and the boys rushed toward the yard. She stayed back a ways while the three boys came right up to Moojie. Sarru'kan, with his viper arm tattoo and belly scars resembling a pox of insects, looked the part of bad news.

"You better get out of here," Moojie said. "My grandfather's not nice."

Sarru'kan waved away a fly. "I am not nice, either. You see, Claw Hand, not only am I rather handsome, but I am also a great sorcerer. My powers are varied and vast, purely supernatural in form, and often deadly by design. There was a time when I prevailed as a demigod. I lived in the shah's palace, dressed in finery, feasted from golden platters, and damsels clawed each other for the privilege of serving me. I have been known to conjure hurricanes and sink ships, to invoke bat plagues and cat plagues and locust plagues, and if you cross me …."

"You smell like onions," Moojie said. "Would you mind not breathing on me?"

"You see, I know all about you. Worldlings are not interested in sorcery except for personal gain. Sadly, this has made me into hunted game. I have been forced to hide like a prize tiger."

"W-what are you doing here then?"

"Ladyship lured me with kindness. I gave up the royal priesthood for a greater cause."

"Greater cause," Moojie said skeptically.

"To protect our kind. To teach noble values. To show the world how to use supernatural power for peacekeeping."

"Really?" Somehow Moojie couldn't put Sarru'kan together with noble values. His ears tingled. It was the same sensation he got when his mother was rushing out of the house to her death. And when he and his father waved goodbye to Auntie Tilda at the train station. But the kindness in Sarru'kan's eyes looked genuine.

"I-I'd be obliged if you were to leave," Moojie said. "Pappy's coming back any minute."

"Come, Sarru'kan!" Babylonia called out.

Sarru'kan gave a snort and left with the others.

Moojie wondered what Sarru'kan's problem was. From the minute they had met, he seemed to have it out for Moojie. A sinister idea came to him: *What if he was to help Pappy nab the scarred banshee?* He worked it out in his mind. He would get the mayor involved so there would be no killing. They could nab Sarru'kan, and haul him off to jail. One fewer obstacle, one fewer rival.

Just then Manish came catapulting across the field with his spear, over the cornrows, arms flailing, legs akimbo. "Prometheus the fire-lighter!" he yelled, and then he landed with an awkward thump on the ground, arm snapping like a piece of kindling.

Moojie rushed over to him.

"I think it is broken," Manish said, cradling his arm and sucking air through his teeth. His lower arm certainly did appear to be broken, his hand twisted into an unnatural position.

Sarru'kan and the others came back to see what had happened. Babylonia got down on her knees next to Moojie and gently brushed Manish's hair out of his face.

"Go fetch Ninti!" Sarru'kan said to one of the boys.

"Fear not, dear Manish," Babylonia said. "Mami will soon be here."

Manish bit his lip and tears leaked out of his closed eyes.

"It's okay, Manny," Moojie said.

"Stay out of this, Claw Hand." Sarru'kan shoved Moojie aside. "This does not concern you."

Babylonia gathered Manish into her arms and held him close while uttering a quiet prayer. Moojie searched his memory to repeat what had happened with Elsie the cow when she was in trouble. He couldn't recall what it was, exactly. So he took Manish by his good hand, and got very, very quiet inside. Manish began to relax and his breathing slowed and Moojie said, "It's already done." He didn't know why he said it; the words just said themselves. Then Manish's arm snapped into place. Wide-eyed, he held it out, wiggled his fingers and rotated his wrist. "Prometheus!"

Babylonia stared at Moojie. Sarru'kan inspected the arm, looking more skeptical than surprised. It seemed neither Babylonia nor Manish were surprised at all that the arm had been restored—a little bruised, but perfectly aligned and flexible again—but the fact that *Moojie* had healed it seemed to astound them.

When Moojie got back to the cabin he shut himself in his bedroom. What exactly had happened? A miracle, for sure. Like the cows. But how? What sort of power was it? He knew it was within him. He was only beginning to suspect that it was more powerful than anything he could understand. And, he reasoned, if that power could set a broken arm, why couldn't it heal his legs? *What if I just surprised everyone and threw away my crutches?* The thought terrified him. One must be quiet in order to witness miracles. That's what Ninti had said. There was no mistaking what had happened to Elsie and the calf and Manish's arm. And there was no mistaking he had something to do with it.

In the fervor of excitement, he wanted to put his power to the test. He closed his eyes and tried to call back the feeling he got when he was with Manish. He waited. It was but a few minutes before a wave of heat radiated out his chest. He took off his leg braces and stood, grasping the chair. Then, he let go. On his own, he stood for a few seconds. On his own! He tried to take a step, lost his balance, and crashed to the floor. "I could use a little help," he said, glaring up at the ceiling.

Chapter 3

*Which records circumstances pertaining
to the day when the snotty Markhams
inadvertently lend Moojie a hand*

Bound for the moment by the torment of his limitations, and at the same time exercised over the triumph of Manish's healing, Moojie took the opportunity to minister to Hocus Pocus. When he touched her swollen, arthritic knees, Pappy's King of Pain Relief liniment left a perfume of ammonia, turpentine, and camphor on his hand. Determined to test his power, he closed his eyes and bowed his head and opened to the mysterious force that had recently prevailed upon him. He breathed in and out, and the warm sensation flooded his body. Before long, there was a pair of soft lips and warm breath on his head. Hocus seemed to be pleased.

The vultures were back, wide-circling over the fields. Black crows gleamed on the cabin's tin roof, swooping casually at sun-worshiping blue bellies. Under the oaks, the cows had stopped cowing. In the stalls, the goats had stopped goating. That morning, it took Moojie four verses of "Frère Jacques" and two "God Bless Americas" on the kazoo to incite the pigeons to return to the loft.

"You're comin' on deliveries today," Pappy said from the porch, startling Moojie.

"I don't want to go."

"Did I say you had a choice?"

"The villagers stare at me."

"You can wear a blinder."

Moojie wanted to argue, but this fateful Thursday morning, it was too hot in the valley and the wind had picked up; it seemed to whisper a message to him, an invitation with a whiff of mystery.

They arrived in San Miguel just as the astronomical clock struck eleven. The villagers seemed to be drugged by the cold white fog coming off the ocean. In a stupor, they strolled aimlessly along the boardwalk, past the gift store, past the bakery and the green grocer's, as if they were passengers on a ship lost at sea.

On either side of Flum Street were signposts:

NO ICE CREAM CONES

NO UNDOCUMENTED ALIENS

NO POMPADOUR HEELS

NO MUSIC WITHOUT A PERMIT

NO SPITTING

LAMPS OUT BY 9 P.M.

Mr. Abu's teeth gleamed through fig-colored lips as he popped outside his store to greet the buckboard. He plunged a brown hand in Moojie's direction, a four-fingered brown hand that showed no indication of there ever having been a thumb, which always took Moojie by surprise as he shook it because the green grocer was famous for his green thumb. There was something special about Mr. Abu. Moojie had known him since he was a baby. Every time he had visited the store with his mother, this hair-oiled man with skin the color of almond husk greeted him with a bow. And a gumdrop.

"This is a very good day," Mr. Abu said while vigorously shaking Moojie's hand. "An auspicious day, indeed."

The word "auspicious" made Moojie tingle from the feet up. It was a word like hands reaching out and shaking him by the shoulders, a word that pried open some delightful hidden door to his soul.

Who can figure whether it was fate or coincidence or heavenly intervention that caused Moojie to go to the village that day? It's difficult to say. In matters of superstition and synchronicity, the San Miguelians were well-informed, but such big words were new to Moojie. If anything, he seemed to possess a talent for being in the right place at the wrong time. Or was it the other way around when Pappy stopped in at Tilly's and Moojie decided to wait in the buckboard across the street in the park?

There Moojie sat, watching the waves lap the beach off the end of Flum Street. The ocean had always terrified him. He imagined a thousand glowing eyes under the water's surface. And as he was sitting there waiting and watching, out from the shrubbery appeared Greta and Uma Something, a mother and daughter who the villagers had nicknamed "the trolls" because they lived under the park bridge. Moojie remembered the way the San Miguelians had jeered and teased Greta when she was a young lady, living like a hobo. They tossed bread crust and coins at her as if they were a carnival game. Moojie's mother had stood by and said, "Let that be a lesson to you, my little nougat. Either in this life or the next, we all must pay for our sins."

Greta, now a mother, pushed a two-wheeled cart onto the park lawn, her young daughter trailing closely behind. The cart was loaded with knick-knacks—strung acorn necklaces, buckeye napkin rings, pinecone candleholders—probably to sell. Face lined and thin as a broomstick, Greta must have aged a hundred years since Moojie saw her last. Uma skipped in circles around the cart, blond hair thick as a scouring pad, skin the color of stoneground wheat.

Royce and Bentley, the snotty Markham brothers from Wimbley Wood, lit upon the scene with their black dog and mob of school buddies. Across the park, they gathered in a huddle, whispering and jabbing each other, up to some nasty purpose. The dog charged at Greta, who scooped up her daughter and ran until she ended up backed against a rock wall, facing the fanged, snarling beast. The Markham boys and their friends whistled and slapped their hands and made smart-aleck remarks. "Boy, ain't it a dog's life," and "I'll be doggoned." Harharhar.

Watching this scene stirred up a dark, forgotten bile in Moojie, a memory of the time the Markham brothers had locked him in their potting shed. And as he watched them now, bullying Greta and Uma, he couldn't stand by. This time, a wave of courage and strength overcame him. Maybe stupidity. He stepped off the buckboard, lost his footing, and fell to the ground. Unable to reach his crutches quickly, he seized a buckeye and lobbed it at the dog, but missed, hitting Bentley square on the behind. Instantly the boy and his pride of hooligans turned and charged toward Moojie.

By the grace of heaven, Pappy strove onto the scene.

The mob jumped backward and the dog hid between Bentley's legs. Pappy crushed out his cigarette with the heel of his boot and said something to the boys that Moojie couldn't hear, something made crystal clear by the jab of a finger in the air, causing them to fall over themselves running away.

On the way back to St. Isidore's, Moojie had a new appreciation for Pappy; in fact, he was bursting with optimism, like rolling down a grassy knoll, like a sky full of buckeye blossoms, like bugles and kazoos sounding off.

It was that very night when Moojie awoke out of a dead sleep with a brilliant idea. He went to his desk drawer and took out the pouch of seeds Ninti had sent to him. It was the strangest idea a crippled boy ever dreamed up, and yet, it seized him entirely: he would grow watermelons for Greta and Uma! Yes, he would feed the poor mother and daughter, and prove to Ninti that he, Lord Littleman of San Miguel de las Gaviotas, could absolutely, undeniably, live by The Code!

Chapter 4

A reliable chronicle of the sage discourse that passes between Moojie and the man-pig, and other ordinary events

The growing season was coming to a close so Moojie had to get to work immediately. He didn't know the first thing about planting watermelons, but he knew the seeds couldn't take root in stone-hard dirt. Clearing a space in the growing patch with one arm made grueling work. All the next morning, he hoed and raked and dug with the fervor of two men, and nearly popped a cork when he looked up and noticed a shiny-snouted, rosy-cheeked pig standing in the cornrows.

Pappy didn't have a pig.

Moojie looked up the valley, thinking maybe this critter had escaped from another farm. When he turned back it was gone. Instead there was a short, stout man with pink cheeks coming toward him. Around his waist was a linked belt made of shiny metal lids from cans, and tucked into it a scrap of wood. Gray-streaked hair drawn into a ponytail, two curls hanging on either side of his face, white dot on the forehead: Imi'tittu, the older. As he drew closer, Moojie could see his own frowning face reflected six times in the shiny belt.

"Ask a question and life will show you the answer!" Imi'tittu said. "Good day! May I lend a hand?"

Moojie wiped his sweaty forehead with a dirty hand. "Ground's too hard," he said.

Imi'tittu's face was long, blanched, and flat-cheeked, not unlike Hocus, kind, aloof, and sad. He pursed his lips, pink and bright, and pulled the wood scrap from his belt. "Would you care to move things along?" he asked. He bent forward and rolled his hand, in the manner of addressing a king, his pinkish-orangish eyes twinkling with the affection of a shoat gazing upon a pigling.

Moojie turned toward the cabin, scanning for Pappy.

"From where I come," the visitor continued, holding up the wood scrap, *"epinnu"* is the word for this sort of thing. Your word is plow, is it not?" He knelt on the ground next to Moojie, knitting his wiry, white eyebrows as he studied the wood. "I believe, my lord, the secret lies in the lie of it."

Epinnu. Moojie thought it was much better than *plow* because *plow* sounded like tired oxen with loose swinging throats. But working a plow wouldn't be any easier for Moojie than one-armed digging. "Afraid that won't help," he said, holding out his left arm. "I'm all, you know, catawumpus."

Imi'tittu's face rose like a surprised pink sun. "Nonsense! Why, Ladyship reports that you are, in fact, quite extraordinary."

Moojie went all bubbly inside. Bubbly and quiet.

"Catawumpus? Yours is the strangest of languages,"

Imi'tittu said.

"As in square wheels. Or crooked flagpoles. Or messed up things."

"As in fathers and sons."

Moojie straightened to the level of Imi'tittu's gaze. What did *he* know about his father?

The small round man giggled and snorted. "Catawumpus. I should hope to avoid any occasion for such a word."

"W-what language do you Light-Eaters speak?" Moojie asked.

"Why," Imi'tittu's eyebrows rose, "we speak any language we choose." He pointed to his temple. "A matter of opening the faucet."

"I-I want to learn to do that."

"I fear at this point, t'would be impossible. You see, you cannot achieve this yet because your mind is, in a word, *applesauce*."

Moojie had no idea what he meant.

Imi'tittu looked seriously at him. "My lord, can you be trusted?"

Moojie said yes, but at this point even he didn't know to what degree.

"So you want to feed the poor, dear lady and her daughter?" Imi'tittu asked.

The way the Light-Eaters read his mind was getting obnoxious. Moojie showed Imi'tittu the seed pouch, and asked, "Why is it you read people's minds sometimes, and other times you don't?"

"Ah, it is not an exact science. You see, there are an infinite number of mental frequencies occurring at all times. It takes a good deal of effort and a lot of quiet in one's own mind to 'single out' one individual's frequencies. It does happen sometimes, that one picks up a thought here and there, without effort."

"I want to learn to do that."

"The biggest juiciest behemoths this side of the Nile!" Imi'tittu said, looking at the seeds. "Indeed, the ground must be prepared before planting."

Moojie took up his shovel.

"My lord, you mustn't speak of your plans to anyone. It could endanger us."

It felt as if Imi'tittu wasn't telling him everything. Moojie wanted only to prove himself to Ninti; he had no plans to make trouble for the Light-Eaters. He had seen well enough what his grandfather did to the cougar. So he weighed the risks of carrying out a secret plan, the danger of being found out and getting the strap, of having to sleep on straw and eat hog jowl gravy in a boy's home for the rest of his life; he weighed the significance of these risks, and understood that life surely wasn't plum pudding because any day he might also be sent back to Mother Teagardin, and then there was the hopeless state of his body, which made everything seem more dangerous, and he blurted out:

"Why not?"

"Very good! Then, you must know that whosoever shall swear by our friendship," Imi'tittu said, "shall also swear by our mission. May we be assured that you will not betray us?"

"No, Sir," Moojie said. "I mean, yes, Sir."

"Now, tomorrow we will plow the ground and plant the seeds, and you will in good time see watermelons you have never imagined."

Moojie's heart danced with excitement. Imi'tittu drew his arms around him and *hugged him,* filling Moojie's heart with so much joy that when Imi'tittu let go, he was standing on his own. No telling how this happened. Moojie had dropped his crutches and was just standing there. Startled by the unexpected realization, he started to fall and Imi'tittu caught him. *Whew! That was weird.*

For the remainder of the day, Moojie could barely conceal his excitement. Just once he wanted to see the expression on Pappy's face, looking up from the porch rocker and seeing humongous green watermelons tumbling down the driveway toward the cabin. Just once. He counted the seeds twice. They were like thirty little black teeth. His mind spilled over with new ideas: new possibilities, new prospects, new beginnings. And the very thought of the Light-Eaters made his heart surge with hope. He listened to the sound of that surging.

The next day, while Pappy slept in late, Moojie and Imi'tittu worked secretly behind the shed, chiseling and hammering the scrap of wood, a bit here, a bit there, adding new parts, rearranging the configuration this way and that. "Hurry," Moojie kept saying. "Before he wakes up." They settled on a configuration of an upside down double cross with nails for claws. They attached the plow to the saddle on Hocus Pocus, and she pulled it across the patch to break up the tough ground.

"Let's get on with the planting," Moojie said anxiously.

"All in good time, my lord. We must bless the seeds first. Above all, we must bless the seeds! They may look lifeless; however the whole of life is right there, waiting for the opportunity to show off. Come now, let us praise the Source of life."

It occurred to Moojie that the chubby gladiator could be crazy as a bedbug. But for some reason Moojie went along with him. What did he have to lose? Though he had no idea who or what the Source was, he was willing to give it a try. He counted out ten seeds and held them in his warm hand. "I praise the Source of life," he said.

"I-I thank the Creator of these seeds because no one thinks seeds are very smart or even holy, but they can grow into amazing things we can eat and share, while humans can only grow bodies that probably taste l-like horse leather. I-I thank the great maker of the moon and the sun and the sea for these nice seeds. Amen." And with that he felt light as ether.

"Very goodly done!" Imi'tittu said. "Now let your mind rest. You see, one must lose oneself, lose one's body, forget about the world altogether."

"We better get on with it. Unless you want to lose your body when Pappy shoots you."

"Bring him on!" Imi'tittu laughed.

Moojie shushed him.

"All right, after you plant the seeds," Imi'tittu said, "do not dwell upon them, except to water and bless and praise them and their Source. Give thanks for the laws that turn them into food."

Into the freshly tilled dirt went the ten Ali Baba seeds. Moojie watered and covered them with straw, and he and Imi'tittu hopped to their feet excitedly, as if they might just sprout gold.

"I must be off, "Imi'tittu said. "But first, a riddle! Are you ready?"

"Y-you better get out of here."

"There is a green house," Imi'tittu said. "Inside the green house a white house. Inside the white house a pink house. Inside the pink house many babies. What is it?"

"Please, get going!" Moojie turned, starting for the cabin, and bungled straight into Pappy's crossed arms.

"Stand back, boy," Pappy said, rushing past him.

Imi'tittu sprinted to the other side of the patch.

"Curse you!" Pappy said, chasing him. "As God is my witness, you're a dead man!"

Around and around the brambles they went, Imi'tittu

laughing like, well, a pig, snorting and squealing and trotting, until Moojie poked a crutch through the brambles and tripped Pappy, causing him to dive head first into the tomatoes.

Before leaving the magical, mystical garden, Imi'tittu spun about-face, bowed to Moojie, and said, "Watermelons, my lord! The answer to the riddle is watermelons!"

"You all right, boy?" Pappy asked, panting and leaning on an elbow in the dirt. "Dad blame it! McTavish was right! They'll steal you blind given half a chance." He looked down the point of his finger at Moojie. "If it's the last thing I do, I'm going to throw that hobo and his species into the brig and they're gonna live out their days on watery beans and rusty water."

Broken by the fervor of his praise for life, Moojie's spell of hopelessness and despair had disappeared. That night, and all through the next day, he imagined a universe of magic, of freedom and purpose, a future world of wonders. From a sullen, lazy boy, Moojie Littleman had transformed into a force of light, combing his hair, tucking in his shirt, silently praising the seeds up and down, praising them until he nearly burst a seal. Moojie Littleman, Lord of the *Epinnu*—motherless and as good as fatherless—went about his chores, imagining the possibilities: great mounds of swirling green houses, and inside them white houses, inside them pink houses, inside them little black babies.

Chapter 5

Bells ring and watermelons come tumbling through the Valley of Sorrows

The seeds took but three days.

On the third morning, when Moojie went to check the garden patch, he stood aghast. There before him lay more than a dozen fully grown watermelons clumped together like green dinosaur eggs. Seeds to sprouts, sprouts to shoots, shoots to vines, vines to leaves and buds, buds to fruit, in only three days! Had Father Time stepped out for tea?

He sniffed, tapped, and turned the watermelons to check for ripeness, just like Imi'tittu had told him to. Were they sticky? Was the color even? He thumped them, listening for the hollow sound. He turned them over, checking for yellow spots where they had touched the ground. Yes, they were ripe indeed! He let out a hoot and Millie-Mae barked. The goats in the field broke into maaing, the pigeons squeaked out a chorus. The sky shone bright and the clouds hummed with praise. *Watermelons! Fat, juicy watermelons! Magical watermelons!*

Pappy flew out the cabin door in his skivvies and boots, coffee mug in one hand, shotgun in the other. He hastened to the growing patch. "What is it? What happened? I'll blast those scalawags!"

Moojie pointed at the watermelons.

Pappy put his mug on the post and slowly uncocked his rifle. He stared dumbly and scratched his belly. "Well," he said, "I'll be dipped!"

That night a barn owl screeched outside Moojie's bedroom window. Moonlight pressed through the glass and soothed his burning eyes—eyes that had glimpsed heaven and were swimming in the afterglow. Phineas came purring to the cot and jumped up to lick Moojie's face, as if he understood. As if he could lick away Moojie's longing to share the good news with his friends.

Moojie wound his mother's music box and lay back on the cot. "Mamma," he said, hoping she could hear him, "something happened today." Her way of responding whenever he did anything surprising would be tears. Her lovely tears. He wanted to tell her he had been given a wand, a magical, mystical wand, with which he could sprinkle dust and turn little black seeds into great shining green houses. *Whoosh! Watch this, Mamma!* I will turn the dry fields into streams that flow to the sea and paint the grassy fields with wildflowers. And she would say *Bravo, Moojie! Bravo!*

Everything felt different that night: the trees, the sky, the stars, the moths, the bats—everything. Different and the same. It didn't make sense, and it made perfect sense. Magic was everywhere. The sun and the stars, the planets, galaxies, seas, and mountains; the people, the creatures, even the tiny seeds, were truly, suddenly, magical. Ladyship Ninti and Imi'tittu had opened his eyes. They had introduced him to a new world, a thrilling world of rolling green planets and pink skies and black stars. He laughed aloud. He was Aladdin, living in a world rubbed out of a lamp.

At sunup the next morning, the twins came to see Moojie in the barn as he was milking the goats.

"Salaam," they said, hands folded, heads dipping.

"Shh!" Moojie said. He looked outside to make sure the light wasn't burning in the cabin, then went back to his milking stool next to Rainbow, the goat.

"That's Pearl," he said, nodding at the other doe. "You can milk her."

"Me first!" Manish said, shoving Shar to the side. He grabbed a bucket, got on his knees, and started milking.

"Quiet!" Moojie whispered loudly. "You know, y-you shouldn't come here anymore. Why do you keep coming?"

There was a sound outside the barn and the pigeons stirred in the loft. Moojie held up his hand to silence the twins. He heard nothing more. "I-I know you can hide in your cave," he said, "but that doesn't mean you're safe. Pappy has been keeping strange hours lately. You never know where he's going to be."

"Sarru'kan can make the cave entrance disappear," Manish said. "It's only visible at dawn, when we all come out for sunlight."

"Go. Tell Ninti. Tell her it's not safe to open the cave in the morning unless I-I sound the kazoo three times," Moojie said. "When I blow the kazoo, that means 'all-clear.'" He shooed the boys out of the barn.

When Moojie went into the cabin, he didn't see Pappy

sitting in the dark.

"I'll take a cup of coffee," the voice came from the wingback chair.

Moojie jumped, completely taken aback. His grandfather hadn't been awake that early in weeks.

"Any sign of the Hostiles?" Pappy asked.

"Actually, th-they aren't really Hostiles, Sir, they're something else." Moojie's pulse was speeding, his hand trembling as he lit the lamp.

Pappy's jaw went askew under his mustache. "Oh, flip me, boy, you been fraternizin'."

Moojie shifted into defense mode. "You said I was free. *You* lied! I-I'm not free. I'm like one of your pigeons!"

"If I was your father—" Pappy began, eyes unflinching.

"You're not my father," Moojie interrupted.

"Why, you little ungrateful sneak!" Pappy stood and lifted Moojie by the collar off his feet and raised a hand to strike him. All at once Phineas came out from under the sofa and sunk his claws into the back of Pappy's legs, sending him recoiling. He dropped Moojie, swirled about-face, seized Phineas, and pitched him across the room.

Silence rose like a red tide between Moojie and his grandfather, poisonous and sour-smelling. Moojie felt a little sick, his head throbbing. "I-I may not be th-the smartest boy in the world," he said, "but I'm not a frater-fraternizer. Mamma said I should spread kindness in every direction, a little kindness could change the world. The world needs more kindness, she said."

Pappy stalked out the door. Wincing and cursing his back, he began to load Moojie's watermelons onto the buckboard.

"Wait! No!" Moojie said, voice cracking.

"They're going to the green grocer."

"No! You can't … they're for the poor people!"

"We ain't no breadbasket of the Confederacy," Pappy said.

"They're mine, y'ole coot!" Moojie couldn't control himself. With one hand on his crutch, he tried to use the other to unload the watermelons. One slipped from his grip and broke open on the ground. He grabbed another.

"Someone's gotta take you down a notch or two," Pappy said, jerking the melon away from him, causing Moojie to lose his balance and fall. Pappy loaded the rest of the melons, climbed onto the wagon seat, and snapped the reins. "You took me for a fool, but I ain't no fool. If it weren't for my back, I'd be on that mountain today, roping Hostiles. Tell your chums in the hills I will soon deliver them to the edge of doom."

Pappy was gone until very late that night. Moojie realized he must have been eavesdropping outside the barn when the twins were there that morning. He must have overheard everything that was said. In a desperate attempt to win back his grandfather's approval, Moojie had fed and groomed the critters, flown the pigeons, mucked out the stalls, and even washed the dishes. All afternoon, he had scuffled the length of the porch, back and forth, muttering and scuffling, counting off the hours. He played Caruso on the gramophone, wrung his hands, and scuffled some more. He lit a cigarette and burned his finger on the match. Through the window, Phineas eyed him as if he were a dog. Moojie turned up the volume, Caruso's voice rising over the valley as the sinking russet light drained from the sky—slowly, like red oil.

Chapter 6

Moojie's marvelous afternoon with Babylonia

Moojie rode to the cave at dawn the next morning to prepare Ninti for the unexpected.

"He means to come after you!" he said, when Ninti and the twins came outside to greet him. "It was different before. He and McTavish used to talk and joke with each other, a-and they laughed a lot."

"And what has changed?" Ninti asked.

"Pappy's crabby now, just serious, you know, plotting."

"And what is he plotting?"

"I don't know. Y-you've seen the hole in the field, haven't you? The one they were digging till Pappy hurt his back. I went out there the other day. There's a tunnel and a locked door at the end of it."

Ninti lowered her eyes and folded her hands together. She didn't seem to know what to say.

"Many good thanks, my lord," Manish said. "Have

you noticed anything else?"

"Pappy goes t-to the village and he gets the people riled and pretty soon they're going to come after you. I-I've got a bad sense about it."

"Riled? What does that mean?" Manish asked.

"Yes, what does it mean?" Shar repeated.

"What did you hear, my lord?" Ninti asked.

"'*Afterclaps.*' They kept saying it l-like it was secret code. '*Afterclaps.*'"

"And what does it mean?" Ninti asked.

"I-I don't know."

"And?"

"Pappy said he was going to round your butts up."

Ninti looked wistful.

Moojie was still sitting on Hocus. "I gotta go. The old man will be waking up soon. I-I'll find out what I can."

Ninti said quietly to herself, "We are so close … so close."

"Close to what?" Moojie asked.

She didn't answer him.

"Let me join you now," Moojie said. "I-I won't let him hurt you."

"My lord, it will never work," Ninti said. "Alas, it is not your destiny …." She went back into the cave.

"Not my destiny! What did sh-she mean by not my destiny?" Moojie asked the twins.

It cost Moojie two squares of *sukulutu.*

"Well," Manish said, "it concerns your father."

"Papa?" Moojie said.

"Are you a peacemaker or not?" Manish asked.

"Aye, are you or not?" Shar said.

"The only kind of peace he'll get from me i-is a piece of knuckle sandwich," Moojie said.

"You must make peace with him, at least in your

heart, or you will both be doomed to suffer," Manish said.

"Guess we're cooked then," Moojie said.

"What about your quest?" Manish asked.

"Aye, what about it?" Shar asked.

Whereas Moojie was once brimming with hope, he was at the moment unable to lift his own hand for the weight of his flagging enthusiasm. Quest? He just wanted to be loved.

It was raining lightly when Pappy left for the village late that morning.

Babylonia sidled into the yard, and went straight to the chicken hutch.

Moojie sneaked up behind her and she jumped back in a fright. "I saved the blues for you," he said. He offered her a scuttle. She filled it with blue eggs. Moojie insisted upon giving her a ride back to the cave. They rode double on Hocus, across the field and through the woods, her arthritic joints going *clickity-clackity* all the way. Sitting up front, Babylonia held Pappy's red umbrella, and Moojie reached around her to guide the reins. She smelled like honey.

"How is your watermelon crop?" she asked him.

"Well—" he said.

"Who have you fed, my lord?"

"Well, it's complicated," he squirmed. He didn't want to appear a failure to her.

"What about your grandfather?" she asked.

"Actually," he said, "he's quite sad. He doesn't have a girlfriend." Goose bumps ran over his arms as he spoke about himself in disguise. He had the feeling of flying on a magic carpet.

"Well then, you must find him a girlfriend," she said.

The rain let up and Moojie couldn't help but run a hand along Babylonia's hair. She squirmed a little, gave him the umbrella, and took the reins.

"Careful," he said, "Hocus spooks easily."

The pine-scented air around them became filled with dragonflies, thousands of blue dragonflies, like transparent flying flowers. Moojie's world was transformed from something worrisome to something magical. Awestruck, he and Babylonia rode along with their hands outstretched to touch the vibrating wings. They came upon two handsome ones, a young man and a maiden, kissing under a tree.

"I think it's a good omen," Moojie said. Why he said that, he didn't know. Babylonia dug her bare heels into Hocus. She seemed in a hurry to get back to the cave.

As they rode up the mountain, there were no prosaic words to describe Moojie's state of mind. He was a poem. He was fire and light and dynamite. He had been watching for signs that she cared for him as more than a friend, and he now was beginning to think it was possible. Before she got off Hocus, Moojie took out his red pencil and drew a heart on the underside of her wrist. Her eyes lit up, but then she abruptly got down and said, "Go, I pray you!"

"But I like you. And the others, I like them, too."

"My lord, I owe Sarru'kan my life. You see, he rescued me from the emperor, and who knows what might have happened had he not been looking after us all this time!"

"Can't you just say thank you?"

She lowered her eyes.

"I don't get it. Do you love him? Tell me you love him and I'll forget about you."

She didn't answer.

"I-I've got something to say," he said. "I've been a-a bad person most my life. If I hadn't been so messed up, my mamma and papa would probably still be here. But I've changed, and …."

"Pray pardon, I must go—" she said, and ran into the cave just as Sarru'kan came outside.

"Upon God's teeth," Sarru'kan said to Moojie, "if you do not stay away from Lady B., I will turn you into a newt." He backed into the cave, and before Moojie's eyes the entrance fizzed and crackled and transformed into a wall of granite.

Poor Moojie. Poor clumsy, lovesick Moojie. He dreamed that night he was walking the plank of his own misguided ship, and when he jumped into the ocean, a dark-haired mermaid came to greet him.

Chapter 7

Wherein is recounted the desperate means by which My Lord tries harder to win the approval of the Light-Eaters

With renewed enthusiasm, and ignited by the promise of love, Moojie planted another watermelon crop. Since Pappy had relied on him to pick the vegetables and fruit for market, Moojie didn't expect him to come to the patch unless he drew attention to it, which he knew not to do again. Moojie plowed the ground, planted ten more seeds, did a little praising, and planted ten more. His last twenty.

The twins arrived early that morning, anxious to show Moojie something.

"Many good thanks and hearty greetings, my lord," Manish said. He unfolded a tattered page that had been ripped out of a medical encyclopædia, a picture of three contorted, scaly creatures—not human, not animal, not vegetable—who could have been the cousins of Cyclops.

"The work of Sarru'kan," Manish said.

Moojie studied the picture.

"My lord," Manish said, "before your grandfather came here, the ranchers tried to rope Sarru'kan like a bull, and Sarru'kan summoned the spirit-demon, that is to say, the six-headed serpent Nahzi, and cast a terrible spell upon them, changing them into monsters. These are pictures of them before they joined the circus."

Moojie's heart went out to the strange miscreations. He knew what it was like to be a freak. "Sarru'kan doesn't scare me," he said.

"But he has done worse!" Manish said. "He once exploded the eyeballs of a band of hunters upon the mountain."

"Eyeballs!" Shar said, pointing to El Serrat. "On the mountain!"

Moojie wondered if this explained the story of the hunting party that had ended up as lunch for the vultures.

"Methinks you had better keep away from Sarru'kan," Manish said to Moojie.

"I can handle him," Moojie said.

"You ought not offend him," Manish said.

"Ought not!" Shar echoed.

An inexhaustible optimist, Moojie shrugged it off. But the news did put Sarru'kan into a different perspective and Moojie was determined to find out how he operated. He took out some chocolate and held it up. The twins grabbed for it. "Nuh-uh," he said. "First, the coin trick."

"I cannot explain how to do it," Manish replied. "Just try to understand. Everything is light."

Shar interjected, "It is not the coin that appears, but a part of oneself."

"Be careful," Manish said. "Sarru'kan is a powerful

magus, able to summon spirits from the vast deep. What is your word for magus?"

"Upchuck," said Moojie.

"Is that French?" Shar asked.

The next time Moojie saw Sarru'kan, he was at the creek making paper with Babylonia and the twins. Moojie called out for him, and when he turned around—by force of will, and summoning the power of his mind—Moojie extended his mighty righty, held his breath, and concentrated with all his might. Imagine his surprise when he opened his palm and found a squirming yellow, white-and-black-striped blob in it—a live caterpillar!

"Ah!" Shar exclaimed.

Visibly surprised, Babylonia and Sarru'kan approached Moojie.

"*Ellu!* Ha!" Sarru'kan snorted. He examined the caterpillar and, in a low, gravelly voice, a voice spiked with malice, said in French, "Maggots have no magic."

Having had French lessons from his mother, Moojie understood perfectly what Sarru'kan said. And yet, he remained transfixed on the caterpillar. *Did I do that?*

Sarru'kan cocked his head and continued speaking in French. "He is a worm, just like that filth in his hand!" And then he jerked away one of Moojie's crutches, causing him to topple to the ground, sat upon Moojie's back, and slurped a fresh plum. Moojie squirmed to get out from under his weight. He reached behind himself to grab an arm or a leg. It was pointless. He was helpless as, well, a worm. He floundered, stupidly at a loss for words, and when at last something came out, it wasn't what he expected. Out poured a stream of words—wet, buttery *French* words! "Nothing is wrong with being a caterpillar, or a worm since they're beautiful, and if it wasn't for them, flowers wouldn't bloom and there wouldn't be any color in the spring." The phrases just gushed out, clear and sparkling. To think that at one time his tongue had been Sleepy the Dwarf! He even surprised himself.

The twins backed away. "Sahib is unclogged!" Shar whispered. Babylonia blinked with astonishment. Sarru'kan stood, speechless.

And then, from the trestled bridge, the sound of wagon wheels.

The Light-Eaters disappeared with a *whoosh!* behind the granite outcropping, sweeping away their footprints in the sand with lilac switches. Was Pappy coming? Had he seen them? What would Moojie do if he had? The last thing he needed was to be skinned alive.

Moojie trekked up the trail toward the cabin, still stewing about Sarru'kan. A diabolical idea came to mind, a plan that would put the magus in his place once and for all: What if he snitched on the clan? Ha! What if Pappy knew what was *really* going on at the creek and in the fields when he was gone? There came an awful tightening in his throat. The spot of light came back into his field of vision, like a sunspot in a camera lens. Everywhere he looked, it followed his line of sight. Everything outside him—the shrubs, the creek, the woods—appeared to be transparent, nearly formless and colorless. Aggravating.

He stumbled into the yard, heart thumping, brow dripping, just as the wagon rolled in. The driver had on a dark shirt like Papa used to wear. For a minute, Moojie thought it was his father. His breath flew out of him.

No. It wasn't Papa. It was Moojie's grandfather. And the spot of light was gone.

The idea of using magic to win his place in the tribe burned inside Moojie. With a fervent desire to know more about the miraculous caterpillar that appeared in his hand, he opened *The Waltzing Lobster* and flipped through the pages feverishly, looking for clues. He studied pictures of prehistoric cave art, ancient maps, constellations, and clay tablets. The secrets of the universe were right at his fingertips, in little black letters, sentences and paragraphs, and yet for him they were still illegible, as hard to follow as ants running across a surface of water. He closed the book in a rage, cursing himself for ever believing he was gifted.

He was shaken by the image of Babylonia walking away from him at the creek, saying "Beware the equinox." Spring was yet to bring about so many unknown changes. It pained him to think of what lay ahead. If the future were an ocean, he was standing at the center watching it freeze from the edges toward him.

Chapter 8

The handsomest watermelon in the world

Watermelons! Miraculous watermelons! Stunned, Moojie stood motionless at the gate of the growing patch gaping at the yield of his three-day crop. He counted at least forty Ali Babas, but what surprised him most was one watermelon off to the corner by itself—a whopping gourd the size of a pig!

How the devil am I going to hide that from Pappy?

He expected Pappy to be a problem when he came back from the village—but Sarru'kan? He didn't see it coming.

By afternoon, word of the miraculous crop had already reached the cave. Moojie didn't venture to guess how. Sarru'kan showed up, like a rune or a curse, like a horrible newspaper headline, all bold and ciphered. Accompanied by his two chums, he marched directly over to the behemoth melon, and with one swift stomp of his foot, severed the vine from the mother plant. He shoved

Moojie aside and sent the melon rolling across the yard, roaring with laughter after it flattened a blue belly.

"Knock it off!" Moojie croaked. He started toward them angrily.

While the others held Moojie off, Sarru'kan straddled the melon pretending to ride it, then he hopped off, pointed his spear at it, and uttered something incomprehensible. The air turned green, and the wondrous Ali Baba shook and rocked and burst into a hundred pieces, each transforming into a pink toad.

The hot fury came over Moojie. "He's all smoke and mirrors," he said. Breaking away, he pounced upon Sarru'kan, knocking him to the ground, wanting him to choke on the dust till his body had no breath left in it, wanting to leave this brown worm to cook in the sun and be eaten by vultures. Out from the shade and into the stark sunlight they rolled, pitching side-to-side, gasping and grunting like dogs. Moojie was volcanic, Sarru'kan monkey fast, sinewy, dark, slippery. Sarru'kan threw Moojie onto his back and tried to pin his arms but Moojie heaved him off and straddled his chest, pinning him with his knees.

Just then, the twins came bounding across the field on their spears. "Prometheus the Fire-lighter!" they sang, while vaulting through the air. Manish took such a wild, bounding leap over the fence that he landed in the horse trough. *Kersplash!* The last thing Moojie remembered was Sarru'kan throwing him off, hopping to his feet, and taking a Herculean swing with his arm.

When he came to, Moojie's world was fuzzy and upside down. He lay on the ground cradled in Babylonia's arms, looking up at Ninti, and twin moon faces, and a friendly blue dragonfly flitting and bobbing overhead. Babylonia was whispering a quiet prayer in their language, a lovely-sounding prayer, that Moojie assumed was reserved for saints. Only one person in his life had ever cradled him the way she had that day. His mother. In six years, he had become so accustomed to the absence of affection, that the experience made his heart dance inside his chest. He reached up to touch her face, the face of an angel.

She stiffened and stood abruptly.

Shar brought water from the trough in cupped hands to rinse Moojie's bloody nose. Manish drew a bamboo comb through his hair. Then the twins started collecting watermelons seeds from the ground. The older named Kisha was not pleased about the pink toads congregating in the yard. Moojie caught a glimpse of her raising her shoulders at Ninti, opening her hands, and jutting her chin toward Sarru'kan. She hadn't said it aloud. It couldn't be broken down by logic; and yet Moojie heard her thoughts: *This is the best we can do?*

"Sarru'kan!" Ninti roared. The thunder in her voice could command an army.

Sarru'kan swaggered over to her, rubbing the scorpion scar on his navel.

"Dear one," Ninti said, "should you continue in this manner, I will take it upon myself to endow you with an unbearable skin condition." She then sent him glistening into the field—hair smoothed back, dark, shiny, trailing down his back. "Into the woods for mushrooms," she said. "Nothing with gills, my sweet!"

"Lord Sarru'kan, Savior of the New World," Kisha said sarcastically. "A bear cannot carry an egg upon a spoon."

"He makes a fine warrior," Ninti said. "Who else will protect us?" She surveyed the yard and motioned for Babylonia to follow Sarru'kan.

"Have you no other family?" Ninti asked Moojie. The

twins helped him to his feet and gave him two handfuls of watermelon seeds.

"One aunt. She hates goats," Moojie said.

Ladyship studied him closely, bearing an expression that fell between consternation and pity. "And, what of your quest to feed the poor?"

"Take all the watermelons y-you want," Moojie said, pointing a crutch at the growing patch. "Let's call it done."

"My lord," she said, "is there no one in the village?"

"WHAT?" His voice a scrape of tin.

"Peace," Ninti said, raising a hand. She had a way of calming him like no one else. She would say, "Peace peace," and he felt he might lift off the ground. Or she would begin a sentence with, "It is written …." and her words, honeyed and woodminty, smelling of citrus and dark earth, caused great hope to surge through his body. And Moojie would think, *I can do this.*

Ninti took off her medallion and put it around his neck. On one side, there was an image of a seated man wearing a nimbus and holding a book. On the other, were the very faint words: *IS, XS, basile.* Moojie took the gesture to mean that Ninti had accepted his offer to give the clan food as proof of his willingness to honor the first rule of The Code, and that finally his wish to join them, to belong to a real family with brothers and sisters and cousins and uncles who accepted him—the only thing in life that mattered—would be fulfilled.

"So when can I move in?" he asked.

"There is yet the second rule of The Code."

"Is this thing magic?" he asked of the medallion.

"Oh dear, no! It is very old and very real."

"When are you going to teach me the coin trick?"

"My lord, let us not speak of coins again. I teach miracles, not magic. Continue your quest to feed the poor. It is a noble one."

Moojie could only think of Babylonia's touch. Even in the midst of that joy, he knew he would have to go back to his grandfather's cabin and return to his own room, where the only signs of affection ever came from a pair of pumping cat paws.

"Forget it. Forget about the coins. Forget about the watermelons. I don't believe in miracles anyway," Moojie said. "This world is impossible. I'm sick of impossible! I-I just want to be happy."

A long silence.

"Good," Ninti said. "We are finally getting somewhere."

"My lord is becoming mindful," Manish said.

Watching Ninti leave the yard, Lord Littleman, Lamptosser and Footdragger, dared to think he had just earned a halo. He closed his hand gently around the old medallion as if it were a holy relic, and tucked it inside his shirt.

Quickly, he rolled the watermelons from the growing patch into the barn with his feet, one by one, as if they were green soccer balls. Since coming to St. Isidore's, his right arm had doubled in strength, and he had learned to handle a pitchfork while balancing on one crutch. And this was what he was doing, throwing straw over the watermelons to hide them, when Sarru'kan grabbed him from behind by the throat. Moojie dropped the pitchfork, lowered to his knees, and with one great, godlike spasm, flipped Sarru'kan over his head and onto his back, took up the pitchfork, and pointed the prongs directly into Sarru'kan's stunned face.

Sarru'kan held out his hands to concede defeat.

On his way out of the barn, he turned back. "Mark these words, Claw Hand, you will never, and I mean never, be one of us."

Chapter 9

*In which Moojie finds a cohort
for his watermelon scheme;
and other amusing details*

Moojie, whose stubborn determination had relied upon the genius of nature and God's good grace, realized he would need another kind of help getting the watermelons to poor Greta and Uma in the village. He found the solution to his problem in the west field, amid the rattlesnake grass and hot sage that smelled of bitter tea, amid the apiaries—Zagros, Lord of the Bees.

"Salaam, sahib!" he said, as Moojie approached him on Hocus.

If anyone wanted to go to the village, it was Zagros. Every time Moojie saw him, he pumped him for news of the outside world. Wearing a ridiculous feathered head-dress, Zagros slinked around the hives in the manner of a genie or a wild cat, talking excitedly. "I had a vision last night!" he said. "It must have been the village. There were men and women singing in the church, walking in the park, kissing in the rain." He opened a hive and pulled out a honey-dripping, bee-covered frame. The bees didn't seem to mind his doing this. They flew off and settled on the next closest hive. Not one stung him.

"Well," Moojie said, "there's no church-dancing or rain-kissing in San Miguel. A-and loitering is against the rules ...."

"But one *must* loiter," Zagros said. "In a land where people dress in their dreams and sing like magpies, one must!"

"Does N-Ninti know about your visions?"

"Of course she knows. Ladyship knows everything. She never says anything; she just gives me that look." He made his eyeballs go in circles.

Moojie laughed.

When most of the bees had left the honeycomb, Zagros put the wax-laden frame into a collecting bucket and replaced it with a fresh one. "I tell you," he said, "living in that cave is worse than horse feathers. So what if I go back to being a mortal? So what if I go another round of death and birth, so what? It is my choice to make, mine alone. Every day, a million choices. Sometimes they stack up behind each other, as if behind a closed door, and then one day the lock can hold no longer."

Moojie had never thought of it that way. "Okay," he said. "Here's one for you." He proposed a plan to have Zagros help him secretly smuggle watermelons to the village.

"Zounds! When do we go?" Zagros asked.

"Tomorrow morning. By the way," Moojie said, "if it isn't too much trouble, do y-you think you could get my name right?"

"What is the matter, sahib?"

"My name i-is Moojie. Not sahib. Not Claw Hand. Just Moojie."

"Moojie is not a real name."

"It was real to my parents."

Before sunup the next morning, Moojie milked the goats, flew the pigeons, and sounded the kazoo three times. His handwriting had improved with practice and he was now able to leave a legible note for Pappy: *Gone to check cows.* He and Zagros loaded three watermelons onto Pappy's buckboard, between the seat and the hay bale that was always there to hold supplies in place. Then they climbed up, coiled themselves around the melons and took cover under a tarp.

And they waited.

"What is the matter with the mother and child?" Zagros asked.

"They don't have proper beds."

"What is a proper bed?"

"I don't know. They don't have any money."

"What is money?"

"Oh boy."

"What news do you have of the cities?"

"McTavish says they're building underground trains now."

"Where?"

"On th-the other side of the world I guess."

"What about new inventions?

"Some talk about 'hamburgers,' some kind of new-fangled sandwich."

"What's a sand—"

"Shh!"

They fell asleep waiting.

It was afternoon by the time Pappy bungled out of

the cabin, loaded the milk cans onto the far end of the buckboard and climbed on. Behind him, Moojie and Zagros lay still as stones, corralling the watermelons. Pappy picked up McTavish and more milk tins. They made their usual stops, then left the buckboard at the horse trough in the park, and went into Tilly's. Like a clock.

The boys waited under the tarp until nightfall, keeping a wary eye on the men through Tilly's window. Zagros could hardly contain his senses as they flew out of him to savor the sights and sounds and smells, as he took in the window displays, the painted street signs, the men and women strolling along the boardwalk dressed in vests and bowlers, buttoned boots and feather hats. He gasped when a strand of electric lights blinked on outside the La Pâtis-serie window, illuminating mounds of Sally Lunns spiced teacakes, Graham Gems muffins, cinnamon swirls, and rock crystal candy.

"Bless me Moses!" he cried.

"Quiet!" Moojie said. "More than a few people would like t-to see you hanging by the neck."

"Sahib, I am famished," Zagros said.

Having never seen the clan actually sit down for a meal—except to sample wild berries and fruit, Moojie still half-believed they were man-eaters. "What do you eat anyway?"

"Light beams," Zagros said, spitting out a piece of straw.

Moojie rubbed his nose. "Liar."

"I never lie."

"Babylonia eats eggs."

"Never!"

"Well, wh-what's she doing with all the blue eggs?"

Zagros chuckled. "Look who is in love! Ah, yes, the lovely Lady B., she came to earth like the North Star.

Sometimes she shines too bright and sometimes she cannot be seen at all."

"Not so loud! Anyway, sh-she hardly even notices me."

Zagros lifted the tarp, letting in light to take a closer look at Moojie. "You do dress rather plainly, sahib."

"This i-is how I dress." Were dungarees unfit for Lady B.?

"Where I come from, sahib, love is a riddle."

They were quiet for a while.

When it was dark enough, Moojie went to fetch Greta under the park bridge. She was sitting with her daughter before a puny fire, stirring a tin can over flames. "You don't know me but—"

"I know you!" Greta said, visibly delighted. "You're the one we used to see in the park."

Moojie re-introduced himself and she invited him to sit and stay a while.

"I'm sorry ma'am, I-I'm in a bit of a hurry. But … well … see … it's like this: I've got something for you."

"Oh?"

"I-if you wouldn't mind bringing your cart, I'll show you."

Greta and Uma pulled their little cart across the park to the buckboard and Zagros started passing down the melons. Astonished, Greta hugged and kissed Moojie's cheeks.

"Biggest juiciest melons this side of the Nile!" Zagros said.

Moojie then tossed his crutches into the cart and helped to push it back to the bridge where Greta held out a nickel to pay him.

"Oh, golly, no!" Moojie said. "I-I don't want your money." He was ashamed that he and his mother hadn't helped her when she was younger.

"I heard your mamma died," Greta said. "Are you farin' okay?

"Well, I miss her every day, you know,"

"Yes, I know."

Nervous about being left behind, or worse yet, being caught giving away watermelons, Moojie lumbered back to the wagon. And Zagros was gone. Not under the tarp. Not on the street. Nowhere. Sick with worry, Moojie imagined his friend cornered at knifepoint by the superstitious villagers or whisked off to the jailhouse. He called his name. He sneaked past Tilly's, made one quick pass by the bakery, and circled back to the buckboard. Shaking mad, he climbed back onto the wagon.

Not two minutes before Pappy came out of Tilly's did Zagros jump under the tarp. Moojie had a mind to rail at him, but had to hold his tongue all the way home. But as soon as Pappy unhitched the burros and went inside the cabin, the words blew out of Moojie's mouth like a bellow.

"Gaw! Y-you could've been left behind! What were you thinking?"

"Sahib," Zagros said, "I saw the future, I saw it in the lights! Did you see those swirly rolls and crisscross buns? My life will never be the same. Zounds, how I yearn to crawl inside that food and dance!"

"Yep. Just as I thought. You're crazier than a fruit fly on a picnic table." Moojie was too exhilarated to stay angry. All he had to do was reflect on the moment when Greta saw the watermelons and hugged him, and whizz-bang, he was already setting his sights upon the next escapade. Moojie Littleman, Lord of Misfits, Savior of Trolls, lacking in the world's most valued possessions, and giving away what little he had on the enterprise of knight errantry, and Zagros, his loyal squire, of a less practical aspiration, yet important nonetheless, had together in a magnificent way, succeeded in feeding the poor!

Despite Pappy's vigilance and Sarru'kan's needling, Moojie and Zagros made a dozen more deliveries. It was sort of a good thing that Pappy had been hobbled with back problems, a good thing he liked his whiskey. If Moojie were to tell his grandfather the truth—that he had been spending every free minute of his time making inroads with the reviled tribe—no telling what he might do. To that end, Moojie developed a mastery for skirting his questions.

"Any sign of the bloody Hostiles?" Pappy would ask. "Footprints at the creek? Missing eggs? Trails in the grass?"

"Sir," Moojie would say, "y-you wouldn't believe the stag I saw in the woods!"

Or, "Say, we're near out o-of chicken feed."

Or, "This blasted heat beats all!"

Moojie's despair over losing his mother and father had slowly given way to new hope. He secretly believed the tribe would be his next family. That was one reason that he never questioned Zagros when he offered to help him get together with Lady B.

The afternoon Moojie set out to woo the enchanting Lady B., an autumn chill slipped into his bones. Sarru'kan had no hold on her. With a little advice from Zagros, Moojie was going to present himself as a proper suitor, and win Babylonia's heart. After giving the melons to Greta and Uma, he felt better about himself, a few inches taller and more grown up, and a good deal more optimistic about the future. Sitting high on Hocus Pocus, he arrived in the south woods, shirtless and sun-bronzed, a great warrior's face streaked with ash and berry juice, white-spotted and topped off with the monumental feather headdress—Zagros had promised this would take Babylonia's breath away.

She was right where he said she would be, leaning against the great oak, spear in hand.

"Zagros said I-I'd find you here," Moojie said.

"He was supposed to meet me here," she said, holding up her spear. "For practice." She looked past him to the field.

"Well, I was hoping to …."

The great oak broke into sudden laughter, leaves shaking and acorns falling, and out of its branches dropped three handsome ones. Sarru'kan and his ghouls.

"What have we here, a peacock disguised as a rooster?" Sarru'kan doubled over, slapping his leg. The others were laughing, too. Babylonia put her hand over her mouth, hardly concealing a pretty little guffaw.

Just what Moojie needed to make a good impression, to look like a moron in front of Babylonia *and* Sarru'kan! Immediately, Moojie thought Zagros had set him up to be the brunt of an awful prank. He couldn't look at Babylonia. He couldn't even see out of his eyes, they were so full of embarrassment. "Never mind," he said. He turned Hocus around and set her to a furious trot, her bloated belly vibrating with age as she charged back to the cabin. Fuming, he went to the horse trough and scrubbed the paint off his face.

Zagros slipped into the yard carrying a watermelon. "What news, sahib? Did the fair lady swoon?"

Moojie threw the headdress at him. "Gaw! I must have rocks for brains."

Zagros held up the watermelon and looked at it closely.

"Vegetable of the gods," he said.

"It's not a vegetable, it's a berry. Sh-she laughed at me."

"Some maidens have no taste."

"Sarru'kan put you up to this." Moojie tromped toward the cabin.

"No, sahib, upon my word, never! You looked magnificent! What happened?"

"Cheese and crackers, I'm stupid."

"Sahib, did you not know? Without being stupid, you will never know love!"

Chapter 10

An account of the unmerciful Sarru'kan
who has it out for Moojie

For a whole week, Moojie would not deem to show his face to the clan. It was enough for him to sit on the porch rocker rolling and smoking Pappy's tobacco, watching the autumn sun draw its gilded curtain across summer. Lulled into a warm lethargy, he let his eyelids drop, and fell asleep for who knows how long.

The wind kicked up. In the field, Hocus Pocus started bucking about, snorting, rearing her head, the wind playing wildly through her mane and tail. Moojie knew Hocus well enough to suspect something was amiss—for in all his years of living at St. Isidore's, he had never seen her budge without a certain degree of persuasion. Millie-Mae barked and whined on the porch next to him. Percolating and flapping their wings in the loft, feathers flying, feed spilling, the pigeons had broken into panic.

Dread crawled up Moojie's spine and spread between his shoulders, pushing them upward.

An oily darkness blotted out the afternoon sun, and in the air above the cabin, only there, and nowhere else, there appeared a dark, oblong cloud. Further up the valley, the sky was blue. There was a crackling, tinny sound as the wind hurled itself at the cabin. Scanning El Serrat with the field glasses, Moojie half-expected to see a wildfire. Something high on a peak caught his eye: Sarru'kan, Lord of Magic and Master of Caprice. The tip of his spear was directly pointed at Moojie, belching great quantities of boiling smoke out the end, and the air above the dairy turned thick and sour, greasy even, the color of blue velvet. The wind blew dirt and hay and leaves at the cabin, making Moojie lose sight of both the mountain and Sarru'kan. Then the darkness began to spiral, like a tornado, expanding at the top, rising and swirling, splitting into a half-dozen trajectories and each one taking the shape of a serpent's head. A hot wind smote the cabin. The tin roof flapped and the walls creaked and strained. Six serpents' heads turned and looked directly at Moojie. There was an icy void in his throat. Were Sarru'kan and his evil twin Nahzi going to destroy the cabin?

Asleep in his wingback chair, an empty whiskey bottle next to him, Pappy hadn't so much as stirred. Moojie didn't dare wake him since he would just grab the rifle and gun down the whole clan. Evil, sorcery, black magic, whatever it was, Moojie had never seen the reach of this power, but he was determined to stay calm. He closed Millie-Mae in the barn and crossed the yard. The trees rustled, and the rooster crowed, and the words rung out inside his head: *Stand unmoved before the perverse and the crooked and you will know the power of love!* Where had he heard that before? He couldn't place it. Ears ringing, electricity crackling all around him, a downward pressure flattened him from above, making it impossible to reach the porch. It closed in on all sides of his body, and he couldn't move.

He clung to something Ninti had once said: Evil has no power unless you believe it does. Refusing to be impressed by Sarrukan's show of force, he pressed on toward the cabin. Inside, he went straight past his sleeping grandfather, into his room, sat on his cot, closed his eyes, and ignored the whole spectacle. Unmoved. Peace. Peace peace peace. Unmoved.

The noxious cloud soon lifted above the valley, up and over the mountains, and sunlight again flooded the dairy. Hocus Pocus resumed grazing, and the pigeons went back to babbling.

Moojie went outside and scanned the mountain again with the field glasses. What had ended the whole, greasy, boiling display of magic, he couldn't explain. But it felt good and right and fine, like spring rain and birds singing and sunshine dancing upon the laughing creek. From the high crest, Sarru'kan was glaring at him, shaking his head.

"What you lookin' at?" Pappy asked from behind him.

Moojie jumped. He had to think fast.

"Vulture," he said. "Just another dagnabbed vulture."

Chapter 11

*The dreadful and unforeseeable conclusion of
the watermelon capers*

For a while after Moojie clashed with Pappy over the
watermelons, his grandfather was on him like a tick on a
dog. At least, when he was conscious. Something had
changed. It was a wonder he didn't ship Moojie off. He
pestered Moojie to ride the exercise bike. He hounded
him to shine his boots, to comb his hair. He insisted that
Moojie accompany him on deliveries. But then a letter
would come from Auntie Tilda, and Pappy would throw
it into the stove and, instead of threatening to get rid of
Moojie, he would wax philosophical over the virtues of
self-discipline and the price of freedom. The only threats
he made were aimed directly at the clan. But ever since
he had been dogged by back pain, sometimes to the point
of lying prostrate on the floor for hours, he had been
unable to carry out his threats. For weeks, the work in

the east field had been abandoned, and he hadn't ridden up El Serrat.

In an effort to appease Pappy, Moojie went along with his demands. Despite Moojie's stiff legs and cramped arm, he was getting around better, and had slowly gained strength. Dairy work had served him well. "Sometimes good things aren't what they're supposed to be," he told Phineas. He rarely thought of his father or of going home. He wasn't a foolish boy anymore. He was a young man.

As the year's end drew closer, Moojie dreaded the coming spring and the ominous earthquake of earthquakes. The world was speaking in omens now: a rainstorm caused Copper Creek to swell up like a great wounded dragon that bled into the fields, gushing in a rapid course down the center of the valley, taking with it sand and rock, its red clay banks exposed and smelling of blood. Raindrops the size of strawberries pummeled the cabin. Freak lightning storms, suicidal squirrels drowning in the water trough, and bats tumbling through bruise-colored clouds.

St. Isidore's Fainting Goat Farm had gone to pot. Manure and pigeon droppings now splattered the yard. Wadded paper, metal cans, and bottles spilled from overturned garbage cans.

Zagros came to the barn early one morning.

"Sahib, speak to me, speak of the world," Zagros said, as he watched Moojie milk the goats. "Tell me of the northern city."

"I don't know. Mamma said it had music halls and trolleys and gunslingers and gold diggers."

"What about the merchants and the exotic finery from foreign kingdoms? What about the spices and perfumes?" Zagros appeared electrified.

Moojie wanted to ignore him. He had closed up his heart and locked it tight. He didn't know who to trust anymore.

"What about the poor lady and her daughter?" Zagros asked. "What about the rest of the melons?"

"What about you wandering around the village a- and getting us both strung up? What about you setting me up for the ha-ha funny joke, dressing me like a fool?"

"It would no doubt please Ladyship."

"Forget it. It's too risky. I-I'm not doing anything but keeping out of trouble."

They made five more watermelon deliveries.

Zagros had convinced Moojie that he had no part in any prank, that Moojie was more than fetching decorated as an ancient warrior, and that Sarru'kan had acted out of his own dark purposes. In the end, friends and allies were as hard to come by as family, and friends bound by secret acts of kindness could make an unstoppable team.

Why would he think anything could go wrong?

On the night of their last delivery, Moojie sensed that Zagros had changed. Or had Moojie changed? He wasn't sure.

As usual, Moojie got up early and sounded the kazoo three times, while Pappy was sleeping. He did his chores, and then he and Zagros loaded the last melons onto the buckboard.

"So," Zagros said, "how goes the quest for Lady B., sahib?"

"Great, thanks to you."

"Aye, waiting for love is like waiting for yesterday."

"Yep."

"A riddle, yes?"

"Maybe."

"And?"

"Well, i-if love is the greatest power in the universe, it must be equal t-to the biggest number. And th-that number has to be a number that all the other numbers can fit into, right?"

"Big enough to include all the stars, all the galaxies, and every living thing."

"I got it, then," Moojie said. "I-I got the answer."

"We do not have all night." Zagros seemed in a hurry, nervous, jumpy. As they stood next to the buckboard, he scratched his head and sniffed his nose incessantly.

"Well, then I-I reckon love is the number *one*," Moojie said.

Zagros paused.

"Ha! Sahib *is* unclogged!" He patted Moojie enthusiastically on the back, knocking him off balance.

Prior to fetching Greta at the park, Moojie reminded Zagros once again to keep close watch on Pappy through Tilly's window, and to sound a robin's call if it looked like he was coming outside. "Stay put," Moojie said. "Don't forget the villagers have it out for you."

Zagros grinned and gave him a salute.

Whenever Moojie returned to the gas-lit village of seagull and moss-splattered centuries, he took stock in the fact that he'd been around the village most of his life and still didn't feel as if he belonged. With few exceptions, the villagers had always treated him as an outsider; they couldn't seem to get past his mixed blood or physical differences. He saw himself as a seed without ground, a rootless thistle. This was what he was thinking when he returned to the wagon, and found Zagros gone—again. He called out for him, but to no avail.

Moojie climbed under the tarp. Hours passed. The town clock struck midnight, and Zagros still hadn't come back. Beset with worry, Moojie took little comfort in the sugared night air or the childhood memories of his mother strolling his pram through La Pâtisserie's scintillating aromas. With every passing set of footsteps that didn't belong to Zagros, his stomach tightened.

When Pappy finally gangled outside, climbed onto the buckboard, and snapped the reins, Moojie was beyond furious. He silently cursed Zagros and himself. *How could I have let this happen? I knew he was up to something. Why didn't I keep an eye on him?*

Once back at the dairy, Moojie waited in the buckboard until Pappy doused the spirit lamp in the cabin. Alone, and in a vexation of spirit, he waited. How was he going to tell Ninti that he had lost Zagros?

Chapter 12

Window of heaven, Cave of Fire

Despairingly, Moojie rose from his cot before sunup, blew the kazoo three times, and charged up the side of El Serrat on Hocus Pocus, packing two tins of goat's milk and a basket of blue eggs. Unable to recall exactly where the Cave of Fire was located, he zigzagged and backtracked so many times he lost his bearings twice before getting to the entrance.

"What do you do when there isn't a door to knock on?" he asked Hocus.

She walked directly into the cave, down a dim passageway to a sort of antechamber. From there, Moojie just let her go until they reached the end of a tunnel where there had been a hint of light. They came to the opening of a gigantic cavern. Moojie had to dip his head down to avoid hitting the overhang as Hocus sauntered right into a scene bustling with Light-Eaters. Illuminated by oil lamps that hung from posts embedded in the walls, there were olders, handsome ones, and youngers alike. They were hunched over makeshift tables, squatting on the dirt floor, and circling the fire pit, all engaged in different activities, which they stopped immediately in order to stare up at Moojie and Hocus Pocus. Wide-eyed Moojie was appalled at what looked like a grisly gallery of human skulls hanging from wall hooks. If he didn't know better he might think they were busy with the ghoulish chore of dismembering their next meal. He laughed when he realized the heads were merely gourds with cut-out holes that looked like mouths.

"Sorry," he said to the group. "I-I should have knocked."

The air stunk of mushrooms, wood smoke, and orange peels, of old treasure chests and dark secrets. Black roots reached through the limestone ceiling like wild hairs growing between teeth. A fire pit glowed with embers at the center of the cavern. At a table made of an old door, Imi'tittu looked up from a scroll, dipped a feather quill into a pot, and winked at Moojie.

"Would you care to pull up a chair?" Ninti asked Moojie. Everyone hissed and buzzed and went back to work.

Moojie got off Hocus, unstrapped his crutches, and gave Ninti the eggs and milk.

"Clever," Ninti said. "You sounded the kazoo to make certain we opened the cave." Moojie wondered if Ninti knew there was a salamander on her shoulder. "We were just finishing our work before going out to greet the sun," she said. She had him rinse his hands in a wooden bowl filled with water, something the Light-Eaters always did upon re-entering the cavern.

"Winter is upon us," Ninti said. She then held up a long, thin knitting project. Was it a broomstick cover? Whatever it was, she went back to work looping and knotting the yellowish wool with a small bone, maybe a bird's rib. "I believe you call it a sock," she said.

"A zucchini sock," Imi'tittu said.

More hissing and buzzing.

Off to the side, Moojie spotted a mound of blue eggs nestled atop a straw mound, the keepers that he had marked with red hearts. It was a comfort somehow. Nearby, the older named Kisha was twisting wool onto a top-whorl spindle. Next to her, two fellows were weaving grass mats, and an older was piling dried grass with a crude wooden rake. Shar was rolling beeswax into candles, the smallest youngers were dipping their fingers into a honey pot, and a maiden with a baby slung across her shoulders ground a mortar and pestle. She stopped, chewed a bit of fig, and slipped it into the baby's mouth.

Pappy would flip his pancakes if he ever saw this!

"His name is Shemman," Ninti said of the baby. Moojie leaned forward to have a closer look. The baby's eyes, wide-set and overlarge, looked like a goat's—the palest of blue, iceberg blue. Had Moojie not been anchored on his crutches, he surely would have fallen backward because a booming male voice came out of that baby's little beak, saying: "Greetings, brother. I have cast a fire upon this earth and I shall guard it till it blazes!"

"Whoa! That doesn't sound like a baby!" Moojie said dumbfounded.

"You mustn't let appearances fool you," Ninti said. "Shemman is older than all of us by star years."

Babylonia and Sarru'kan came into the cavern. One look at Moojie, and Sarru'kan withdrew into the shadows with a mocking snort. Babylonia's braids were coiled about her head, made into a wreath decorated with wildflowers. Moojie couldn't take his eyes off her as she poured orange-scented water from a clay pitcher into a wooden box and rinsed her feet. His heart turned to a lump of ice cream, scooped and melting.

"You see, my lord, we are very busy," Ninti said.

"And very clean."

"A riddle," she said. "What is greater than love, and more wicked than the imagination; the poor have it, the rich need it, and if you eat it you will die?"

Oh boy, another cannibal joke. Moojie thought a moment then shrugged his shoulders.

"Nothing!" she laughed. "Nothing is greater than love; nothing more wicked than the imagination; the poor have nothing, the rich need nothing; and if you eat nothing you will die!"

She grinned. The salamander on her shoulder grinned, too.

Muddled and misty and full of butterflies, Moojie asked, "W-Why do you always talk in riddles? Why not j-just say what you mean?"

"Ah, this I do," she said. "I mean what I say. That is the same thing."

"It's not the same thing," Moojie protested. "I-If that was true, then to say *I see what I am* would h-have the same meaning as *I am what I see.*"

Babylonia peeled a fig with her teeth. Moojie sighed, feeling stupid. Again.

"I need to talk to you …" he said to Ninti, "… it's about Zagros …."

Sarru'kan came up from behind and jostled Moojie, causing him to drop one of his crutches and knock a lit candle onto the floor. Quickly, Ninti and the twins doused a fire in the straw.

"Are you all right, my lord?" Babylonia asked Moojie.

"Yep," he said. "Just clumsy." He wasn't going to give Sarru'kan the pleasure of being noticed.

Ninti offered him a bamboo culm with a deer antler fastened to the end. "Imi'tittu made this for you. It is for earthquakes." He laid his crutch aside and took the bamboo as a staff. She looped his left arm around her waist and, seizing an oil lamp, led him into a passageway off the cavern. He accidentally trod upon her feet. Oops. Sorry. Well. Like his feet, hers were hard to miss.

"I-I've got something to tell you—" he started again.

"Aye, we are aware that your grandfather is in pursuit of us. Your daily 'all-clear' signal is most helpful. We do require sunlight to survive, and of course, one can never predict the behavior of humans. Secrecy is crucial to our survival."

Moojie hesitated to tell her about Zagros. "I understand," he said. So much was happening, there were so many complications to their friendship, he just didn't know how to tell her the bad news. What if she got angry and banished him?

The air smelled of water, wet clay and bone. Streaked and calcified, the limestone walls appeared to be crying, and water seeped underfoot as they sloshed along the eerie underworld passage. They came to a low-ceilinged cavern with graffiti-splattered walls, hundreds of white hands drawn in double white lines, reaching upward, like ghost gloves, and pictograms, symbols and shapes scratched into rock. A collection of large earthen jars sat off to the side, some lidded, and some stuffed with paper scrolls. And just ahead, this chamber opened to another that was lit with the eeriest electric blue light.

"One can find truth in the tiniest bit of dust or in the grandest scheme of a galaxy," Ninti said, pointing to a black spiral on the wall.

"The beginning of the universe," Moojie said, thinking it looked like an electron.

"Very! You are wise beyond your years, my lord." He was surprised to hear this. For so long he had struggled to read and write, and had always believed that he was mentally inferior.

Ninti's shadow rose into the white haze above them, as if the lamplight had smudged her shadow onto the rock wall. Even if she were a cannibal, Moojie was beginning to trust her not to eat *him*. He leaned forward to get a peek into the blue-lit side-chamber, but she steered his attention back to a picture of a collapsing building, waves, tossing boats, and what looked like an astronomical chart.

"Before modern civilization," she said, "the sages read the history of the universe in the stars. They charted the zodiac to predict events. See here, this chart marks the next opening of the matrix, that is to say, the portal. It will open directly above this mountain, at the Circle of Trees."

"Oh yeah, the Circle of trees!" Moojie said. He recalled what his grandfather, a fount of archeological knowledge, had said about the site being a place for ritual sacrifice.

"It is a sacred site," she said. "Every solstice and every equinox, we return to the meadow to re-establish our contact with home."

Overcome with curiosity about the blue chamber, Moojie wasn't really listening. He leaned in its direction to try to see what was inside.

"My lord," she said, "pay attention. You must beware the pandemonium."

Moojie had grown a little skeptical about all that talk. "You sound like Father Grabbe."

"The Earth may thunder and rumble and lions may rattle in their cages, but you need not fear," she said.

"So when the end comes, what are we supposed to do?"

"Stand unmoved before the perverse and the crooked."

Moojie's hands tingled. There it was again! It was as if Ninti, and the past, and the future, were all speaking to him in a language he hadn't mastered.

"My lord, be of good cheer!" she said. "There was light before there was sun. There was light before the stars, and before the seas." Her hands moved with her words, rolling about each other, undulating, diving, soaring like two lovebirds tying invisible ribbons around his future. As if the world falling apart was akin to a Fourth of July party, where people blow holes in the sky with fireworks and dance on tables and make fools of themselves, then wake up in the morning to a new day.

"What's in there?" Moojie asked, pointing to the blue chamber.

She gestured for him to look. Peering into the small opening, he was astonished by what he saw. There was a collection of strange plants growing out of the rocks like sea anemones: all emitting tiny, blue spores of light that rose and dissipated.

"We must get back," she said.

"Wait, please, I-I've got something to tell you! It's about Zagros." That finally got her attention, and Moojie was able to explain what had happened the night before. When he was finished, he watched for her reaction. She just looked at him—her eyes, sharp as a clean blade.

They returned to the main cavern and Ninti announced to the others that it was as they had suspected, Zagros had chosen to return to "the human equation."

Gasps all around.

"What?" Manish cried.

"Are you sure?" Imi'tittu asked.

"What ever happened?" Babylonia asked.

"He wanted to go to the city," Moojie said.

"You lost our brother?" Manish asked.

"Let us not make hasty judgments," Ninti said. "Zagros chose his own path. We are all free to choose. We must pray that he be guided safely home."

Sarru'kan remained unusually quiet in the corner by himself, sharpening the tip of his spear against a boulder.

"I-I wish I had never asked Zagros to help me," Moojie said. He wished he knew the difference between being stupid and brave.

"Where you been, Littleman?"

The voice in the barn gave Moojie a horrible start. Standing next to Hocus Pocus, he turned around to see Pappy smoking in the doorway.

"Roughly, uh," Moojie said, "here and there."

"What's that you got around your neck?"

Moojie realized that Ninti's medallion had come out of his shirt. He went pale. As soon as he found his voice, he set about spinning a tall, involved tale that had something to do with the old well pump, and his discovery of the necklace when he was cleaning out the main line, and then his thinking maybe it had belonged to a prehistoric hunter that aliens had lured into a flying saucer, or maybe it belonged to a cowboy who got into a boat and sailed from San Miguel to China, where a secret army of assassins took him hostage.

"Why if that ain't the biggest load of all-fired hogwash," Pappy said. He swept a hand across Hocus's back. "She's hot. She's hot like she's been ridden farther than the well pump. Hot like she's gone up the mountain." His eyes widened. "Is this how you thank me? By lying? You been up yonder with the riff-raff, ain't you, boy?"

"Well." Moojie's head was throbbing. He searched his brain for what to say. How was he going to get out of this one? "See, sir, I-I wanted to catch one of those devils myself. I spotted one this morning and chased him up El Serrat. I know y-you don't want me going up there, but I came this close to grabbing him by the hair, got right up next to him. Dang, he was fast!"

"Hm," Pappy said. "What'd he look like?"

"All scars a-and mean-eyed, like the devil."

"Yeah, I know the one."

"This close." Moojie showed the measure of an inch with his thumb and index finger.

"Listen, boy. You got no business goin' after them Hostiles. You wanna hunt, shoot a few squirrels. Leave the big game to me."

"Yessir." Moojie's pulse was still bouncing.

On the way out of the barn, Pappy dropped a glowing cigarette ash into the straw and a little fire started. Moojie burned the cuff of his trousers stamping it out. He was getting good at putting out fires. But Pappy wasn't the only fire-starter. Having been to Tilly's Tavern, Moojie knew he was only one of many.

Chapter 13

*Of what befalls Moojie and his trusty
squire Phineas at the hands of
Captain Finnegan*

Pappy crept around late that night, a phantom in socked feet, sipping a steeped concoction that caused a green, hovering haze throughout the cabin.

In the morning, he poured boiling water into a tall ceramic mug with a hinged lid. "Cracked corn," he said to himself, as if reacting to his own thoughts. The ingredients were lined up on the kitchen table. He drizzled maple syrup into the mug, grunting and wincing with every move. "Three pinches cayenne. One gunpowder. Stir."

"Can I help, sir?" Moojie asked.

"Nope."

Pappy took a pinch of chewing tobacco from a tin, and added it to the concoction. The look on his face said everything, skin blanched and sweating: the torment of pain.

Phineas came out from under the table, stringy, brown, and fur-clotted.

"That cat needs brushin'," Pappy said.

"H-he won't let anybody …."

Pappy let out a moan and, with lightning-bolt action, took Phineas by the scruff of his neck. Eyes bulging, teeth and gums bared, Phineas hung helpless in mid-air while Pappy rummaged through the kitchen drawers with his free hand.

"Let go of my cat!" Moojie said. He grabbed at his grandfather's arm, knocking him backward. Pappy winced and, still gripping the cat, got hold of a pair of sheep shears. Cursing, grimacing, eyes glinting with madness, he marched out to the porch and sat down heavily on the rocker. He flipped Phineas onto his back, pinched his head between his legs, and fleeced him to the quick— neck to tail. Phineas snarled and growled and spat, his brown fur rising on the chilly morning air.

"Gaw, stop it!" Moojie cried.

Hairless as a Chihuahua, Phineas got loose and raced back into the cabin. The furious Moojie followed him into his bedroom and slammed the door.

"I'm the end of the line, boy!" Pappy said.

In the silence that followed, Moojie worried that he had just as good as signed off his own exit papers. And he was beginning to believe Pappy had been right: for every blessing there was a curse, for every curse a blessing. Pappy, his guardian and jailer. The Light-Eaters, friends and foes.

Moojie reached under the cot, lifted Phineas up to his lap, and stroked his ears the way he liked. "I-I should have done this sooner. Watch out for vultures." He opened the window and let Phineas go free. "Go get her, Phinny.

Show her what you're made of." He looked up at the white clouds, imagining the great disaster ahead. He thought about Greta and Uma in the park, cooking over a fire, and the unsuspecting villagers going about their business. He thought about the clan, up in the cave, doing something else altogether, carrying out some sort of pre-historic congress.

"Pappy's wrong," he said aloud. "He is not the end of my line."

Chapter 14

*Cripes, she's back; a lumpishly awkward reunion
wherein Auntie Tilda tries to extricate young
Moojie from the extremely questionable
circumstances at St. Isidore's*

She came like early winter, without welcome, as if her charm bracelets sounded the change of seasons, marching across the yard in button boots, African bubu and kufi, flaming hair and freckles, smelling of talcum powder and vinegar. Since the funeral, she had doubled in bulk and bad tidings. She nearly suffocated Moojie in a hug. "Dear lad, dear, dear laddie," she said, rattling her charm bracelet. "I'm appalled to say the least. You living out here with the rusty cannon."

"I'm fine, thank you, Tilda," Pappy said sarcastically. "And you?"

"What business do you have raising a child?" she asked.

"He ain't complainin'."

"You're talking like a cowboy. Have you forgotten your homeland? Bloody fool. Anyone can see the lad hasn't been eating. And look at his hair."

Moojie hadn't noticed until then that he had gotten thinner and his hair had grown past his shoulders.

Pappy made sardine casserole for supper, and the grownups emptied two bottles of wine that McTavish had made in his dairy cellar. Wine-softened, Auntie Tilda took on a different demeanor, and it wasn't long before she and Pappy were commiserating like long lost girlfriends. Pappy complained about the heat, his back, and the Hostiles. Auntie Tilda mourned her wasted youth, and the end of the smalt mines, far and be gone. Next thing you knew, they were lamenting the potato famine in Ireland and howling "Danny Boy."

After supper, Moojie went to his bedroom, but he spied on the grownups, listening anxiously for any indication of change to his situation. He wouldn't allow himself to be frightened by what they decided, and was already searching his imagination for new, deviously brilliant ways to delay their decisions. He could pretend to be sick or maybe arrange to fall and make it look worse than it was, but then he would be made to endure any manner of Pappy's home remedies and who knows what kind of regimen. Surprisingly, they didn't talk about him at all. With his future in the balance, they were carrying on as if it were a nice, cozy family reunion. Millie-Mae made like felicity, circling the kitchen, Oh boy, oh boy, oh boy, while they reminisced and revisited and recalled the old days, giggling until breathless, and toasting their "airlocked" selves.

"You know," Pappy said to her, "my ten children, your nieces and nephews—I mean the ten that are left— they've become strangers to me. At the funeral, they were *polite.* Like infantry."

"God knows, you were no saint as a father," Auntie Tilda said.

Pappy turned away from her. "Eh, they deserted me. All but Katie. I get sick every time I think of her forever in the dark."

Auntie scooted to the end of the sofa and dabbed his tears with a tissue from her sleeve. "There, there, dear. Not to worry. If only you knew what death was like, you'd be on the boat today—all light and loveliness." She rose and snooped inside the icebox. "Turned goat's milk. Stale zucchini bread. A hunk of chocolate bitten into? For the love of God, Sean, how do you expect to take care of the boy?"

"Take the bed. Ask me in the morning."

"School? What about school?"

He flipped his arm over his eyes. "The boy can run dairy. He don't need school."

"'Tisn't right, I tell you, 'tisn't decent."

"Eh, he's all right, Tilda."

"Well, for your information, Henry has given me his blessing to take the boy to Ireland. I'd like to enroll him in a proper boarding school where he'll learn to dot his 'i's and cross his 't's."

There it was. Worse than anything Moojie had expected! Disaster!

"What the—?" Pappy rasped, scrambling to get to his feet.

"All right, all right," she whispered harshly, flopping her hands up and down. "No use getting aerated. You'll wake the boy."

"I-I'm already awake," Moojie said, clomping into the room.

"Oh, there's the dear," Auntie said.

"I'm not going." Moojie said.

Auntie looked at her watch. "No, you're not going anywhere just this minute, dear. 'Tis very late. Off to bed with you. We'll chat in the morning. I have a good bit of news to share."

"Is Papa back?" Moojie asked.

"Well, no," his aunt said. "I mean yes. I mean …" She prodded Moojie toward his room.

"… I have a letter."

"You're not taking me t-to the Steel Barn," Moojie said, refusing to budge.

"Of course I'm not," she said. "I wouldn't have it. Not to worry, now. Sleep tight."

"You're not taking me anywhere!" he said.

Auntie Tilda looked at Pappy, as if to get some help. He escorted her to his bedroom. "Tilda, take my bed. Get some rest."

"Wait—" she started to say, but he closed the door.

Pappy looked in at Moojie standing next to his cot, a shadow of dread and despair. "We'll talk in the morning," he said. "Get some sleep." And shut the door.

Moojie stood there, hovering like the ghost of himself, until he could stand no longer.

At sunup, Pappy was still asleep on the sofa. Moojie covered him with a blanket, made coffee, and went outside to tend to the critters.

Soon enough, Auntie Tilda bustled out to the yard in her bubu, hair a crown of flames. "Well, well, well," she said, "Captain Finnegan's living off the fat of the land, isn't he?"

"Watch," Moojie said, pointing at the pigeons circling overhead, "th-they move together," he said, "like one bird, l-like they have the same mind." He blew the kazoo, but only once, to call the pigeons back to the loft, careful not to give the "all-clear" signal to the tribe.

A cold gust swept through the yard.

Auntie Tilda squared Moojie's shoulders and held him against her great undulating belly.

"Poor lad. Auntie's going to straighten things out for you. You'll see. Your daddy wants what is best for you. You belong with me in Ireland."

"No Ireland!" Moojie shouted. He slogged back to the cabin.

Auntie came inside, poured a mug of coffee and put it on the low table in front of Pappy. He squinted. Her scrutiny fell over him like a dark curtain. "You'd think he was still in Ireland," she said to Moojie, who was standing against the wall, looking like a half-crazed owl from lack of sleep.

"Hell will freeze over before I-I go to Ireland," Moojie said.

Auntie Tilda tossed her shawl over her shoulder. "Desperate times call for drastic measures," she said. On with the kufi and out the door she waddled, waving to Moojie as she drove away in his father's buggy.

She was back the next day, with her drastic-measures smile and a basket of freshly baked scones.

"I should have stepped in sooner," she said to Moojie. "I should have taken you after the funeral. But I didn't know your father was going to … to … anyway, I've wanted a child all of my life and by God you deserve a better home than this."

"Nothin' doin'!" Moojie thundered. "I-I'm not going! I have friends here. I don't know anybody in Ireland." Shaking from head to toe, he hammered his crutch on the kitchen floor. He came dangerously close to divulging his plans to join the Light-Eaters.

"Why, this bloke is out of control!" Auntie Tilda said to Pappy.

"Can you blame him?" Pappy asked. "He's got an idiot for a father and a gasbag for an aunt."

Moojie lumbered outside. Down the ramp he flew. He lost his balance and barreled into the side of the pigeon loft, got up, and stormed to the creek, where he hid behind the granite outcropping until nightfall. Until, starry and bright, the constellations were beset with agitation, and his aunt grew hoarse from calling out to him.

Claiming to have no choice in the matter (being born under the sign of Aries), Auntie Tilda would not be dissuaded. Next Sunday, she came buggy-trotting to the dairy again to take Moojie away. But this time Pappy had padlocked the Isidore's gate, and she got stuck trying to pass through the boards, spitting out a litany of curses— enough to turn the air blue. Pappy and Moojie rode the buckboard to the gate to try to talk some sense into her.

"Top of the mornin', Tilda," Pappy said, "Have you been to church, yet?"

Auntie Tilda extricated herself backward from the gate, grunting daintily. She glared at them and climbed back onto Henry Littleman's buggy. "I'm going to get an axe," she said.

"Dotty as a bat," Pappy said to Moojie. They watched from the porch as Auntie Tilda hacked through the boards with an axe. "Wait in your room. I'll deal with her."

Though unsure of his grandfather's motives, Moojie took consolation in the joining of forces against the tenacious, Irish starfish, and listened through the bedroom door as Pappy offered Auntie a cordial greeting, served tea, and then delivered a final opinion: "The boy's better off here. I have chickens."

"I won't be put off any longer!" Auntie Tilda spat, and came banging on Moojie's door. "I want to have a word!"

Moojie threw open the door. "Forget it," he said. "I-I'm not going. I'll decide where I'm gonna live!" With all his sad, heavy, despairing heart, he still hoped to build a future with the clan. Shuddering, he thumped past her, straight out the cabin door.

It happened again. It was as if Moojie was transported back to his childhood as he tried to calm down, and couldn't. He had half a mind to get on Hocus and gallop away—but then the other half was misfiring, incoherent, scrambled. A surge of electricity burned up his spine. He couldn't stop it, couldn't will it away. He lost control of his power. All around him the wind kicked up. Dust started spiraling off the ground, first taking up leaves and sticks, then buckets and chickens. To his absolute astonishment, he unleashed a raging tornado.

Pappy and Auntie watched from inside the cabin, their appalled mouths fallen open.

When it was over, Auntie Tilda went outside and patted Moojie on the head. "'Tis more than obvious you're not eating enough starch, dear. I'll be back with papers."

Chapter 15

*Moojie learns of the Second Rule of the Code
and turns an eye to his dubious future;
the resurrection of Anahita*

It rained for twenty-nine days straight. There were no periods of respite. Courses of lightening and thunder rattled the Valley of Sorrows and sent mud sliding down the face of El Serrat. And yet, weather was the least of Moojie's concerns. He had ridden Hocus up the mountain several times in search of the Cave of Fire, but the Light-Eaters were concealing the entrance behind the spell of invisibility, even where he was concerned. He suspected Sarru'kan to be the culprit, he and his trusty six-headed, sidekick Nahzi. Still intoxicated by desire for Babylonia, and desperate for a new life—a *real* family—Moojie rejoiced when at last, one December morning, he found Ninti and the twins in the woods.

"Hail, Lord Littleman!" the twins chimed and clapped

when he rode up.

"How good of you to come!" Ninti said, twirling wild mint between her fingers.

Moojie stared at her, disbelieving how old she was.

"Old as God," she said, "and young as the new-fallen snow."

"You're reading my mind, again!" He laughed and shook his head. He was overcome with relief that they were friendly and didn't seem to hold any malice for the mishap with Zagros. The fragrance of mint reminded him of his mother's garden—a far away and long ago garden.

Ninti and the boys studied him. They looked a little surprised. Had he said something amusing?

"Well?" he persisted, thinking it should be obvious. "You know who I'm looking for, don't you?"

All he had been thinking about lately was Babylonia … Babylonia prancing through the grass, Babylonia picking flowers, Babylonia tossing a spear, Babylonia, his mystery, his quiver, his stomach cramp. It was of no importance to him if she was a Hostile or an Akil-Nuri, or some kind of egg-thieving alien species older than a dinosaur. What a strange new feeling this was!

"She and Sarru'kan are at the Circle of Trees," Ninti said.

"Great," Moojie said, bristling with jealousy.

Ninti looked at him strangely. "You are aware that he plans to marry her."

Babylonia marry Sarru'kan? What? "I … I—"

"Come, let us walk," Ninti said. She and the twins strode alongside Hocus to the great oak. Moojie dismounted and took up his crutches. "There is something you need to understand about Babylonia, about us," Ninti said. "Before we came here, we chose our bodies the way worldlings choose a carriage. Except we do not need a horse to pull us."

The twins giggled and buzzed.

Moojie thought a minute. "So what are you saying?"

"I am saying that if you were to be with Babylonia, here, on Earth, you would grow old and she would remain young."

"So then ... are you saying that if we left the Earth, it would be different?"

"Aye, in the fifth dimension, one does not have the sensation of a material body. Without matter, age is irrelevant."

Right. I'll just sit with that one for a minute.

"But does Babylonia actually *want* to marry Sarru'kan?" he asked.

"You will have to ask her."

Everyone went quiet.

"My lord, "Ninti said, "have you not noticed that you are speaking clearly now?"

Moojie was surprised. "I—hey, you're right. I'm not stuttering!"

"You see, miracles can happen," she smiled.

Moojie was delighted for a moment, but his spirits darkened again at the thought of Babylonia betrothed to Sarru'kan. "What good is talking going to do?" he asked. "Talking won't help me."

"Pish posh, there is work to be done! What of your quest?" Ninti asked.

"I don't need a mission, I need magic."

"My lord," she said in a grave tone, "I want you to listen to me, and listen closely. Ultimately, every worldling has but one true purpose: to become conscious of and to express the patterns of love. For heaven's sake, mercy is far more powerful than magic."

He narrowed his eyes.

"I shall give you a riddle," she said. She tossed a pebble

into the air and it landed in the dirt. "Can you see gravity?" she asked, quite seriously.

Gaw, another joke.

"And yet," she went on, "you are certain gravity exists, are you not?"

"I already know about that. It's in a book."

"In fact," she pressed on, "you might even stake your life upon it."

"Ever seen a square watermelon?" He had a riddle or two of his own.

"Listen closely, my lord," she said. "Time is running out."

"What about the coin trick?" he asked, not listening to her, at least not registering that he should be. He believed the only way to earn his way into the clan was to perform dazzling spectacles and displays of power. "I want to read minds. I want to tell the future—"

"Are you going to continue to waste my time?" Ninti straightened.

Moojie made note of the tight exasperation of her mouth. "Sorry. It's just … I want to prove I can do anything Sarru'kan can do."

"There are much more important things to prove, my lord. You have a source of power within that transcends you. It is not your human will. This power is aligned with the entire universe; it is the energy from which all of life arises."

Manish retrieved the pebble Ninti had tossed, and she lobbed it into the air again. This time, it stopped midair, spinning in place above Moojie's head like a little planet.

"What the—?" Moojie asked.

"It is a big step from goat farming to riddles, and from riddles to love," Ninti said. "Pay attention, dear: your mind is a garden. If you do not pay attention, your neighbors will trample upon it, beasts will devour it, and dogs will poop in it."

Moojie stifled a giggle. *A mind full of poop!* The twins covered their smiles. The pebble continued spinning. Moojie's hands and feet were tingling. He glanced at the country road, checking for Pappy's wagon.

"You have prepared your garden well," she said. "You have grown fine watermelons and given them to the poor. I applaud you. Shall we move on to the second rule of The Code?"

Moojie inspected the spinning pebble and leaned sideways to look for strings or magnets.

"Now," Ninti went on, "gravity is the most powerful force in the physical universe, is it not?"

"Right."

"Wrong. What is more powerful? Think. What can subvert even the law of gravity?"

Was this the deciding moment? Was it a twist of fate that Moojie had to come to this very scene only to find that the secret of life is hidden in a spinning rock? Mulling over the question, he thought of the way gravity kept the continents from flying off the face of the Earth, and how it stopped the planets and stars from slamming into each other, and he came to the conclusion that there was only one way to subvert the law of gravity: "Magic!"

The pebble dropped onto his head. *Plunk!* Shar and Manish wheezed and sniffled. Very big smiles and very big teeth.

"No no no, that will never do," Ninti said to Moojie. She pointed to her temple. "Quiet your mind, my lord, give it a rest."

"Are you going to show me how to grow watermelons out of my head?" he asked with a sarcastic grin.

The twins snorted. Manish slung an affectionate arm around Moojie's shoulder. Millie-Mae strode up to them.

She delivered a live blue belly on the ground near Moojie, and chased it as it fled away.

"The answer is love," Ninti said. "Love is more powerful than even gravity. And, that is what leads to the second rule of The Code: Make peace with your enemies."

"What?" Moojie asked. For some reason, this immediately bothered him.

"Let us sit," Ninti said. She and the twins settled on the ground, against the trunk of a great oak. Moojie lowered into an awkward pose, legs bent to one side, arms to the other side, a tortured pose as if he were hanging sideways off a saddle.

"Close your eyes," Ninti said. "Just breathe."

Moojie closed one eye. The other eye, a rogue pirate, kept a look out. Noises, words, wildfires, electrical storms stampeded through his head. What would his grandfather do if he found him consorting with the enemy? And where the devil was Babylonia?

"Calm your mind," Ninti said. "The noises are just thoughts, little birds in a cage. Forget about them. Forget about your body for just a minute. Allow life to be as it is."

What she was saying came as a strange comfort. Moojie would always remember the seraphic light filling her eyes, and the weight of her long hand on his shoulder when she, bearing the burden of human stubbornness and the fury of the ages, said: "Be still, my lord. Believe in the power of mercy, for it is the key to happiness."

Moojie closed his eyes again, mind slowing. He became suddenly aware of what seemed to be the greatest obstacle to his happiness: Sarru'kan.

"Well?" Ninti prodded him. "Do you want gold coins or miracles?"

Chapter 16

Which chronicles a startling incident to imply that there are greater miracles than magic coins and spinning rocks; and other unfortunate events

Due to back problems and the unusual cold of winter, Pappy had never returned to the work in the east field. But every now and then, he openly declared that his physical condition would not deter "Operation Afterclaps." Moojie could only hope that the delay would extend until the vernal equinox, when everyone would be too busy cleaning up after the big quake to bother with the Light-Eaters.

Ordinarily he took great care to conceal his despair from his grandfather. But the ripples of light that had been so omnipresent during the summer were now being battered by hailstorms, and St. Isidore's night skies were stained and starless as squid ink. As he sat on the porch rocker watching the frozen hailstones wear away the corners of the outbuildings, Moojie, a young man now, needed someone to help guide him through the darkness of his heart. His aunt would be back any day, and with legal rights to take him away.

When the storm let up, Pappy, who had been drinking and sleeping for the better part of three weeks, stumbled outside and floundered into the rocker next to him.

"So," Moojie said, "I count about fourteen pigeons now. Thirty-nine goats. Two cows. Two Burros. One horse. One dog. And I don't know how many chickens ... I'm wondering, do you love them?"

"What?" Pappy asked.

—"I mean, you love critters because you feed them, right? And keep them safe. But how do you, you know, love a girl?"

Captain Sean Finnegan took a swig from his crock, paused, and said, "Same as a critter."

Moojie's head was in the clouds. "Love is a miracle."

Pappy blew a raspberry through his lips. "Don't know nothin' about miracles. Ain't it enough to be a man?"

Just then, a large, pale creature loped out from behind the barn and into the field. A cougar? Moojie stood slowly.

"Flippin' faeries!" Pappy sprung out of the rocker, ran inside, and came back with the shotgun, firing into the night's shadows.

Moojie made no attempt to try and stop him this time. He knew the cougar was out of range, but a pure, clairvoyant recognition told him that it was Anahita. The last time he had seen her, she was a carcass swirling in the creek. How could she be alive? His wild questioning relied on the power of the stars and the mercy of Mother Nature as an explanation. He came to the astonishing but logical conclusion that it had been the work of Copper Creek, the laughing current over mossy rocks must have brought her back to life.

The next morning, at sunrise, Moojie was crossing the yard on Hocus Pocus, planning to go find the clan and show them a little magic of his own, when unexpectedly, something dropped down from an olive branch, hanging upside-down like a giant overripe olive. Sarru'kan! Hocus reared up with a fright. Moojie tried to rein her in and Sarru'kan seized him from above by the hair. Moojie stifled a scream. The pain was unbearable. He reached up and twisted Sarru'kan's arm with his crushing right-handed grip, causing him to let go. A clap of thunder rumbled up the valley as Moojie rode into the woods undeterred.

The spirit of independence had loomed up inside Moojie, as surely as his shoulders and arms had begun to force the seams of his deerskin shirt. He found Ninti, Imi'tittu, Babylonia, and the twins in the woods near the great oak. After bowing to them, he whipped out a yo-yo, and gave a demonstration of the One-handed Star. "All a matter of physics," he said. "What goes around, comes around."

The youngers shouted with glee and swarmed after him. Babylonia and the olders just smiled and continued gathering mushrooms, which had squirted out of the soil, fat and wet, overnight.

"I saw Anahita," Moojie said, testing them. Imi'tittu nodded. So it was true, she was alive!

"What else? What other magic?" Manish and Shar clamored after Moojie.

He took out his mother's music box and held it up. "This," he said, quite seriously, "isn't a toy."

"Ahh," said the twins.

Babylonia looked over with an expression of curiosity. Coy-smiling, she walked over to him. He leaned down from Hocus to show her the box. Her face was so close he could smell her breath—golden, like honey, like freedom. What was she doing to him? Something in her eyes. Mischief? He didn't know. Girls.

Just then, Sarru'kan came thundering onto the scene. Moojie plunged the box into his pocket and said to Babylonia, "Actually, it doesn't want to sing right now."

"Come now, Claw Hand. You are among friends here," Sarru'kan said.

Moojie lit a wooden match against his denim jeans and held it up. "Magic!" he chirped, feeling rather proud of his contribution to this lost civilization.

Sarru'kan sniggered, waved his hand in a circle and held it up, a flame popping out of the tip of his index finger. "Magic!"

The twins reached up, trying to get into Moojie's pocket.

"Careful!" he said, swatting them away. "If you make the box mad it'll never sing again."

Before Moojie saw it coming, Sarru'kan vaulted over the hindquarters of Hocus, landing square behind him on her back. In two exacting moves, he spirited the box right out of Moojie's pocket.

"Our torchbearer," Imi'tittu scoffed, as he and Ninti watched this. "What was it you said? Sarru'kan serves with selfless devotion …."

Sarru'kan jumped off Hocus, shook the music box and put it to his ear. Moojie snarled, lowered his head between his shoulders, vulture-like, gripped his crutch like a jousting lance, and charged. Sarru'kan ducked and howled with laughter as Moojie swung the crutch at him, lost his grip, and dropped it. Moojie turned Hocus around and made another pass. He threw a right hook, but Sarru'kan got hold of his fist and held it like a vice.

"… and abundant restraint," Imi'tittu continued.

Moojie pulled free of Sarru'kan and this time took *him* by the hair. "The box or your hair!" He put his heels to Hocus and dragged the growling, spitting magus a ways, until at last he surrendered the box by tossing it into the air. Moojie caught it on the fly. His moment of triumph was short lived, however. Ninti, Imi'tittu, Babylonia, and the twins just stood there looking at him as if he were a festering canker sore.

Breathless, Moojie's eyes stung with embarrassment. For the first time, he could hear *their* thoughts: *the box or the clan*? It wasn't an easy decision. The music box had been his most significant tie to his past, to his mother and father, to home. He wanted to keep it, the way one guards a happy memory—forever. To go back to the cabin, wind it up, and let it soothe his weary soul. But now he was faced with an impossible decision: if he was he going to prove himself worthy to the tribe, if he was ever going to impress Babylonia, he had to be willing to give it up.

"All right," he sighed. He held out the box to Sarru'kan.

Sarru'kan walked right past him. "You are a fool, Claw Hand, if you think you can buy my favor."

By then Moojie's body was beginning to feel like a weather-beaten glove that no longer fit his hand. He went back to the dairy and undertook a campaign to overcome his limitations. Secretly, he practiced standing in the barn, with Millie-Mae as his sole witness. He fell. He got up. He fell and got back up, again and again. Pretending that the gassy, blond mutt was a blushing maiden, he said, "Would you do me the honor ... will you take my hand in marriage?" He lay in the barn straw, grinning a foolish grin, imagining Babylonia in a wedding dress, imagining a new life with her and the others, until his eyes became crossed and Mamma's voice inside his head broke the spell: *First Moojie, you must learn to dress yourself.* It was a matter he had to resolve, once and for all.

In the privacy of his bedroom, he took out his old laces and put them back on his shoes. He was going to tie them come hell or high water, a mean task with one disobliging hand. *Over, under, pull it tight, make a bow and loop it to the right.* Over and over again, three times then five times and ten times. Good Lord knows how many times he tried. When he had had all he could bear of failing to get it right, he invented a sort of double-knot, a whatnot-knot, he called it, and left it at that.

From then on, Sarru'kan took every opportunity to rankle Moojie. In the darkest hours of the night, he sent serpents into his dreams, "For to be a wonderworker," he said, sarcastically, "one must be impervious to venom." Moojie knew it was Sarrukan's handiwork that put Elsie into a trance of mooing outside his window in the wee hours. Who else could make vultures drop live mice upon Moojie's head as he rode the exercise bicycle? Sarru'kan, wizard of aggravation, vexation, and shape-shifting, everywhere and nowhere. He could appear as a bat in the barn rafters or a snake in the grass. Here one minute, gone the next. Sarru'kan outshone Moojie in every degree of magic and brilliance and never missed an opportunity to disparage him for daring to co-mingle with a superior race. The evil of Sarru'kan's purpose might have succeeded had Moojie taken him up on a dare to fly off a cliff. This bothered Moojie more than he let on. And yet he, a goat in the midst of frolicking unicorns, plumbed new fathoms of self-determination. Sarru'kan was simply not going to get the better of him. Unless of course, he got the better of him.

Before the bathroom mirror Moojie pointed at himself with a toothbrush, and said, "Praise the spirit!"

in French. He spat on some baking soda, made a paste, and rubbed it onto his forehead. "Praise the light!"

Millie-Mae yelped three times as if to sing Alleluia!

Moojie turned around, mortified to see his grandfather standing behind him.

Chapter 17

Cracked corn, thieving mollygrubs,
and the end of hornbumps

Nostrils flaring, Pappy's eyes nearly popped out of his skull.

"It's supposed to bring good luck," Moojie said about the white dot above his eyes.

"Why, I ought to—" Pappy reached for him clumsily, but Moojie darted under his arms and stumbled into the kitchen, putting the table between them. "You get on that horse, go up that godforsaken mountain, and tell those vagrants if they aren't gone by the time I get back, I'll use dynamite to send them home."

Moojie marched outside, climbed onto Hocus Pocus, and left. The Cave of Fire never seemed to be in the same place twice. Zigzagging and backtracking, Hocus Pocus was sucking air by the time Moojie reached the bamboo blind. Of course, since it was the afternoon, the cave wasn't visible. "Mrs. Ladyship!" Moojie called out. He waited and called again. The air crackled with electrical impulses. Finches exploded out of the bamboo. The hillside rippled as if it were turning into liquid, waves of energy radiating out from a center point, and soon the opening of the cave appeared. Shar came outside with Shemman in the sling. "What news, my lord?" he asked with a sugary white grin.

"You and the others had better leave. Isn't there another cave around? I mean, if you don't get out of here, it's the end."

"Brother, have you found the beginning?" Shemman asked.

"No," Moojie said.

"Why, pray tell, are you talking of the end?"

"Um, yeah, well," Moojie said, "I really need to talk to Ninti. It's important." He dismounted this time before going inside.

Shar led Moojie and Millie-Mae into the cave. Sarru'kan came rushing in behind them holding up something in his hand. A dead pheasant. "Praise the bounty of earth's treasures!" he trumpeted. Sarru'kan was bigger than Moojie remembered. This thorn-in-one's-side—slashed by scars that he himself had carved with a hot blade—gave Moojie the creeps.

In the cavern, Sarru'kan's pheasant whipped up a lively reception. Olders and handsome ones alike examined the bird, clapping their hands, cheering, and buzzing.

"All hail Sarru'kan, Supreme Upchuck!" said Manish, pulling open the pheasant wings and inspecting the feathers.

Moojie stifled a laugh. He cleared his throat and waved his hand to get everyone's attention. "Yep, everybody, I've got something important to tell you."

No one heard him over the ruckus. Ninti was fixating

on Sarru'kan's bird and its glorious feathers. The smallest youngers were choking Millie-Mae with affection and rummaging through Moojie's pockets. Kisha grabbed them away. *"Ellu,"* she said in a disapproving, but familiar tone. Sarru'kan had used that word when Moojie made a caterpillar appear magically out of his hand. *Ellu* wasn't anything to be proud of. Moojie gathered that much. "Um, anybody here care about getting blown up?" he said loudly.

The clan had begun to sing loudly in their language and the youngers danced a goofy jig around the fire pit.

"All for a dead bird?" Moojie asked. It was as if he were invisible.

"And yet, of far greater beauty than your puny eggs and soft fruit, Claw Hand," Sarru'kan said.

Millie-Mae growled at him. Sarru'kan dropped into a squat, snarling and showing his teeth. He raised his hands above his head and opened them outward like a praying mantis. Millie-Mae whined and lowered to the ground with bassett hound eyes.

"This is about Zagros, isn't it?" Moojie asked. "They blame me for losing him."

"It wasn't enough that you and your grandfather shot Anahita. You had to—"

"What?"

"Alas, you couldn't kill her, could you?"

Moojie reached out to Ninti as she passed him. "Lady-ship, I don't think you understand. My grandfather is getting dynamite. Do you know what that is? It's like a volcano in a stick."

Ninti stoked the fire pit. "Not to worry, my lord. The pheasant is a good omen. We will eat well tonight." She and the clan encircled the pit, holding hands. They sang in their language, faces aglow in the firelight.

Moojie trudged out of the cave, shaking his head.

Sarru'kan followed him. "They are hungry. Do you blame them?" he said.

Moojie was taken aback by his frankness. He mounted Hocus.

"It was good of you to warn us. Perhaps you *can* be trusted after all. I shall return the favor. I will tell you how to prove your loyalty to the clan, once and for all."

He had Moojie's attention.

"The dairy has many goats, yes?"

"Right."

"If you could but spare one goat, I would accept it as a peace offering, and you will have my blessing. We will be as brothers."

"Just one goat," Moojie said.

"Just one."

"They're hungry," Moojie reasoned with Hocus Pocus on the way down the mountain. "A measly pheasant isn't enough to feed twenty. A goat would surely fill their bellies. And Babylonia, well … *feed them and keep them safe.* That's what Pappy said about women."

Chapter 18

Goat Soup

Seduced by the temptation to prove himself, and by the promise of living in a new world where all he had to do was sprinkle magic seeds on the ground and he could grow all the watermelons his heart desired, where all manner of wonders and friendship and family could be had, Moojie seriously considered Sarru'kan's proposal.

The buckboard was still gone when he got back to the dairy. He went directly to the rifle cabinet, heart pumping, body taut as telegraph wire. *One measly pheasant isn't enough to feed them.* He fastened a rifle sling to the shotgun and loaded it. A goat would be magnificent; a rip-snorting peace offering that would surely impress them all.

Shotgun strapped across his chest, Moojie trundled out to the GOAT LOCKER and stood before a dozen bulging eyeballs, leaned against the siding, and lifted the shotgun to his shoulder. It would be so easy to give them a goat, wouldn't it? But in the end, he didn't trust Sarru'kan at all, and he had no notion to pull the trigger. It came as a complete surprise when Millie-Mae stormed into the barn chasing after a lizard, knocking him off balance. The shotgun's kick threw Moojie backward onto his behind. And there in the straw before him lie Rufus, a crumpled, lifeless heap. Some of the other goats fainted immediately, just plopped onto their sides, rolled over, legs pointing into the air. Others stampeded outside, eyes goggling, mouths agape.

Moojie's ears were deaf with ringing, and when he took inventory of what he had just done, when he saw the bloody hole in Rufus' neck, he felt sick, mortified. In fact, he almost fainted, the way he did when Pappy slaughtered the chicken.

Soon enough, clan members arrived, a torrent of long feet, flowing hair, and white spots—the twins, Ninti, Imi'tittu, Babylonia, Sarru'kan, and others.

Outside the barn, it started to rain.

"Was that a gunshot? Are you all right?" Ninti asked.

Upon seeing Rufus dead, Babylonia and an older woman fell back and whispered a prayer.

"I didn't …." Moojie murmured.

"My lord," Ninti said, "what have you done?" There was a terrible empty ping of disappointment in her voice.

Moojie floundered, his head reeling.

Sarru'kan shook his head and sighed. "*Bravo, mon vieux.* Merry Christmas."

Ninti closed her eyes. It seemed as if she were praying. And then she shook her head. "It is no use. The goat-spirit does not want to return. I cannot revive the body." She lowered her head and left.

"This is a sad day," Manish said. "You killed brother Suhurmas."

"It is no use, my lord," Imi'tittu said. "Our ways are not your ways."

The clan gathered away, crossing the south field in solemn procession.

Moojie was alone again, woefully alone. Moojie Littleman, Lord of the Plow, Destroyer of Homes, Goat Killer. Who would love him, not as a cripple, not as a son or a grandson or an orphan—not as a special package of problems or a sad, lonely story, but for himself? Would anyone ever love him for his tender, kind, strange, ordinary Moojie-self?

Rain slammed onto the yard late that day, trees and sheds slouching under its weight.

Around that time Phineas showed up at the cabin, his fur growing back, long and silvery. Sopping wet, he looked like a lady's wig. Moojie took him inside and dried him off. "I did a stupid thing, Phinny. You just won't believe what a huge, whizz-bang stupid thing it was. I mean, you might think Pappy messed you up with the haircut, but that's just peanuts next to what I did to that goat."

Chapter 19

Wherein Pappy has a serious conniption fit
of his own, and other incidents worthy of note

Rain hammered the cabin roof as Moojie cleaned the shotgun. Pappy had come back to the dairy with three crates of dynamite, the fragrance of moonshine all over him. By then Moojie had concocted a story to fix things.

Pappy came inside, slugged a shot of whiskey, and gave Moojie a nod of approval. "Good, boy. One hair, one speck of sand in the barrel, and you ain't gonna hit an elephant even if it's standing on top of you."

"Yes, Sir."

"Those gallinippers!" Pappy growled. "You say one came looking for handouts?"

"Yes sir. An ugly kid with scars."

"Yeah, I know the one."

"He was in the barn," Moojie said. "So I got the shotgun to chase him off."

"Then?"

"He tried to grab the gun and it went off."

"You didn't believe me when I said they were no good."

"No, Sir. I'm a bit slow, as you know." Moojie's mind was racing. He refilled Pappy's shot glass.

"Yes, a bit slow," Pappy said. He swallowed the golden elixir and Moojie poured more.

"I'm a simple man," Pappy said. "I live a simple life. I ain't asking for much. I gotta right to live alone on my own land, my own way. That's all I ask."

"I'm gonna get the kid with the scars," Moojie said, putting the rifle away.

"I s'pose you think you can catch a weasel sleepin', too."

Pappy was edgy as a jackknife. Moojie recognized the intense look on his face, the same he had had before his last meltdown. Pappy paced back and forth, leather heels striking the oak wood floor. The ticking clock grew louder, the drum inside Moojie's chest pounded, and great thundering Jesus Pappy lashed out at the old clock, sending it crashing to the floor, a spray of broken glass and coiled springs.

Pappy took Moojie by the collar. "Boy, are you with me or against me?"

"Um, well, you know …."

"Where. Are. They?"

"The cave, Sir." Moojie assumed Pappy would never be able to find it.

"Lie to me and I'll pack you off to that fruitcake aunt of yours, I will." Pappy's voice was jagged and bitter-smelling. He let go of Moojie.

"Get some sleep," Pappy said, looking over the rifles.

It was deep into the wee hours before Pappy got up from his wingback chair and staggered to bed. And the minute he did, Moojie went out to the kitchen and got the jar of kelp flakes off the shelf. *One hair, one speck of sand in the barrel, and you ain't going to hit an elephant, even if it's standing on top of you.* No one was going to die. No more dying. No goats. No Hostiles. No elephants. He carefully poured kelp flakes down the barrel of each rifle.

Chapter 20

Qarradu's tree

At first light three days later, the posse arrived at St. Isidore's. McTavish and the villagers came in buckboards, buggies, and on horseback. Mounted on Aggie the burro, Pappy greeted Mayor Bingo. Moojie was watching from the porch as the mayor, sitting erect on her magnificent steed, lit a smudge wand and waved it in the air toward the mountain. "Red energy," she said. "Flesh-eaters."

A shiver went up Moojie's spine, a premonition of tragedy. Phineas must have felt it, too. Hunkering down under the pigeon loft, his tail was twitching, and his eyes were wild.

"Mount," Pappy, Captain Sean Finnegan, said to Moojie.

Two minutes later, Moojie was on Hocus Pocus, crutches fastened, .38 in hand.

"The best battles are always fought at sunup," Pappy said.

He sounded the kazoo three times. Moojie cursed himself inaudibly. Gaw! There he goes with the all-clear signal again! But there was no need to be concerned, right? What harm could Pappy do with a rifle full of kelp?

"I made a promise to your father, boy," Pappy said. "I promised to look after you as I would my own son. This morning, I will make good on that promise."

Whoa! That was something to hear! Was this why Pappy had never sent him to the Steel Barn or back to Mother Teagardin? He had given his word—and kept it. All at once, Moojie was flustered and confused and unsure. He wanted to call off the posse.

"Wait, maybe ...." he started to say. But it was too late.

Pappy waved his rifle and roared, "East field!" and he and McTavish led the marching villagers through the red-misted dawn, looking more like gravediggers than dairy farmers in their hooded ponchos.

Moojie had overlooked one small detail: the dynamite.

He rode up next to the mayor, unable to tell the difference between the beating of hooves and the thundering of blood through his veins.

"I thought weapons were against the village law," he said.

"We're not in the village, son."

When they arrived at the hole in the east field, McTavish disappeared underground and came up with rifles, which he passed out to the villagers. The mayor refused, waving a derringer. While McTavish and Pappy stuffed dynamite into saddlebags, Moojie prayed that the clan had been alert enough to make the cave entrance invisible. *What a mess! What an all-fired, bag of nails, hog-stinking, britch-tromping mess!*

Millie-Mae put her nose to the ground and took the

lead. She knew the drill. How many times had she obediently sniffed out the Cave of Fire? Umpteen times. And yet, obedience can't anticipate trouble; obedience can't sniff out unexpected twists of fate.

Breathing fast, Moojie prayed to the saints. He prayed to his mother. He prayed to the stars, to the sun, to the Source of all life. He prayed until he and the posse reached the third bench in the mountain, near the cave.

The bamboo blind was just above them, and directly behind it the cave entrance couldn't have been more visible.

Moojie felt the blood drain from his face.

"Cover me from below," Pappy said. He dismounted and hiked up the incline toward the bamboo blind, which was just outside the entrance, saddlebags over one shoulder. McTavish hiked to the area above the cave. Every three paces, he heeled strung-together dynamite into the ground. Pappy waved the villagers off to either side of the cave. Slowly, ever so carefully, he approached the bamboo. A tempest of wild finches rushed out of it, and everyone jumped, then they jumped again when Ninti peered through the bamboo.

"*Qarradu!*" she said.

Pappy staggered backward, aimed the shotgun at her and pulled the trigger. Nothing happened, nothing but the dry thud of steel against steel, hammer to receiver. He lost his footing and before you could say whoopsie daisy, went tumbling head over heels down the steep incline, over leaves and rocks and rotting branches, twigs snapping like bones, shotgun now firing a puff of green dust into the air—all happening as if in slow motion, Mayor Bingo reaching helplessly in his direction, McTavish shouting something, and then Pappy's skull coming to a swift *crack!* against an old, burly oak tree.

Moojie lost his breath. Something about that *crack!*

sounded like the whip of the Almighty, putting the finishing touch on his own dark joke. Horrified, he rode down the hillside, dismounted, and collapsed onto the ground beside his grandfather. McTavish was already there, stuffing his poncho under Pappy's head.

Pappy's eyes were open and glassy. He was whispering. Moojie lowered an ear to hear what he was saying.

"I can't feel my legs," he said. "Listen, boy, if I don't make it—"

"What?" Moojie could barely make out what he was saying.

"You were like a son to me," Pappy said. "I never could get the hang of sons."

"I'm going for help," the mayor said. "Cover him!" She rode off.

Moojie ripped off his shirt and lay it over Pappy's chest. Eyes closed now, brow creased, his grandfather bore the look of a bad dream. His lip had been split open, his nose gashed. A tangle of twigs and leaves in his hair. Blood flowed out of his head onto the poncho, bright red and swirling with stories. He smiled. "Hey, my back don't hurt." Then his eyes went dull and sunk back into his head. "Tilda," he whispered, "you were right about the light. 'Tis lovely." And he was gone.

McTavish checked his pulse and shook his head. He closed Pappy's eyelids.

"NO!" Moojie howled. "PAPPY, NO!" Shaking uncontrollably, he tore grass out of the ground with his hands. "Why couldn't you just leave things be?"

McTavish put a consoling arm around him. He signaled for a villager to bring over his crutches. "I'm sorry, lad. I'm truly sorry." Then, he signaled for the villagers to bring the clan down from the mountain.

"You had us going for a while," McTavish said to Ninti.

Sarru'kan growled and lifted his spear. McTavish turned and shot him in the arm. Sarru'kan dropped the spear and grabbed his arm.

"Don't bother trying any witchery on me," McTavish said. "I'm taking the whole of you bampots in. Dead or alive. Time to atone for your sins."

Moojie got to his feet and charged over to Ninti. "Do something!" he said. "Bring Pappy back!"

"My lord, we cannot help him," Ninti said. "Not here. Not now."

"But you said nothing was impossible. What about, what about, miracles?"

"We once tried to make peace with him. He has never accepted our help. Why would he now?"

It looked like Pappy was napping. Moojie touched his freckled hand. Still warm. He pictured his mother meeting Pappy in the afterlife. He imagined her cry of surprise.

It seemed like forever before the mayor came back with the sheriff, the doctor, the priest, and the undertaker. In fact, the entire emergency department of San Miguel showed up, including the barkeep, the baker, and a half-dozen fishermen, hoofing it across the field, crushing new grooves in the wet grass and flushing out the wild turkeys. The doctor lifted Pappy's eyelids to look at his pupils. "Well, Captain," he said, "I'm afraid you've run out of rope this time." The sheriff cordoned off the area around the great oak, giving the tree the look of guilt.

Father Grabbe knelt down, crossed Pappy, then stood. "I suppose this means the Christmas pageant will be cancelled."

Looking like lambs marked for slaughter, the clan obeyed the sheriff as he waved them onto a buckboard. The twins were holding Babylonia's hands. "*Dondé estan las flores violetas?*" said Manish, blurry-eyed. Where are the purple flowers? As the deputy and three armed villagers drove the wagon away, the injured Sarru'kan mouthed the word, *"Ca-ter-pil-lar"* at Moojie.

When the sheriff questioned him about the events leading to the captain's death, Moojie could hardly speak. "We rode out this morning a-and …." It was all he could say.

"We were within our rights, Sheriff," the mayor broke in. "The suspects were trespassing." She emptied the derringer's bullets into her purse.

The villagers lay Pappy's body on a stretcher and carried him across the field. Millie-Mae followed alongside, nudging Pappy's hand with her nose, as if expecting a pat on the head. The stretcher slid roughly onto the undertaker's buckboard. Wood against wood. Splinters. Like Moojie's heart.

"It's a shame, a crying shame," the mayor said. She turned to Moojie. "Sonny, go get your things together. You're going home."

In a state of shock, Moojie rode back to the cabin and stuffed some clothing into his satchel. He couldn't bear being in the cabin alone, fearing Pappy's spirit might walk through the kitchen looking for whiskey. So he went out to the yard. The pigeons were still as lead, the goats hiding in the barn. Hocus came up from behind and nudged him. "Fresh out of carrots, Hokey," he said. She blew air between her lips and joggled her head in the direction of the chicken hutch. "What is it, girl?" Inside the hutch were six blue eggs. He guessed she was telling him to take them with him. It didn't make any sense. He took them anyway.

III

The Long
Crooked Mile
to
Unforeseeable
Complications

Chapter 1

Christmas under the red skies of
San Miguel de las Gaviotas

Auntie Tilda opened the door to number 11 Wimbley Wood to greet the mayor and Moojie. Surprised to see them, she collapsed against the bookcase when she heard the news about Pappy.

The kitchen floor had grown dull over the past six years, and the cookie jar was empty. Mildew and the faint odor of porridge came hissing from the walls like ghosts of the past. While making tea, Auntie Tilda reassured the mayor that she would look after Moojie. That was all he heard of the conversation. At the kitchen table, before an uneaten kipper sandwich, that was all Moojie heard. He was menaced by the ticking clock and the pounding waves nearby. By the image of Pappy on the stretcher. He had never thanked his grandfather for taking him in. But that had always been Moojie's way. He wasn't used to saying thank you to anyone. At least he could have thanked Pappy for not sending him away—for keeping his word. It was more than he could say for his father. He wished the whole world would blow up—the world of Impossible Beginnings and Sudden Endings, of lost days, hours, and minutes. Of things never said.

Auntie Tilda came back to the table. She opened a weeks-old newspaper from San Francisco. "Bloody treaties," she said. "What good does it do? You give savages new schools, new clothes, their own land, you teach them to read and write, and what do they do in return? Is it any wonder they get locked up?"

"They were my only friends," Moojie said.

"You still have a father."

"Right."

"What in the name of Saint Peter happened at that dairy?"

Moojie didn't answer.

"I suppose it'll all come out, one way or another," she sighed.

At first Moojie felt relieved to be back home, but soon the familiar surroundings and the little things, like a photograph of Papa standing behind Mamma with baby Moojie in her arms, made him ache more than ever for the family he once had known.

He was alone in the world now, except for a phantom father and a meddlesome aunt. This realization fell upon him as thick as a rug. He hadn't cried much about Pappy, not because he was brave or happy to be alive, nor because he had returned to Wimbley Wood, though it was quite nice. He hadn't cried because at the moment his tears were frozen in his bones.

The whole world had come into question. Family, relationships. Wasn't life supposed to come fitted with them? They shaped the universe; without them, moons and planets and stars would be orphans lost in space. Without the earth, there would be no sun. Without bees, no flowers. What was a boy to do when he failed so miserably to belong? These thoughts weighed in at a price—*would-have, should-have, could-have* thoughts. Where would he be today if he hadn't shot Pappy's goat? Where would the Light-Eaters be? He should have done something to keep Pappy home that terrible morning.

"Your father," Auntie Tilda startled him by her voice, "the poor fool's gone to seed in grief. But he'll be back, lad. You'll see."

Moojie didn't believe her. Anyway, time was running out. The new year only days away, the spring equinox coming in March. "I had a dream last night," he said to his aunt. "In the jungle, even tigers get eaten."

"There are no tigers near the ocean," she said. "And even if there were, there are no jungles around here, and anyway your grandfather is gone now, but he would have been the first to shoot a tiger, the bloody fool."

A single tear ran down her cheek as she studied Moojie over the top of the paper.

"How do you do it?" she asked. "How do you always make me feel like a child again, willing to believe in miracles?"

His parents' bed had been precisely made, clean tucks and sharp corners. His mother's vanity table, just as she left it nearly seven years before: perfume bottles lined up neatly before the oval mirror, a science book left opened, face down. In the closet, a pair of pink toe shoes hung over a hook, pale and limp as dead angels. Her dresses, aprons, skirts, and blouses were ordered by seasonal colors, spring to winter. Moojie buried his face in them. There came tears that he quickly wiped away.

Startling himself in the full-length mirror, he saw how he had changed. He looked like a hobo, and felt more

like Pappy than he wanted to admit, brittle and jagged—
a codger, a prickly old codger.

Outside, in the garden, the grass had dried up. Dark
buds clung to the shrubs, not living buds but long-for-
gotten gems, garnets, on long spindly limbs. Un-budding
jewels. There were no bees or hummingbirds since there
were no flowers for them. Hard and heavy, many buds
had fallen to the ground, dull red stones in sallow fog-
light. A quiet crow took them in its beak to bury in the
ground.

Dinner was lukewarm chicken soup, Irish soda bread,
and long stares.

Was Auntie Tilda the only real family Moojie had
left? He wished she'd been present when he was born,
instead of living on some green rock in Europe. She would
have seen him crashing to earth like a shooting star and
she might have saved him from being a foolish son. Maybe
she would have grown to like Pappy and his pigeons.

When he could no longer bear his own quiet desperation, Moojie told his aunt everything. He told her of the
Cave of Fire, of Anahita, of the magic watermelons and
Greta and Uma in the park. He spoke of Zagros, and the
friendly dragonflies, and magic coins popping out of the
Light-Eaters' hands, and of the six-headed serpent spirit
named Nahzi.

"And Ladyship Ninti … she can see the future and
the past, you know, and the Light-Eaters can speak any
language they want, and they never age."

"You have a diabolical imagination," Auntie Tilda
said.

"But it's true!"

"And I suppose they can read minds as well—"

"Well—"

"And there's a Loch Ness monster in the bathtub,
too, I imagine."

Moojie wished he hadn't left *The Waltzing Lobster* at the dairy because grownups only believe what they read in books. "They aren't made up," he said. "They aren't even Hostiles. They're angels."

"Banjax me," she crowed. "I feel a lot better with them locked up in jail!"

"Well—"

"No use plowing the clouds," his aunt said, bristling. "Let's get back to real things. Like our trip across the pond. How would you like to see the morning dew sparkle like little diamonds upon the emerald pastures?"

Moojie stood clumsily with his crutches.

"Come now, no use getting your knickers in a bundle," she said.

After supper, Moojie and his aunt sat before the blazing fireplace. The warm, orange light softened Auntie Tilda, her great shoulders surrendering to the sofa's cushions. "'Sometimes one's fate resembles a fruit tree in the winter.' Why does that quote keep coming to me? 'Tis all hitting me now, like the stacking of trains: the loss of your mother, my little Katie, and the death of your grandfather. I shudder to think my time is coming, and I've never even been in love. I would have liked to have my own children, you know. Life. 'Tisn't all beer and gum drops, is it?"

"I reckon families are like stars," Moojie said. "When they don't expand they collapse."

"Mine never was much of a family anyway," she said, wiping her eyes with a tissue.

"What about the dairy?"

"Lord in heaven, one thing I'm not is a farm girl. You mustn't fret, though. Mr. McTavish is looking after the critters."

Moojie opened a book of calligraphy from the side table, and read aloud, slowly and precisely, as if he were a schoolteacher: *"Even a stone will respond to love."*

"Wait," said his aunt, dumbstruck. "You can't read!"

"The Light-Eaters taught me more than how to grow watermelons."

"And I suppose they can make the sun rise in the morning, too."

"Auntie, without the sun they will die. They won't last but a few weeks in that jailhouse. I'm not going to let that happen."

Chapter 2

Pappy's last will and testament;
beauty lays its sharp knife

In accordance with Captain Sean Finnegan's last wishes, Mayor Bingo had stopped the grandfather clock in the cabin before he was buried to confuse the devil and give his soul time to make it to heaven. In case that failed, he was buried facedown with his loaded shotgun so he could enter the gates of hell shooting.

Auntie Tilda—back to her usual bossiness, and clutching her humongous handbag—made ready to storm the jailhouse. "At the end of the day," she told Moojie, "I may be a lost ball in the high weeds, but I have a dogged reluctance to accept failure."

Moojie saw they were a lot alike.

For such a short person, everything about Auntie Tilda was big. Big earlobes, big earrings, big dresses. Big talcum-dusted bosom. That morning she grew even bigger. She had appointed herself chief umpire of justice for the demise of Captain Sean Finnegan. "I want every one of those dossers to get it in the neck," she said, as if she had forgotten all that she despaired of Pappy.

Moojie, who had never been in a jail all his life, had packed his satchel with something for Ninti before leaving for the village.

It was Christmas Eve, and San Miguel de las Gaviotas had transformed into a great uproar of costumed wise men and robed apostles, dogs and sheep and goats, decorated floats and carts and buggies. The mayor's band was setting up a stage in the park, while children dressed as angels danced to fiddles, and nearby grownups who looked like Roman soldiers sang hymns and carols. There were colorful paper lanterns in the trees and open fires and kettles of hot cider. Dressed as Herod, Mr. Ruple, the jeweler, walked on stilts above the crowd. Ernie Love, the courier, sputtered by, a crotchety old shepherd on a motorbike.

At the jailhouse, Father Grabbe squawked through a megaphone: "My faithful lambs, he who has ears to hear, let him hear what the Spirit says unto the churches: I, Jonathan, who am your brother and companion in tribulation, have been put here in this village, to warn you of the synagogue of Satan, who say they are peacekeepers and are not. Let it go on record that we will no longer abide the curse of the savages."

"Praise the Lord!" the villagers answered back.

"Let us rip Satan from the cloth of the Earth!"

"A-men!"

"My dear, earnest moppets, you know where *she* abides!"

"Out with the demon!"

"The spawn has lain inside the earth a thousand years, and will soon hatch and take wing!"

"Hatch and take wing! Hatch and take wing!"

In his gray sweater and white collar, the priest looked, Moojie thought, just like a pigeon. "It is written right here," the Father said, opening the Bible, "Six o six o six. Plain as your nose. The trumpets are sounding. Oh, for the power of his holy rod! We must now go forth in courage to destroy the Sumerian devils. We must act swiftly, for the year of Our Lord 1906 is well nigh upon us. The Hostiles must be brought to justice for the death of Captain Sean Finnegan."

Moojie clung protectively to his satchel as he and Auntie Tilda pushed through the throng.

It came as a complete surprise when the mayor, still in her bathrobe that late morning, announced that the Captain had willed the whole of his property—the buckboard, the critters, a modest sum of money, and even his gramophone and ukulele—to Moojie.

"Whoa," Moojie said. "What am I going to do with all that?"

"It's too much for someone such as yourself to look after," the mayor said. She turned to Auntie Tilda. "Inasmuch as his next of kin are not stepping forward, may I count on you to look after the boy?"

"I can take care of myself," Moojie said.

Auntie Tilda studied her fingernails and then offered a little *humph.*

"You're not of age, sonny," Mayor Bingo said. "Well, Professor Pettibone, what will it be?"

"All right," Auntie said. "But I'll be pushing up posies before I work on that filthy farm. No goat-milking. No stable-mucking. You can put that in writing!"

"That settles it then," said the mayor, signing and stamping the will.

Moojie stood to his feet. "Seeing as I'm the landowner, I demand to see the prisoners."

Mayor Bingo looked surprised. She stood and looked out the window at the street scene. "I hate to be the one to tell them the pageant will have to wait. It's madness. Everyone's gone pot-wallopers. The tea leaves said it was coming." She scribbled something on a piece of paper, went into another room, got dressed, and Moojie and Auntie Tilda followed her outside where she nailed the note to the Town Hall door.

Emergency Meeting
Agenda:
St. Isidore's vs. The Hostiles
Town Hall
Sundown
(No guns. No liquor.)
Your Beloved Bingo

Mayor Bingo, Professor Tilda Pettibone, and Moojie sidled through the horde outside, past the freakish scene of Saint Nicholas nailing together the joints of the gallows; past crucifix-waving elf-picketeers festooned with placards and garlic strands. Past Father Grabbe who was instructing a young girl in the manner of pinning dollar bills to the robe of a life-size mannequin of the Virgin Mary. Past a clump of angels and shepherds chanting: NO MORE EARTHQUAKES, NO MORE BEES, HEMP THE HOSTILES, GIVE US PEACE! Ernie Love drove his motorbike up to Auntie Tilda and handed her a petition calling for the immediate execution of the Hostiles. She signed it and raised a dainty fist at the gallows.

Mottled with lichen and moss, the jailhouse was the natural wonder of two hundred one mostly sunless years. *Calico Jack* was chiseled in the keystone over the entrance, the name of a notorious pirate who built the jailhouse from his wrecked ship and dry-stacked granite from the hills, only to become its first inmate. Standing at the entrance, an armed deputy asked the mayor to hold his cinnamon swirl while he unclipped the key ring from his belt. He unlocked the great wooden door, and down the corridor went the three visitors, single file, shoes *clipclopping*, crutches *tiptapping*, over the polished tiles.

"They don't speak English," the mayor said to Auntie. "But if it'll make you feel better …."

Auntie Tilda entered the dim cell. The mayor stopped Moojie and pointed to the satchel. He opened it to show that he was carrying a small scuttle full of blue eggs.

"They like eggs," he said.

She waved him in. Ninti and Babylonia were sitting opposite each other on fold-down cots, alert and docile as doves. Auntie Tilda wasn't going to waste any time. She marched right over to Ladyship. "Time for you and I to have a little chinwag, woman," she said. "I'm bloody steamed about your shenanigans. You're some kind of witch—a hard case all around, and I don't give a hen's tooth if you can't speak English. You will hear what I have to say. I've a good mind to give you a royal bashing right now. Driving poor Finnegan to his wit's end."

She pulled Moojie from the shadows. "And the boy. The boy's lost a grandfather. Now what's he got? A life gone to pot."

"Easy, dear," said the mayor.

"If I have anything to do with it, she'll swing from the gallows," Auntie Tilda said. Red as a hot radish, she turned to leave.

"It won't be long now," Ninti said softly, her hands folded in her lap, like a nun. "The stars and planets are aligned."

Nearly out the door, Auntie Tilda froze mid-step. "Wait a minute. She's speaking English!"

"In or out?" The mayor asked, rattling the keys.

Auntie Tilda slowly turned back. "In."

"The angel's comin' down from heaven," a woman shouted from the corridor, "and he shall lay hold of the serpents and cast them into a bottomless pit!"

"Mother!" Mayor Bingo said to the woman. She turned back to Auntie. "Five minutes," she said, before bolting the door.

"Just what branch of the devil are you?" Auntie asked Ninti.

Dull-eyed and lacking in vibrancy, it was apparent to Moojie that Ninti and Babylonia were suffering from being locked up.

"It was written long ago, in the stars," Ninti sighed.

"What's she going on about?" Auntie Tilda asked Moojie.

"Better listen," he answered. "It's about the village going to hell and gone."

In the harsh light, Babylonia remained serene and aloof as a cat.

Ninti rose to look out the barred window. "We were so close. And the village will be gone soon."

Auntie Tilda looked as if she'd seen a ghost. She clutched her handbag—wild hair, starfish mouth, pointy little feet. "What is she saying? Mayor!" she called out.

The astronomical town clock struck high noon. Moojie placed the eggs on the cot next to Babylonia.

Mayor Bingo unlocked the cell door.

"It wasn't supposed to go this way," Moojie said to Babylonia.

"Come now, sonny," said the mayor.

"I'm going to get you out of here," Moojie whispered to Babylonia. "Count on it."

Outside the jailhouse, Auntie Tilda took one look at Moojie and said, "Oh, no you don't. I see the look in your eyes. Count me out, lad."

"They didn't kill Pappy. I was there. It was an accident. And if I'm not wrong, when you signed up to be a teacher, you agreed to uphold the truth much the same way the politicians don't."

She sighed.

"One way or another," he said, "I'm going to that Town Hall meeting, and if you give a tinker's cuss about justice, you will go, too."

She looked at the sky. "I need time to think." She turned her nose in the direction of La Pâtisserie. "First, a cinnamon swirl."

Chapter 3

Moojie and his aunt are hereby incited to come to the defense of Ninti and the Light-Eaters

The Town Hall, a converted hay barn, built of massive black oak timbers fitted together with double-cross beams, was busier than a hornet's nest in a plum tree. Everyone was there: the mayor, the courier, the barkeep, all manner of San Miguelians, in and out of costume. Moojie and Auntie Tilda sat front and center with the green grocer.

The day before, Auntie Tilda had refused to attend the meeting. She had no notion to mix with the villagers and her bunions were smarting like the dickens. And she had been gloomy as the English sky. But during the night her feet worsened, and she took it as a sign from God to reconsider.

From the podium, Mayor Bingo slammed down the gavel and called the meeting to order.

"First order of business," she said: "A swift warning

and a reprimand to any villager dreaming of taking the law into their hands concerning the aforementioned events of St. Isidore's Fainting Goat Dairy."

"A plague of demons!" Father Grabbe shouted. "The Hostile nations must be stopped or there will be bloodshed. I tell you, they're forming alliances all over the country."

The mayor's mother, Mrs. Latchkey, stood to address the meeting in a loud mayor's-mother's voice: "In the case of Hostiles, first they hypnotize you, then they eat you."

"Good heavens, 'tis worse than church!" Auntie Tilda said.

Mrs. Markham stood in the aisle. Wearing a dress with a scandalous neckline, she raised her hand like a schoolgirl. "Why, it's a matter of sanitation!" she said. Her son took notes—Bentley, the snotty Markham, looking meaner than a two-headed snake.

"Now, I ain't sayin' it to alarm y'all," a local farmer said, "but it be well documented in point of fact, that trouble's brewing in those thar hills. We gotta hang the Hostiles straight off or they's a'gonna call in backups."

"They're rude and uncivilized, I tell you," said the jeweler. "They've been robbing us of *our* milk and *our* eggs."

Moojie saw a rat traipse across an overhead beam.

"Will you listen to him," Mr. Abu, the green grocer, said. "Coming from the very same mouth that hoards all the kidney beans."

Down came the gavel once more. "Order in the court!" cried the mayor.

With alarming intensity, Mr. Abu looked at Moojie, the heat of stars and comets and galaxies coming from his dark eyes. He cradled Moojie's chin with his thumbless hand. "You know what to say, young man. The villagers will listen to you."

Moojie shuddered. Terrified of speaking publicly, he didn't know what he had in mind to say. But, like Pappy, he wasn't born in the woods to be scared by an owl. And sure enough, when he stood to his feet the people went quiet.

"Well," he cleared his throat, wishing he were a poet, "Pappy's death was a tragedy and I'm as torn up about it as anyone. But you shouldn't blame the clan for it, you know, because it was my fault. All the trouble started on account … on account of … well, because I shot his goat. I should be in jail, not the ones you keep calling Hostiles."

Rumblings.

"How can a child with such a face be crippled?" the mayor's mother asked.

"ORDER IN THE COURT!" Mayor Bingo thundered. "I am aggrieved as anyone about the death of Captain Finnegan. Let us not lose what is left of our minds. As mayor apparent, I'm obliged to represent those of us who are out of our minds as well as those who are not. Henceforth and heretofore, let this go on record: I, a public servant, witnessed firsthand the unfortunate events that ended the captain's life. If the present company would care to stop flapping its traps and sit its hineys down, I will, in fact, set the record straight."

The villagers grumbled back to their seats.

"Now, the sun was climbing over the hills …." the mayor began, licking her mouth and twisting out a clever, expert-witness smile. She told the story of how she and the captain had headed up the mountain six mornings before. And it all was true, except when she got to the part where Ninti came out of the cave and Pappy's rifle jammed. "The captain swung around," she said, "and the old crow just up and pushed him to his death."

Auntie Tilda let out a mournful peep.

"So you see, gentlefolk of San Miguel de las Gaviotas," the mayor said, "Captain Sean Finnegan was murdered, plain and simple."

"That's a lie!" Moojie stood again.

"Those savages are going to swing from their necks," the mayor said. "And, you, sonny, are in no position to argue."

The crowd roared with excitement.

"I say put the Hostiles to work building a seawall before we string them up!" someone said.

"Hold on," the priest said. "It's my godly duty to convert their souls!"

"What about vaccinations?" Mrs. Markham said.

Moojie waved a crutch in the air and shouted: "By my word, the clan is innocent. I was there and nobody shoved, nobody pushed. Pappy fell, plain and simple. Anyway, St. Isidore's belongs to me now, and I say the clan can stay as long as they please."

The people clamored out reprisals.

"Oh, wind your necks in the whole lot of you!" Auntie Tilda boomed.

"If Mr. Littleman won't press charges," the mayor said, "I will. On behalf of the citizenry of San Miguel, so help me, I will."

"But—" Moojie protested. He could feel heat rising into his ears.

"I hereby exercise my authority to set a judicial hanging after tomorrow's Christmas pageant. I move that this meeting come to a close. All those in favor—"

"Don't listen to Littleman," Bentley squawked. "He can't even tie his shoes!"

Moojie looked down at his shoelaces, at his whatnot-knots, frying with embarrassment.

"You, lad," Auntie Tilda said to Bentley, "had better

shut your cake hole."

"Who's the bowl of fruit?" Bentley asked, eyeing her red, orange, and green bubu.

The villagers were still at it among themselves.

Auntie bounded onto her feet. "I'm with the lad. He's right!" The green grocer followed suit. So did the sheriff, and the deputy, and one by one, a number of villagers. "Here, here!" they rang out. "The boy is right!"

Mayor Bingo hammered the gavel. "ORDER!"

Order was not a word to describe what followed. There came a seismic rumble of shouting and the hall was transformed into a battlefield of finger-pointing, arm-waving, and tongue-wagging—*Ayes* against *Nays*. The mayor slammed down the mallet and went hoarse shouting, "Order! Order! Order!" and the mallet snapped off its gavel, sailed over the mob, only to land front and center between Mrs. Markham's bazooms!

Moojie spotted McTavish in the back of the hall, face half-hidden under his cowboy hat, jaw clenched, mouth hitched sideways, frozen in time—the look of retribution.

Tilly's barkeep crossed his arms and legs, and shook his head. "Blame the automobiles! They have brought socialism to our doorstep!"

Moojie wasn't ready to die. Not yet, anyway. For the first time in a long while, he was surging with life. Something had snapped loose inside him. Higgledly-piggledy, noise and chaos, it came to him. He knew what he had to do.

He and his aunt pushed through the mayhem, toward the deputy sheriff, who was scrambling to separate the jeweler and a fisherman, two grown men, on the floor pulling each other's noses. The deputy's jail keys fell onto the floor. Bentley lurched in front of Moojie and snarled. Moojie stomped his toe with the tip of his crutch, and Auntie Tilda whacked him on the bottom with her leather bag. "You're a lot of blarney," she said.

Once outside, Moojie held up the keys and grinned at his aunt. "Ha!"

"Dear lord in heaven!"

"I got the Light-Eaters into this mess. I'm gonna get them out of it."

The sky was blushing red with the setting sun as they sidled into the jailhouse. It seemed everyone had underestimated the crippled kid and the loud squatty aunt in tiny red boots. Through the speakeasy on the cell door, Moojie and his aunt could see Ninti and Babylonia sitting cross-legged on the floor, the eggs between them. Together they whispered something and each broke open an egg. Light burst out of the shells, a stunning, blinding light, white as new stars. And they gulped it down, as if it were milk.

"Hold on now while I get the biscuits!" Auntie whispered. "That's light they're drinking. Light!"

Moojie sent Auntie Tilda to fetch the wagon and bring it around back.

He unlocked and opened the cell door.

Startled, Ninti and Babylonia stood and followed him as he unlocked the rest of the cells. He led the clan outside where they piled onto the flat bed of the buckboard.

"Promise me something," Moojie said to Auntie Tilda, as he drove the wagon up the hill to the west end of Flum Street.

"What is it, lad?"

"If we get away with this, promise me you'll teach me to tie my shoes."

"There's a good boy!" she laughed.

Chapter 4

*An account of the events after Moojie returns
the clan to St. Isidore's, with details
equally ludicrous and true*

"For pity's sake, where in the world did you come from? Are there more of you about? And what the ruddy willikers are you doing in that cave?" Ninti remained silent as Auntie Tilda fired questions at her, riding up front on the buckboard with Moojie. He just rolled his eyes and flicked the reins.

"We did not foresee the accident," Ninti said wearily.

"They're going to come after you," Moojie said. "Don't worry, I'll take care of you."

"You'll do no such thing," Auntie said. "We are not staying at the dairy! You'll take your friends back, pack your bags, and say your goodbyes."

In the darkening sky above, a stream of seagulls followed the buckboard.

Moojie snapped the reins and glanced back at Babylonia who was wedged between the twins. It had been nearly seven years since they first met. She hadn't changed, but he had grown muscular, and was catching up to her in height. Was it age that aggravated his desire? He imagined she would always be taller than he was, a tall flame, lithe and soundless and setting everything on fire. So often his dreams had been filled with flames. No, she hadn't changed. He had.

Moojie caught Sarru'kan's eye and turned back frontward.

"So," Auntie Tilda said to Ninti, "you can foretell the future, can you? I suppose you'll be claiming some special connection to the Almighty."

Rubbing her earlobe, tousled and drawn in the face, Ninti didn't appear her usual self.

"Everyone has the connection, my lady," she said. "Did they not teach you that in grade school?"

"They did not," Auntie Tilda said.

"Did your mother—"

"Never."

"How then do you ever lift your moorings?"

Auntie Tilda glanced down at her enormous bosom. "I beg your pardon!"

The conversation parked there for a while and the wagon continued east through the Valley of Sorrows. Meandering in thought, Moojie went over the tragic events of only a week ago, when Pappy rode up El Serrat for the last time.

When the wagon reached the turn to St. Isidore's gate, the seagulls made a great banking circle and headed back toward the coast.

Millie-Mae flew off the porch to meet the wagon.

"My lady," Imi'tittu said to Auntie with his hands folded together, "you have done a good deed for our kind.

Pray, accept my deepest gratitude." Beside herself with uncharacteristic blushing, Auntie and her pointy hands and pointy boots and bumptious bubu seemed out of place amid the cactus and olive trees, as out of place as a starfish in a reptile's terrarium.

Moojie hurried to pass out scuttles to everyone, urging them to go into the cold storage shed and take all the nuts, gourds, milk, eggs, dried fish, and fruit they wanted. A new and implacable sense had charged through him, a shouldering sense. Someone had to look after the clan, someone had to get the Light-Eaters holed up in that cave before the villagers discovered them gone from the jailhouse, and by golly, that someone was him.

Sarru'kan snatched back the baskets from the others and shoved them at Moojie, saying, "We don't need his food." The gunshot wound had disappeared from his arm.

"Thank you, my lord," Babylonia said to Moojie, retrieving the scuttles. "You have been good to us."

Sarru'kan jerked the scuttles away from her and threw them down. She shot him a look of defiance. He lifted a hand to her, and Moojie stepped between them.

"Don't do it," he said to Sarru'kan. "You'll be sorry."

Imi'tittu whisked Sarru'kan away from the scene immediately.

"You mustn't provoke him," Babylonia said to Moojie. "He will cause you great pain."

"Is that why you're going to marry him? So he won't beat you up?"

She picked up the scuttles and went to the shed.

"What about your clothes?" Auntie asked Ladyship Ninti. "We can't have you mucking about dressed like bedroom furniture." Imi'tittu, strolling about the yard, noble and erect in his sacky shirt and coffee-can waist ornament, looked dashed. "And money? You'll need money," Auntie Tilda said, rooting through her handbag.

Ninti waved off her paper bills like they were bad oysters and, guided by starlight, she led the clan across the field toward to the mountain.

"The nerve!" Auntie Tilda said to Moojie, once they were inside the cabin. "'Did they not teach you this in grade school?'" She mimicked Ninti while lighting the kettle.

"She didn't mean any harm," Moojie said.

"Why, she's got the brains of a kipper, she does. She's a troublemaker, like all the rest of them."

"But—"

"I have no intention of staying here. I'm going back to my homeland, and you're coming with me, young man. We'll settle everything with Mr. McTavish tomorrow. He'll look after the goats and such."

That very night, Auntie threw herself into scrubbing the cabin top to bottom, mopping the floors, beating the dust out of the furniture, washing the windows. "Don't go getting any big ideas," she said. "I'm only tidying up. If I don't leave things in order, I'll have to live with the guilt. Now, I'm tired, my bunions ache, and you ought to get packing."

Of course, he did no such thing.

At the moment, Auntie Tilda might have been his only semblance of a family, but he was far from giving up on the clan. They were more like family than she could ever be. All but Sarru'kan had accepted him. They had taught him to read and write, to honor all of life, including the unseen world, and they came fitted with more than enough sisters and brothers and aunts and uncles than he could ever hope for. Ninti and Imi'tittu had helped him master his power, and convinced him that he could help others. The twins had inspired him to laugh again, to douse the world with light. And then, there was Babylonia ....

The stars glistened outside the window, white and flickering, swimming through infinity like bright silver fish in a dark, over-full river, slowly, struggling against the current, never touching each other.

In an effort to forget about the lovely Lady B., Moojie distracted himself by slogging through chores. He greased the buckboard axles, and mucked the stables. He cleared the growing patch, groomed the critters, and rode the exercise bicycle. It was no use. A bird would fly by and he would think of her. She was everywhere—in the keepers, in the drifting clouds, in the winter stars shining down like fireworks captured in time. His stomach would ache, and she was the first thing to come to mind. Auntie Tilda found him lying in the straw with the goats. "Bless me boy, what are you doing?" she asked.

"Taking a nap." For ten days Auntie had plied him with buttered scones to prepare him for the good life of Ireland, and this harassed him all the more. She spoke of proper hygiene and proper table manners, of proper education and proper religious training—all of which went into his brain like water into a chambered shell. And yet, her scheme had outrun any of Moojie's better ideas. Furthermore, the worm of some grand purpose that he needed to accomplish, some quest that required all manner of saintliness, and if he failed, he would somehow be missing the whole point of his life, bore through his conscience. Tortured, feverish, he crept about the cabin in socked feet, feeling the weight of Pappy's torment. He slacked off on chores and rode up El Serrat, just in case the cave was open or Ninti decided to give up her doubts and welcome him to the fold. The cave stayed closed now, invisible, even to him. The granite masquerading the entrance was a cold, sure, solid, flecked husk. He didn't shout or call out. As the granite face held him at bay, he listened through it. He heard a babble of voices coming through the tunnels and passageways. He sent a thousand blessings swirling through the energetic field, and they came back rejected. Still, the door to his heart had swung open, and he was not going to be denied. Even as Auntie Tilda made him drink boiled carrot juice and nettle soup to ward off fever. Even as she pinned to the cupboard two passages on the eastbound train to New York City, where they were supposed to catch the steam liner to Ireland. Even then.

At 5:00 A.M. a noise in the kitchen awoke Moojie. He got up and peered around the corner at Auntie Tilda. All dressed, her trunk near the front door, she was making tea. Moojie was just about to say something, when she took a knife to a scone and cut herself.

"Oie, jaysus!" she gasped.

He bungled over to her.

"My finger," she said, holding a dishcloth around her hand. Pale as a cloud, Auntie Tilda rocked back and forth in her chair, biting back tears. Without giving it a second thought, Moojie covered her hand with his and lay his head against hers. He turned within to the healing force, to call forth the divine pattern of all things, reaching, reaching, reaching, for that feeling, that peace, that pouring-through sensation that had suffused him when the cows and Manish needed help, and then he felt warmth surging out from his chest, and he knew—inexplicably, undeniably—she would be all right.

"It's okay, Auntie. You'll be okay."

She drew a breath and color came flooding back into her cheeks. They stayed with their heads together for a while, and when she removed the bloody cloth from her finger, no trace of a cut could be seen.

"Janey Mac, what the—?" Auntie Tilda exclaimed. She sort of looked afraid of him.

It happened so quickly, so easily, that Moojie was surprised, too. But not as surprised as before. Though he didn't understand how healing happened, he was beginning to get the hang of this sort of thing. It had something to do with forgetting himself completely, and letting life itself take over.

"Is this what love is?" he asked absentmindedly.

Auntie Tilda's expression made him laugh.

"'Tis a bloody miracle!" she said, teary-eyed. "Look at this finger. Look what you've done! You are no ordinary boy, Moojie Littleman!" She eventually settled down with a cup of tea and dropped off to sleep on the sofa.

Moojie's understanding of his purpose was coming into fuller view. Still a mystery, he knew this much: the healing force lay beyond the power of nature and magic. Light, weightless, he went to his bedroom and sat on the cot next to Millie-Mae. "There comes a time in every boy's life," he said in all seriousness, "when he's got to master socks." For years, he had gone without them just to avoid this very moment. He took a pair out of the drawer and with his mighty righty tugged and stretched and convulsed, legs jerking involuntarily out of reach, ripping both the socks, until at last he got them onto his feet. And then he put on his braces and shoes. It took twenty minutes, but, alleluia!, he tied his laces properly for the very first time. No more whatnot-knots, Bentley Markham. So there.

On his way up the mountain the next morning, Moojie was astonished to meet McTavish and several villagers on their way down the trail. They had Imi'tittu. His hands were tied behind his back, and he was walking alongside their burros, tethered at the neck.

Moojie blocked their passage. "Nope," he said.

"Stand aside, lad," McTavish said, holding his rifle casually across his chest. "The law is the law."

Imi'tittu gave Moojie a brief smile, a wink, and a nod, as if he wanted Moojie to let them pass. Reluctantly, Moojie moved aside and the group continued past him down the mountain. Inside he was panicking.

"I know you're in charge," Moojie said to the sky. "And I know you know everything. I'm just a fool, but I'm here to help. By your grace, show me what to do."

Two minutes later, the twins came bungling down the trail. "My lord! My lord!" Manish cried. "Sarru'kan is going to kill them!"

Sarru'kan and three handsome ones had struck out with their spears down another trail to take Imi'tittu back by force.

"Sarru'kan refused to obey Ladyship," Manish said. "He said forget about The Code; violence is the only language worldlings know how to speak."

When Moojie and the twins reached the cave, Ninti was outside watching McTavish and the others cross the lower field with Imi'tittu.

"I have a plan," Moojie said quickly. "Get your spears."

Ninti crossed her arms.

"Trust me," he said, "I don't want to hurt anybody."

She paused a moment, went inside the cave briefly, then reappeared with the rest of the handsome ones and the olders, all bearing spears.

"Hurry!" Moojie said, keeping an eye on the field. "Go down to the first bench. From there, put ten paces between yourselves and wait for my signal. When I blow this," he waved the kazoo, "fire upon the beehives, each of you taking a different one. Go quickly!"

They looked at him as if unsure.

"I promise," he said. "No one will be killed."

They started down the mountain. Moojie rode in the opposite direction to a different vantage point. Just as the posse approached the beehives, Moojie blew the kazoo and sixteen spears sailed over the trees in great, high arcs that came down on the hives, knocking them over and releasing tens of thousands of bees, nasty, fizzing, inciting an assault on the posse. McTavish and the villagers flailed their arms and waved their jackets, their burros bucking and honking, and all together galloping away from the dairy, and just then Sarru'kan burst from the woods, spear held high, bellowing a battle cry, YEEAAA! at no one in particular.

Imi'tittu's laughter bellowed up from the field.

"Hail, Moojie! Lord of the Plow!" Ninti, Babylonia, the twins, and the others cheered and whistled in triumph.

But Moojie knew the trouble was far from over.

Chapter 5

The land of forgotten time and good manners

Dreading what lay ahead for the clan, Moojie told his aunt about the posse and the bees. But instead of offering to help, she became more insistent about leaving for Ireland.

"We both could use a bit of emerald green, yes?" she said. "Go in and start packing because we're leaving on the next train out of here, which is now five days away." She had wakened in a fury that morning, sweeping and scrubbing and putting the kitchen shelves in order. "I don't give a cracker's crumb for this place or the village. And I wish I had a copper penny for every time the villagers asked me why I don't have children of my own! I'll take the cinnamon swirls, but you can have the bloody fog." On and on she bubbled through her orange lips, loud and skirling.

Over his aunt's protests, Moojie marched out of the cabin, got onto Hocus, and rode up the mountainside.

Cave closed. He continued up the trail to the top. Baby-lonia was there, standing inside the Circle of Trees.

"It's almost spring," he said, sitting on Hocus. "I reckon you and the others will be picking berries soon, and making paper at the creek—everything back to normal."

"Aye, nearly spring, and aye, everything will return to normal, but nay, not how you think. We are returning to our homeworld."

"What? No." Moojie was, to say the least, stunned.

"The coming earthquake will at last open the portal and we will rise into the vortex," she said, pointing directly above her.

"You're *leaving*?"

"I believe the English word is *transmigrating*." She was picking olive sprigs and putting them into her skirt.

"Why didn't you tell me?" he asked.

"You helped us escape jail. You helped divert the posse. We are most grateful to you. However, we cannot risk any more trouble."

"It wasn't me, you know," he said.

"Sorry?"

"I didn't blow the all-clear signal the morning Pappy came up here."

"No other soul knew of it."

"I know, I know. But, I think Pappy overheard …."

She started walking back to the cave.

Moojie knew it was useless to try to explain himself. Though he had sabotaged his grandfather's rifles on the day he died, he knew it looked bad. It looked as if he had—either willfully or carelessly—aided the assault on the cave. As he watched her go down the trail, he felt his breath leave him. *Not again. Not bloody again! Another family, slipping through my fingers!* He didn't know the first thing about transmigration, but he called out after her: "I'm going with you!"

For three days Moojie endured the minefield of Auntie Tilda's passion to return to Ireland—the long speeches and blistering admonitions—while secretly planning to ditch her on the train and return to St. Isidore's.

"Today's lesson starts with a pot of tea," she said, pouring two cups. "And then you shall meet the patron saints of my homeland: Brigid of Kildare, Colmcille, and Patrick."

Behind her back, Moojie picked up a knife and pretended to slit his wrists.

"I'm just going to check the fields," he said, heading for the door.

"Oh, no you don't. Come right over here. You'll have time for that later," she slurped her tea, and began to peel potatoes from the great bowl in front of her.

He glanced out the window and sat back down.

"Had it not been for the Troubles and the Sorrows," she began, "my homeland would never have gone to pot. Had it not been for the Protestants, the promise of heaven would be real as rain, true as the crowning of the Glory of His Love, as it was written, world without end."

Moojie imagined stuffing one of those potatoes into her mouth to shut her up. But he didn't have to. A little earthquake shook the table and did it for him. But only for a minute.

Auntie Tilda merely paused, then went back to scraping the potatoes. When finished, she rinsed her hands, and called him over to the sofa. As usual, before reading anything important, she swiped her eyeglasses with her tongue and rubbed them dry with the hem of her bubu.

"I was hoping," she said, "that from today's lesson, we'd both recover a proper sense of faith—or at least to settle on a plan to get away before the so-called end-of-the-world."

It was futile for Moojie to argue. Auntie Tilda would only chop logic or get worked into a froth; in short, drive him crazy. He didn't want to go to Ireland. He didn't want her lessons on churches and religion and saints, and the whip of her voice was more than he could bear. All at once, he popped onto his crutches and said, "I don't need you to teach me about miracles. I've seen them for myself!"

"Yes, well, I'll bet you didn't know the spirit of the dead last-buried keeps watch in the graveyard till the next dead come, did you? Purgatory is a very hot place, and the dead must get water to their loved ones. And when two funeral processions enter the graveyard at the same time, it can get bloody ugly. No one wants their beloved's soul cooking on a hot dosser!"

Moojie slammed his crutch down upon the coffee table. "I'm sick and tired of your voice!" He was yelling now. "And that thing you do with your tongue!"

"What's wrong with my tongue?"

"Every day, all day, blah blah blah blah blah, the saints and the Protestants. Gaw, you'll drive me to drink—"

"Is that right? Why, I'm appalled, to say the least. You could use a lesson on manners."

"You sound just like my father," he spat, and trundled outside.

She opened the door and said after him: "No wonder he sent you away! You're not fit to mind mice at the cross-roads. No wonder he came back and hasn't come for you!" As soon as she said it, she covered her mouth.

Moojie's body seized up. "What?" His father had come back?

"Oh dear. I'm sorry. I didn't want to tell you. I saw him just over a week ago, riding his horse out of the livery stable. I ran after him, but he turned and went down the coast. I didn't tell you because … because … oh, he's such an idiot." She tried to hug Moojie.

He held her off and went directly to the growing patch where he sat in stunned silence under a squadron of flies. Papa had come back to the village and never contacted him! The news wiped out every excuse Moojie had made up for his father. It felt as if a withered limb of his life had just been amputated, the sickly dream of a reunion.

That night after supper, as if to make up to Moojie, Auntie Tilda brought out *The Waltzing Lobster* and asked him to tell her about it. He opened it to the page marked with a bay leaf, the story of the Light-Eaters.

"Hmm," she said, looking it over. She looked up over her glasses at him. "Is this … are they?"

"I'm going to San Miguel tomorrow," he said. "It's time to call a town meeting and square off with the villagers."

So engrossed was Auntie Tilda in the book, that she read it until she dropped off to sleep with it open across her chest. Moojie covered her with a blanket, closed the wood stove, and filled the kettle for the morning.

"Can you forgive me?" she asked sleepily.

"What?"

"I didn't tell you your father was back because I wanted to save you the heartbreak."

"Wouldn't it be strange if I ran into him at the village?" he said.

"He's a disgrace of a father. I'm disgusted with him. I told him so. It's a poor excuse of a man who leaves his son in a dungheap."

Moojie went out to the porch. No sign of life anywhere. Only the stars and the moon. Only the rattling of crickets, and a barn owl sailing from tree to tree as if stealing dreams. Moojie had almost forgotten what Papa looked like—except for the gray-green putty of his eyes.

The next wave of villagers arrived at St. Isidore's wearing body suits, white jumpers, screened helmets and gloves, ready for the bees. It was early morning when Moojie spotted them from the porch as they marched up the long driveway and across the bridge. Moojie counted nineteen in all. Led by an elf-sized person carrying rattles and animal claws, the multitude was armed with garden clippers, ropes, and shovels, and heading straight across the east field toward Pappy's bunker. The gate was locked, but they just passed through the boards. "Everything but pitchforks," Auntie said, watching with the field glasses. "I expect they'll put a period at the end of the sentence."

Moojie looked through the glasses, saying, "We'll just see about that."

"Are you all there? They'll lock you up!"

Millie-Mae circled the kitchen table, claws clacking against the wooden floor. When Moojie opened the door to step outside, she made a mad barking advance toward the mob.

Moojie got on Hocus, circled behind the cabin, and rode out to the bunker, blood rushing through his body and thrumming in his ears. When the posse arrived, one of the tall ones removed his hood. McTavish.

"You needn't concern yourself with this, lad," he said. "No one's going to bother you. It's the Hostiles we're after."

"You're trespassing," Moojie said.

"Don't be getting above yourself, lad. The law's on our side. The government has given the Hostiles a nice place to live elsewhere. If we let them stay, it's only a matter of time before they try to take what is ours by rights."

McTavish went into the underground tunnel and came out with a crate of dynamite. He opened it, stuffed his pockets, and passed out more to the others.

Pigeons. The word just popped into Moojie's mind. He knew by then to never question such distinct messages. He rode back to the yard. Inside the loft, the pigeons were wound up, fluttering and sputtering and pitter-pattering. He opened the cage and they whooshed out, climbing into the sky, circling the yard once, then soaring straight out to the field where they pecked the villagers heads, arms and backs, sending them gaping and yawing back to their carts and buggies, horses and mules.

Auntie Tilda came outside. "What in Bob's name?"

"Ours is not to question," Moojie said with a new appreciation for the pigeons.

"How long do you expect this to go on?" she asked.

He couldn't tell her about his plans. He couldn't tell her that he was only holding off the villagers until it was time for him to leave with the clan. She would split a seam. She would get all worked up, and gnash her teeth, and blow up with hot air, then she would lift off the ground, floating higher and higher, until she split another seam. And then she would come crashing back to earth, whistling like a teakettle. Or something. "I don't know how long it will go on," he said. "But they're like family to me, and I aim to keep them safe."

Chapter 6

The door of doubt and the crackling of moss

They entered March, and the sky blackened with clouds and cold rains came with a vengeance. Moojie thumped about the living room, as water running under the cabin caused the floors to swell and buckle. He wrung his hands, and paced, and cursed the rain, as water from the leaky roof dribbled into buckets. Left to its own devices, the growing patch had turned to sludge. Fences leaned, stalls fermented. The vernal equinox was only weeks away, and Ninti hadn't yet agreed to let Moojie join the clan.

It was crazy to think anyone would actually *want* to get sucked up into the cosmos, never to be seen on Earth again. Moojie had honored The Code; at least, he had fed the poor. Sarru'kan had bullied Babylonia into accepting marriage, Moojie was sure of it. She was more afraid of him than in love. Somehow, it all came down to one miserable question: Would the clan ever trust him? If not, then what? Losing another family would be worse than death.

Sitting in silence and praising the wonders of life was nice—but was it everything? Was Moojie happy? And what about Grace? He mumbled the word like it was a curse. Grace. Ha! Grace had created the world and then gone on vacation. He was an outcast in his homeland, a warrior without a war, a king without a kingdom. He had once believed in miracles. But that was a long time ago.

When the rain let up, he found Sarru'kan and several handsome ones at the creek. They were taking machetes to the shrubs and trees along the banks.

"What are you doing?" he asked one of them. "You shouldn't be here. The villagers might see you."

"Preparations," the boy said, "for the fire."

"Fire," Moojie said sarcastically. "Right. Now we have a fire."

Wearing the same smelly shirt and jeans for a week—smelly, as in sweat and hay and wood smoke—Moojie had just come from working in the garden, his hands muddy, boots caked with manure. He saw Babylonia and was embarrassed by his appearance. She smiled, her eyes shining and soft.

Sarru'kan slithered up to Moojie. "I see how you look at her," he said to Moojie. "Meet me here at sunset, and we will settle the matter for once and for all."

"My lord!" Ninti called out to Moojie.

"I was just …." Moojie held up his dirty hands and pointed to the creek.

She called him over to the rock where she liked to sit, and he was heedful this time not to land upon her.

"Have you given any more thought to The Code, my lord?" she asked.

"Well, I planted some more watermelon seeds but—"

"What I mean to say … your father has returned, and—"

"Gaw, how'd you know that?"

She smiled.

"Right," he said. "You just know. Like the big quake and the end of the world, you know." He picked up a rock and skipped it across the creek.

"You do not want to see him?" she asked.

"I'd take the Steel Barn over him any day."

"Will you never make peace with him?"

"Some doors don't open twice."

"My lord, light cannot pass through a door."

Heat rushed into Moojie's head. "I'm not a door and I'm sick of your riddles!"

"My lord," she said, laying a hand upon his arm. "The constellations are aligned, the time is approaching—"

"Wherever you're going, I'm going with you," he said.

"My lord, it is a very long way back to Earth. And there is the matter of your father—"

"Ha! My father. Are you kidding? Gaw, you said love is everywhere, but it isn't." Exasperated, he started toward the cabin.

At sunset, Moojie stepped outside the cabin. He had mentally prepared for the meeting with Sarru'kan, and imagined with great pleasure the feeling of pummeling his face and rearranging his scars. So pumped up, he didn't even remember walking to the creek, he was just there, all of a sudden, crutches planted in the sand, taut, electrified, ready. And Sarru'kan never showed up. But Anahita, the cougar who was supposed to be dead, did— all muscles and jaws and teeth. Moojie's heart bounced wildly against his ribs, and when she strode toward him, shifting the weight of her muscular body from shoulder to shoulder, he looked left and right, and he said, "Jesus Christmas, there's a nice kitty, you don't want to harm me," and she crept closer to him, head low, eyes fixed upon his face. He backed into the rock outcropping. Anahita growled, showing her mighty fangs, and he held a crutch aloft to keep her away, but she batted it and hissed, and he froze until she turned back toward the woods and left.

Sarru'kan had set him up! In the twilight now, Moojie trekked back to the yard. He paced in front of the pigeon loft, he vented and spat. He socked his left arm and punched his legs. The pigeons flapped their wings in panic. "You have wings," Moojie said, electricity crackling in his head like tin foil. He threw open the cage. "Go on! You can go!" They piled into the back of the cage. And flooding in upon Moojie, to his utter surprise, was a sudden dark, angry, helplessness and despair, engulfing him so swiftly that, as the goats peered out from the barn, the feelings drowned him, and he took hold of the loft's underside with his mighty righty and he threw it over on its side, collapsed onto his knees, and wept from the pit of his soul. The pigeons spewed out the broken door in a gray panic.

Ninti came up behind him quietly, and laid a steady hand on his shoulder.

"Forget about our agreement," he said. "Forget about The Code."

"My lord, what about your quest, your purpose?"

"Right. My purpose." Moojie doubted there was such a thing.

"If your purpose were a loaf of bread, Sarru'kan is but the crust."

"What?"

"Listen to me. You can choose suffering, or you can choose peace. Your greatest purpose is to awaken to your true nature, and that nature is merciful. The one you most despise, the one who in your estimation is unforgivable, is your wayshower."

Moojie sighed.

"Think upon it, my lord," Ninti said, before leaving. "The same lesson will be waiting for you wherever you go. You can reject what I am saying, of course, and take another thousand lifetimes to accept it, if you prefer. It is your choice."

Inside the cabin, Moojie studied his reflection in the bathroom mirror, gazing closely as if looking at a stranger. And he didn't like what he saw.

That afternoon McTavish paid an unexpected visit to St. Isidore's, and when he saw the pigeon loft on its side, he looked at Moojie and said, "I suppose 'twas the wind?"

Moojie felt his eyes burning and he didn't want him to see him crying or blushing with shame. McTavish helped him set the loft upright and back to order.

Auntie Tilda invited McTavish for supper of corned beef and cabbage, and the Scotsman pressed her and Moojie for details about the clan. When had they last seen them? What were their daily habits? What were they after? Moojie pretended to know nothing and was happy at last when Auntie Tilda changed the subject.

"I miss Ireland so. Do you miss Scotland, Mr. McTavish?"

The smells of baked whiskey brack and wild blackberries sweetened the kitchen haze.

"Indeed, I do. What I wouldn't give for a good lump of haggis."

"It's the books I miss, poetry mostly," she said. She recited a verse in Gaelic. "Poetry is a girl's best friend."

"What about you, lad," McTavish turned to Moojie. "Do you miss home?"

"This is my home," Moojie said. In truth, he didn't fully believe it. His place was with the Light-Eaters. But he couldn't say that.

"Your father is sure to come get you," McTavish said.

"Sure," Moojie said, with a puff of irony.

"It can get mighty lonesome out here," McTavish said. "What about a girl? Do you fancy a girl?"

Moojie blushed.

"Crikey," laughed Auntie Tilda. "The lad has a bad dose!"

Wary of McTavish knowing anything about the clan, Moojie grimaced. Auntie Tilda seemed to understand from his look that she had ventured into a dangerous territory. She burst from her chair and scurried over to the wood stove. "Scones?"

Moojie scolded his aunt the minute McTavish left. "You could have given them away!"

"Not to worry, lad. Your secret is safe with me. Anyway, I've got the dear Mr. McTavish twisted about me little pinky," she winked. "Maybe we shouldn't be so hasty about leaving the country. Maybe, we should stick around a little longer."

Moojie grinned to one side. The relief was not uncomplicated.

"It's the pretty girl, isn't it?" she asked.

He bit his lip.

"You know," she said, "sometimes love is like an apple. It's too big to fit into your mouth all at once."

Love. Yes, he'd heard that word before. Here one minute, gone the next. "Gaw, but it isn't right to take the apple from another man's tree," he said.

Chapter 7

Giving an account of the red moon and the next
strange turn in Moojie's adventure

Auntie Tilda's new interest in McTavish bought Moojie some time, but fifteen days had lapsed since the vernal equinox and he was coming unraveled. The pandemonium would be happening any day, the mother of earthquakes, and the portal would open, and the clan was going to leave without him! He stood outside the magical granite face and he called out for Ninti and Manish and Shar, but they wouldn't answer. The March days were long, and thoughts of his mother returned. Late at night, he lit his lamp and took her dusty diary off the shelf. There was an old photograph in it, two pairs of feet, a man's and a baby's. On the back was written: *Papa and Moojie, three days after meeting each other.*

Moojie's ability to read had vastly improved because of the lessons with Zagros and Babylonia, and for the first time he was able to comprehend an entire entry:

> *February 21, 1888*
> *Mother Teagardin showed us to the rectory kitchen. I'll never forget the smell of fresh-baked pumpkin bread and candle-smoke. There were two boys needing a home. One had a fever that day, and one didn't. Mother brought us the healthy one. "May I hold him?" I asked. She handed me the boy, who was just under a year old. He smiled at me and touched the button on my sweater. I stepped to the window to look at him in the light. He had dark hair and steady eyes. Oh my! A sure riffling ran through me, like an inland breeze, and I knew, I mean, I really knew, undeniably, positively, he was already mine. There was a bread knife on the counter. Henry looked at it and said, "Anybody tries to take him, I'll trim their crust." I never loved Henry more.*

It came as a shock to Moojie that his father had once wanted him. It was actually the first time he ever thought about it—*his father had once wanted him.* The grandfather clock—now repaired, thanks to Mr. Ruple—clanged in the late night. Wide awake, lying on his cot, Moojie resisted sleep. He dragged himself to the living room, lit another lamp, and looked at the time: 3:01 A.M., to be exact. *Something's wrong,* he thought, as he stepped outside, into night's ether. It had been a cold, wet spring, wind coming up the valley every day. But the air had suddenly turned warm. And now the world was quiet, eerily quiet, the three-quarter moon spooky red and, as if an angel were bearing forth a great carbide lamp, Mars beamed in the sky. The air hung thick and still and stunk of sulphur.

And the valley had gone still. No din of crickets, no screeching owl, no scuffling raccoons.

The goats were making a commotion, though. And when Moojie went to check them, he found some circling the stalls like bleating anchovies. The fainters had flopped onto the ground, legs pointing stiffly at the stars. Moojie rousted them and herded them all out to the field. From the fig tree, a seagull sounded an alarm. A seagull? Three miles inland? The pigeons, the trees, the rocks, all seemed to be humming. What were they saying? He checked the henhouse. Not one egg had been laid. Woozy and jittery, he went back inside the cabin, got dressed, and waited at the kitchen table—for what, he didn't know.

Auntie Tilda snapped out to the kitchen in her slippers. She lit the kettle. "Look at us, a couple of zombies," she said.

"This is it, Auntie," Moojie said grimly. "Things are about to change."

She peered out the window into the darkness. "We could do with a little less change, could we not?" She filled a teacup with boiling water and dunked her teabag in it. A bible and *The Waltzing Lobster* were stacked on the table next to her. "Would His Mulligrubs care for a cup of scald and a book discussion before the end of the world?"

"No tea, Auntie. No scones. No thank you, Auntie."

Moojie couldn't stir himself to do anything. He had but lost the will to talk. Not even about books. The problem with science was that it explained how God worked but not how to work with God. The problem with the Holy Scriptures was that they didn't teach a boy how to capture a Girl with Starlit Eyes. He had heard about love, but it always seemed as if it were for other people, and there had been no sign of it for him, and this ongoing mystery suddenly caused a weird reaction. As if impelled by some inner demon, he went for the broom-stick. And while Auntie Tilda uttered, oh dear, oh dear, oh dear, he snapped the broomstick in two across his knee, shimmied the grip off Pappy's umbrella, crammed it onto the end of the broomstick, and then rose to his feet, took a step, and toppled over, taking the kitchen table with him. *Flump!*

"Oh, dear God!" cried his aunt.

He put a hand up to stop her from helping him, "Gaw, I can do it!" And he got to his feet and announced, "I'm going to the cave!"

"'Tis hours before dawn! You're crazy, but you're not out of your mind."

Moojie left his crutches behind and balanced himself with his new cane, carefully taking one step, then another, making his way out the door and onto the porch. The lantern shed light on the wild, cross-eyed cat as she scruffed kittens from under the porch to a hollow tree stump. Moojie mistook unripe figs dropping off the tree for stones falling out of the sky, and field mice racing across the yard for rushing water. And was that the ocean he heard—the low timber of a warning, the first rum-blings, faint but coming in? It wasn't going to be like other earthquakes. This one would be a whole different kettle of fish. What would Papa be doing just then, in the village? Sleeping? Oblivious.

"What is it, lad?" Auntie Tilda asked, through the screen door.

"It's starting, Auntie."

"What's starting? Come inside, dear."

"I had the dream again," Moojie said, "the one where a boat lands on my father's house."

He scrambled down the ramp and stopped. He pic-tured the village breaking off from the continent and his father carried out to sea by kelp, roped and dragged through sand like a calf.

"Good heavens!" Auntie Tilda said, coming outside. "First it's colder than an English mother, now it's hotter than an English harlot in Hades." She unwrapped her shawl. "Are your ears popping?"

Babylonia drifted into the dim yard, with Shemman in a sling. Ninti, Imi'tittu, the olders, Shar, and Manish were behind her, a soundless migration of burning torches and bamboo staffs. In the grazing field, Elsie and Odds and Ends whipped into a freakish dance, snorting and stomping their hooves.

"It is time," Ninti said, looking at the stars. "Mars … red moon … nary a breath of wind."

Standing near her, Moojie could smell Babylonia, wild sage and blue sky, the heat from her torch warming the side of his face.

The light in the sky above El Serrat turned gold and began to pulsate softly.

"The portal will soon open, Ladyship," Babylonia said, her voice fragile against the great dark valley.

"Red moon," Auntie Tilda said. "And the rising of sulphur? Surely the signs of evil."

"Silence!" Ninti said. She held up her staff and sniffed the air. "I had a vision last night … a great tidal wave will follow the earthquake … and the sea will take the village."

Her news hit Moojie like a whip. The village, his childhood home—*his father*—about to be history.

Sarru'kan and his chums were standing a little ways away in the darkness, eavesdropping ghouls.

"We must bid our farewells," Ninti said in a disturbingly final tone.

"Wait." Moojie stepped forward. "Wait."

"We have been waiting for centuries," Ninti said. "No more waiting. Today, we go back to our homeworld."

"Saints alive," Auntie said, fanning herself. "Now we

have another world?"

"Are you coming, my lord?" Ninti asked Moojie.

"What?" Auntie Tilda squeaked.

Moojie couldn't explain what had come over him. He had wanted more than anything to leave with the clan, to start a whole new life with a whole new family, no matter what the cost.

"No," he said. "I'm not leaving." He had been awakened by an urgent, soul-deep command. It was crystal clear now. The hand of fate was poised above him, waiting for his acceptance. No matter how much he resented his father, no matter how much time had passed, no matter how much he wanted to leave with the clan, he simply could not choose his own happiness over his father's life.

Chapter 8

*When the Lord of the Plow takes the
leap of faith*

"What in heaven's name are you up to?" Auntie asked, pinning Moojie with wild uncertainty, as the sky smelled sour-yellow, and the cows in the field were snorting and stomping. "Would someone please tell me what's going on?"

"This is farewell," Ninti said.

"I will go to warn the villagers," Sarru'kan said, stepping into the light. He had on a woman's pink blouse that Auntie Tilda had donated to the clan. Taking Babylonia by the arm, he said, "Lady B. and I will stay and join you in the next transmigration—"

Babylonia pulled away. Puzzlement appeared on all the Light-Eaters' faces.

"No, I'm going," Moojie said. "The villagers will never listen to you. And you can be sure as hogs are made of bacon my father won't follow a snake in a lady's blouse."

"Over my dead body!" Auntie Tilda crowed.

"Then, it is settled," Ninti said. "Sarru'kan will go."

"Ladyship," Imi'tittu said, "forgive me, but when it concerns Sarru'kan, you are blind as a beetle. In my humble opinion, he is most impertinent and ill-suited to lead the people to safety."

"You will beg to take back those words," Sarru'kan said.

"And this is how you honor The Code," Moojie said to him.

The clan members seemed to be holding their breath, all eyes on the ear-tugging Ninti. Inside the cabin, Millie-Mae barked and whined.

"Go ahead and talk, Claw Hand. You have failed to honor the second rule of The Code," Sarru'kan said, putting his arm around Babylonia. "We will be leaving in a moment now."

Moojie rubbed his cold hands together. No, he had not proven that he could make peace with his enemies. Babylonia squirmed away from Sarru'kan and sidled up to Ninti.

"Now, Lady Babylonia, now," Sarru'kan said.

"I will not," she said. "My place is with the clan."

"Get into the wagon," Sarru'kan said.

"Sorry, buckeroo, she's made her choice." Moojie said.

"Wait for me in the wagon!" Sarru'kan roared at Babylonia.

"No," she said.

"Do not test me."

"No," she said.

One of Sarru'kan's sidekicks said, "By Zeus, if she were my lady I would turn her into a cat and keep her in a cage until she came to her senses."

"Enough!" Ninti said.

And surprising everyone, Moojie moved closer to Sarru'kan. In sort of a last-ditch effort to prove he could make peace with his enemies, he put all pride aside and extended his right hand to Sarru'kan in a gesture of reconciliation—man to man, one knight to another, one warrior to another.

"Never!" Sarru'kan said. He straightened, as if completely taken off guard.

"Sarru'kan!" Ninti said, her voice bellowing to the hills and back. He shunted backward and, catching on Imi'tittu's foot, fell onto his backside. The twins stifled their laughter.

"My lord," Ninti said to Moojie, "if you choose to go to the village, you have my blessing. Your courage is honorable." She smiled. Was that a smile of satisfaction, triumph—acceptance—at last? "Where is the medallion?" she asked.

Moojie pulled the necklace out from under his shirt and she touched it with reverence.

"Who is he?" Moojie asked of the seated man on the throne.

"Eashoa, the greatest of wayshowers," she said. She kissed the medallion. "Wear it well, my lord."

Ninti called for a three-minute glass, and everyone stood paralyzed with suspense until Auntie Tilda returned from the cabin with one.

"After the earthquake," Ninti said, giving the hourglass to Moojie, "you will have little more than one turn of the glass before the sea covers the village. Go now. Make haste, dear fellow. The angels will guide you." She embraced him.

Heavy with sadness, Moojie just then felt the impact of his decision to go to the village: the loss of his friends. They had been good to him, better than most humans, and Ninti had made him believe there was no end to his goodness.

Pointing her staff at the changing light above the mountain, Ninti cried, "*ATLAKA!* To the Circle of Trees!" She and most of the Light-Eaters started toward the mountain.

Moojie started toward the barn to get Hocus Pocus.

"Stop that train this instant!" Auntie Tilda cracked, marching up behind him.

"It's okay, Auntie," Moojie said, taking her hand. "It's okay."

She sniffled. "Do you know why I came to this, this place? I came here because I wanted to help *you* have a better life. Dear lad, dear, dear lad, I was but a fat, old maid with bunions, and there you were, climbing a mountain every day, while I had only a slope. And now this? I suppose I will never understand."

Babylonia drew close to Moojie and Sarru'kan swooped in like a bat out of a cave. Auntie Tilda gave him a brisk shove.

"I'll handle this," Moojie said. By now, he'd gained more strength and better use of his legs and arms. He didn't consider this a miracle, not in the sense of having been granted a special favor from heaven. It was more that he'd actually forgotten he was crippled.

"Go home," Moojie said to Sarru'kan.

While the others stood by, Sarru'kan threw down his spear and grabbed Moojie's right arm, bent it behind his back, and put a knife to his throat. He cut the medallion off Moojie and threw it into the weeds. "You are not worthy," he said. "I am the new wayshower. You see, I have changed my mind as well. Lady B. and I are not leaving. We will stay here and have children and they will be demi-gods. As in heaven, so on Earth."

"What are you talking about?" Babylonia asked, looking bewildered.

Moojie flipped about face and knocked the knife out of Sarru'kan's hand so quickly that the youth looked boneless, as if someone could hit him and he would go *splat!* But he swooped up his spear and gave Moojie a blow on the side of his head, sending him reeling to the ground.

Millie-Mae burst out of the cabin, charged Sarru'kan, growled and showed her teeth, and he pointed the end of his spear at her like a witch's finger. Flames shot out the tip, singeing the yellow hair off her back. She squeaked and leaped into the horse trough, and when Moojie got to his feet with his staff, Sarru'kan turned the flames at him, reciting some guttural evil. Sarru'kan's arm started vibrating, and he seemed to be fighting to keep hold of the spear. A terrific bolt of electricity hit Moojie square in the chest, the force sending him flying backward onto the ground. First great pain, then complete numbness; Moojie was unable to move a muscle.

"Magic!" Sarru'kan laughed.

Babylonia fetched Moojie's cane and helped him to his feet.

The light glowed green over El Serrat. "You better go," Moojie said to her.

"What are you doing?" Sarru'kan grabbed her arm. "Get away from him."

She shrugged him off.

"You dare to choose sides against me?" Sarru'kan asked.

Moojie lurched forward, and Sarru'kan said "Tut, tut," then gave him another smite of the spear that sent him backward. "Never interfere in a lover's quarrel."

"You're really going to marry *him*?" Moojie asked Babylonia.

She lowered her eyes.

"She wants me," Sarru'kan broke in. "Me. All the

maidens want me. I am not only beautiful, I am powerful. We are staying."

That comment, thought Moojie, coming from a warrior dressed in pink ruffles, hangs in the air the same way manure doesn't.

"Oh, shut up," Babylonia said to Sarru'kan.

Sarru'kan looked absolutely shocked, and gripped her arm. "You *belong* to me."

She struggled to get free. "I will not stay here! Leave me! Go to your other maidens."

"I should have left you at the palace!" he said, eyes flashing contempt.

"I'm going to kill him," Moojie growled, and he shunted forward. Sarru'kan tried to stop him with a riposte of his spear, and Moojie knocked it clear out of his hand with his cane. Sarru'kan came back with a right hook that sent Moojie to the dirt.

"Look at him," Sarru'kan said. "He is but a pathetic worm. He and his pathetic father. Let them perish with the rest of the fools."

"You are not going to stop me," Babylonia said. "I am leaving—"

"You have no choice," he said. "As my wife, you are bound to go where I go."

"In that case, I will not marry you." She broke away from him.

Sarru'kan growled and ran after his spear, but at the same time, the twins, Moojie, and Auntie Tilda rushed in to lock arms, creating a barrier between Sarru'kan and Babylonia.

"You will have to go through us first," Moojie said.

"I will fry you, one at a time," Sarru'kan said. He recited another incantation and waved the spear in a triangular formation. The air thickened with electricity and a great pressure pressed down from above the yard, a galvanizing force.

"Nahzi!" Manish said.

Six-headed, drooling and orange-eyed, the spirit hovered over Sarru'kan then entered his spear.

Frazzled and weak, Moojie stepped forward and croaked, "You and your pet snake aren't going to fry anyone. You're gonna turn around and get the hell out of here." Lord Littleman, Master of the plow, Wizard of Watermelons. Cool as catmeat.

Sarru'kan stood ruffled and pink and exasperated before the others, a towering lout, eyes dark with rage, stark-raving mad. It appeared as though the six-headed serpent had taken possession of him.

"It is the end of Lord Upchuck," Manish whispered.

Sarru'kan snapped up the knife from the ground and threw it at Moojie, and right then, in the blink of an eye, it happened, like the Big Bang, like the birth of a new star, like the cow miracles—in one graceful, instantaneous *whoosh*, Moojie whisked the knife out of the air *with his left hand*. His left hand! Restored to perfection! Grasping the knife, he inspected his hand, turned it over, felt its aliveness. And when he opened it, the weapon had transformed into a live Monarch butterfly.

A hush fell over the yard. And then Auntie Tilda broke into laughter, and the twins buzzed and clapped, and Babylonia remained transfixed on the butterfly, radiating something close to marvel.

Sarru'kan scooped up the butterfly, and stuffed it into his mouth, his hand as fast as a lizard's tongue.

"Dear Lord in heaven!" Auntie Tilda said.

Moojie lurched at Sarru'kan, threw him to the ground, and quickly tied his hands together with the leather thong of the medallion. From inside Sarru'kan, the demon spirit howled and writhed and spit fire through his mouth. Moojie knew he had nothing to fear but fear itself, and as long as he stayed calm, the evil appearing before him could do no harm. He, the twins and Babylonia heaved Sarru'kan onto one of the burros. "Take him to the Circle of Trees," Moojie said to the twins. "Ninti will be waiting."

"Pray, come with us, my lord," Manish said.

"Oh boy. Maybe some day, mate," Moojie said. "Right now, I've got some seeds to look after. You have been a good friend. I won't forget you." He folded his hands and bowed his head.

"I will think of you whenever I see purple," Manish said.

"Me, too," Shar said.

"You but pilfer the good graces of my kin!" Sarru'kan yelled as the twins led him away. "I will conjure fires to roast your flesh!"

The light above El Serrat brightened to yellow, and when Moojie looked at Babylonia's torch-lit face, another wave of sadness came over him. A complicated pause followed, an electrified silence, and rising in the midst, the awful sulphur.

"Stay," he said.

"I—"

"You know, I haven't spoken to my father in years. I could be dead and he wouldn't care. Maybe he is an old coat past stitching up. I could go with you and everything would be good and … and …."

"And?"

"And, I don't know. My father needs me."

"Since he is your father," she said, "he must be a good man."

"Maybe I believe what Ninti told me," he said. "Maybe mercy is the door to freedom. Anyway, it's weird, I just know that if I don't do this, I'll never know what I can do."

"I pray you find it in your heart to forgive me," she said. "I cannot stay because I do not belong here. But neither will I marry Sarru'kan. I have relied on his protection for so long that I forgot my own strength." She put her palm on the center of his chest. "You are a good son."

The light above El Serrat turned pink, and Moojie felt that his heart might burst.

"Make haste Lady B.!" Manish called from the field.

Moojie wondered if he would always love what he couldn't have, and he prayed to Auntie Tilda's patron saint of desperate cases, St. Jude, while he walked Babylonia to the edge of the field. Tears were streaming down her face. He took her hand, and noticed on her wrist a perfect little heart-shaped scar right where he had drawn the red heart months before. "You see," she said, "you have made an impression upon me."

He ran his fingers over the little heart. And he held up his head and squared his shoulders and stood erect, not from pride, but from love, because he loved Babylonia, and he knew that meant he had to set her free, and that was part of his purpose—to love others and to set them free.

He then took his mother's music box out of his pocket and gave it to her.

"I was hoping you might—" she said.

He kissed her softly, the way he imagined warriors kissed their women before going to battle, and all of a sudden, in one magnificent sweep, the torment of the last year was heaped up and lifted away. He shivered from the spine out, a white dove rising like a spray of light, spreading its wings, and the words came quietly to mind: *All is light.*

She disappeared into the foredawn.

On the cabin porch, Phineas and his wild mistress

touched noses and licked each other's faces.

"'Tis suicide!" Auntie Tilda said, as Moojie harnessed Baggie the burro and Hocus Pocus to the buckboard.

"Yeah, maybe," Moojie said.

"Why in Bob's name would you rescue your father?" she asked.

"I don't know. He's family."

"Fish have families. So do bacteria. They don't risk their lives for one another."

"Well, maybe for the first time in my life, I'll be able to help someone have a better life," he said, repeating her very words. "I love you, Auntie."

It was the first time he had ever said those words.

She was a blubbering mess. "I hope you know what you're doing."

"Of course I don't." Moojie climbed onto the seat and jostled the reins.

Chapter 9

Dark night of the soul; details of the rescue,
which give Moojie more mortification than
all his other misfortunes

Three miles to the coast. How long would it take? Was
Moojie going to die? Somehow, it didn't matter to him—
his life so far a book of losses. Moojie felt for the hourglass
inside his pocket, and the buckboard bounced along the
dark valley corridor, due west, Hocus and Baggie pushed
to their limit. Moojie expected trouble from his father.
"Your mother built a house of cards," Henry Littleman
had said just after the funeral. "And you brought it down
all around her."

Ninti called his father "a great hall of mirrors."

"Yep. That's one mirror I don't care to look at,"
Moojie had said.

"It would benefit you."

"Too dark in there."

"We must overcome darkness from within."

"I can't—" he said.

"You most certainly can."

It was the tone of her voice that had said everything. How can a sound tell so much? It rang of faith and expectation and potentiality, of great pealing bells and golden nightingales.

Three minutes. That was all he had from earthquake to tidal wave. Either he had nothing to fear or everything to fear. The world of pandemoniums and civil wars and vigilantes made no sense to him, but it was all he knew. He wished he knew more. The old buckboard careened along, a deliberate plodding wooden ship, hooves pounding against the earth, like the pain in Moojie's head. Every passing minute bore down on him like ten, the end rising up wild before him.

Ahead, a massive, pale creature appeared in the road, a being that could have been a ghost. Moojie quickly reined in the team, and jerked on the brake, and the wagon skidded sidelong into a tree. Through the settling dust, he saw that it was a cougar, Anahita, the immortal Anahita!

Fearless, majestic, she stood her ground, in a way like his mother had—unmoving, as if privately setting her mind to do a thing. In the dim light, their eyes locked, and her illumined amber stare penetrated his, a look that reached inside him so directly that it gave him goosebumps. And then the heartbreaking beauty vanished. Like his mother, like the angels and the stars, like Babylonia, she was gone.

Moojie quickly took off the brake and flicked the reins, "Get moving!" But the team couldn't pull the wagon loose. The wheel had jammed up against the tree. Moojie panicked. What now? What do I do now? He closed his eyes. *Breathe.* He was at the crossroads. *Breeeaaathe.* The world outside looked big and terrifying and he didn't know how to pray or what to pray for, and trying to stay calm, he reached within himself to connect with whatever was greater than any power on Earth, whatever it was that kept the stars and moon and galaxies in order. *Peace. Be still. Still still still.* The air around him was charged with a sudden, gentle energy, an invisible presence, a definite and distinct something much greater than him, but really it was a part of him, and he wondered if it was having a good laugh.

"Is that you, God?" he asked.

The rotting perfume of sulphur rose from the Earth, pungent and nauseating. Moojie got down, leaned a shoulder into the buckboard and pushed; he pushed with all of his might; he pushed with every hob-raising, light-shucking, hemp-stretching particle of his being, "Pull Hokey! Pull Baggie!" The team lifted their heads, dug their hooves into the dirt, the axle twisted, the harness stretched, and the wagon lurched free.

When he reached number 11 Wimbley Wood, Moojie jumped off the buckboard with his cane, goat-god to the rescue. In the front stall, Papa's horse was in a state of agitation. Moojie pounded on the front door of the house, rammed it open and went inside.

"Papa!" he called out.

He searched the house, the bedrooms, the carriage house, the closets. And from the kitchen window, he spotted his father in the backyard, straddling the branch of an oak tree. He rushed to the back door. But a whir of sudden doubt caused him to pull his hand back from the doorknob, as if it were hot. *Why should I help him? He ditched me. Why bother? He might never accept me as a son.* He already knew the answer, but when it came to his father, it was easy to forget. He wiped his forehead with the back of his hand and opened the door.

Once in view of his father, Moojie found himself leery of the man, but for reasons he couldn't explain, he approached him directly. He took a deep breath and saw that his father's tussled hair had turned from brown to white. The buttons on his nightshirt were misaligned, and the fingers of one hand bleeding. Papa? He seemed to be unaware of Moojie, in a trance, spellbound by the little blue and white jar balanced between his legs.

Behind the tree, beyond the yard, the deadly quiet ocean.

"A mapmaker once told me one ought never turn one's back on the ocean," Moojie said.

"Leave me be," Papa said.

Moojie flashed upon the six-year-old memory of just beginning to talk and Papa saying, "You had us all fooled." Yes, he had been cruel at times, and yes, he was a cold turnip, but some inexplicable, nagging summons bid Moojie closer.

The eastern, valley sky had begun to change. An aurora flickered whitely across the face of the red moon. Moojie's heart raced as he shimmied clumsily up the ladder beside the tree trunk and sidled along the branch toward Papa.

"What you got there?" Moojie asked about the object in his father's hands.

"She shouldn't have died," Papa said. "She was far too young."

"I miss her, too." Moojie's eyes welled at his mother's memory.

"I said leave me be."

"I gotta get you out of here, Papa."

Moojie reached out a hand and it seemed to startle his father. He jumped and the pretty jar went crashing to the ground, breaking open, spilling what looked like sand and a locket of hair.

"Snap out of it, Papa!" Moojie said. He grabbed his father's arm, ripping his sleeve, and they both plummeted into the ivy below, Papa landing on top of Moojie like an upholstered chair. Choking on the dust, Moojie tried to throw his father over, but Papa was stronger than he expected, wiry and ornery and fit to be tied. He flipped Moojie over and wrestled him into a chin lock.

"What kind of son are you? You make me wiggy!" Papa said.

"Gaw!" Moojie choked. In one great spasm he threw over his father and pinned an arm behind him, face down. "I wanted to be like you, Papa. Every day, I wanted to go with you into the fields, I wanted to learn about the world. You never took me."

"Yeah, well, everything was fine until ...." Papa's voice cracked.

"I know I messed up ... my body and my mind, they're all messed up. I'm sorry, Papa."

Papa was sniffling. "I still remember the day we got you," he said. "Your mother said, this is the one, and I remember seeing you and having so much expectation, you know, having so much expectation because I was going to have a son. It was so hard. As a father you expect your boy to talk to you, and to walk." He cried some more. "I wanted to teach you, to show you things. People take that for granted, you know, that their kid is going to talk and walk." He pushed his fingers into his eyes, as if to poke out the tears. "Just to talk and to walk. And then you didn't. Then, you started, I don't know, you started breaking things."

"I'm sorry, I—"

"You hated us for it, didn't you? You blamed us for your handicaps. Like we were supposed to make it all better, and we failed you."

What he said seemed to just freeze mid-air.

Though Moojie shared no blood ties with him, he saw himself in his father's torment. Shell-shocked, hair full of leaves, dirt in his ears, torn nightshirt, one missing slipper—Papa looked like a little boy. Something moved through Moojie, a hymn, a symphony, a change of light, like sunbeams through a tree, and the idea of leaving him behind became impossible.

"Whatever happened, you're still my father!" Moojie said. "There's no time to argue about it. You're coming with me." He moved off to the side and crawled after his staff.

Papa tried to scoop up the broken jar and its spilled contents.

"Hurry, Papa. There's gonna be a nasty earthquake," Moojie said.

Papa gave him a strange look.

"I know it's weird that I know this. I'll explain later. Just please believe me," Moojie said, offering a hand to help him get up. Papa lay the hair and ash and broken porcelain on the ground and took Moojie's hand.

When they got to the buckboard, Papa tied his mare to the back. Before he climbed onto the wagon seat, Moojie stopped him, and threw off his shirt.

"What the devil—?" Papa said.

"Give me your shirt," Moojie said, ripping the sleeves off his shirt. Papa stood there stupidly. "Your sleeve! I need your sleeve!"

"All right, for crissakes!" Papa said. And he tore a sleeve off his nightshirt.

Moojie tied the sleeves over the horse's and the burro's eyes. "I know," he said, stroking the agitated Hocus Pocus. "I'm scared, too. Just keep to the reins. I'll get us home."

Just as they came to Flum Street, the earthquake hit and the buckboard jiggled wildly underneath them. Trees swayed, walls tumbled, buildings rattled like teapots, and the street rolled like a shaken picnic blanket. The minaret toppled over, missing the buckboard by a whisker. "Dear God!" Papa howled. The way ahead was blocked by the demolished creamery.

There was no choice but to turn the buckboard around and head straight toward the ocean. Moojie remembered what Ninti had said about the tidal wave and reached into his pocket for the three-minute hourglass. It was broken.

All rumbling and tumbling and toppling stopped and La Pâtisserie leaned like a listing ship in the eerie stillness, wooden planks creaking and stretching. Somewhere in the distance, a baleful scream. A gas line exploded inside La Pâtisserie, firing a blitz of wood and brick and pastries onto the street and boardwalk; a woman staggered, weeping, to her feet; an old man, consumed by the dust of collapsing buildings, choked and vomited. Standing near the rubble that had once been Tilly's Tavern, a man clutched a wooden bucket and fishing rod.

And the ocean started shrinking away from the beach.

"Oh, God, what are we going to do?" Papa said.

"Easy, Papa, easy. We'll get out of this." Moojie tried to stay calm, thinking, *Right now, what I want more than anything else in the world, is to get out of here. To go back to the dairy with my real father, have a nice lunch, and start over as a family. That's all I want. That's all I ever really wanted. So if I whip these reins and push the team, we could get up that hill ahead of the tidal wave ....*

But all around him people were looking for a way out of the village, disoriented, stunned, lost as little birds. How could he leave without helping them?

He reined in the team and waved the woman and old man over to the wagon.

"Are you crazy? You'll kill us all!" Papa said, eyes wide.

The ocean smells mixing with the bakery smoke flooded Moojie's senses—salty beach, burnt sugar, sour kelp slime—the final whiffs of a forgotten childhood. At the end of Flum Street, fish and crabs jumped from the freshly exposed wet sand. Moojie steered the wagon north, then southeast, making his way back along a side street and then through San Miguel Park, where Greta and Uma had once lived, where he had picnicked with his mother.

"We don't stand a chance," Papa said, looking back at the sinister ocean, and Moojie kept saying just one more and just one more, pushing the odds to their limit, and he loaded up five more men, six more children, eight more women, and a dog—"Get in! Get in!"—passengers half-hanging as the blinded team charged up the hill and the stoic village succumbed to the brown-gushing end of creation.

When they arrived at St. Isidore's, the sun had not yet risen. The aurora sky swirled pink and green, and Auntie Tilda came bounding out the door to greet them. "Glory be! You made it!" She looked Papa up and down. "And there's a sight for sore eyes."

"Tilda," Papa tipped his head in a formal manner.

"It's like the dawn of creation!" a woman said from the buckboard as she looked at the still-changing sky over El Serrat.

Moojie found a red bandana in the yard, and knew immediately that McTavish was afoot. Hastily, he unhitched Hocus Pocus. "I know I'm asking a lot of you, girl, but can you do just one more thing for me?" She knelt down, and he flopped onto her back, and they charged across the field under the changing sky. *Would McTavish shoot the clan?* Partway up the mountainside, Hocus was panting and puffing so hard that Moojie got off and trudged on foot with his cane, slipping on loose rocks and tripping on tree roots.

At the Circle of Trees, all twenty of the Light-Eaters were huddled together in the center like frightened sheep, and off to the side, McTavish holding them at rifle point.

Careful not to be seen, Moojie moved behind some shrubbery.

"Okay, Skinny Malinky Longlegs," McTavish said to Ninti, "let's go."

Moojie wasn't surprised that McTavish had come. He had been stalking the clan for months—always sniffing around, in the woods, in the grass, asking questions, a hate-poisoned river that had breached its banks.

Ninti stood fast.

"You'll be going nowhere today," McTavish raised his voice. "You are staying put to pay for your crimes. Come on, all you hoolie hoos, up on your hooves!"

The wind kicked up, the sky started swirling, and McTavish charged toward the clan. "You think I'm bluffing?" he said, pumping the forend of his shotgun. The clan dropped to the ground.

"We have no quarrel with you, my lord," Ninti said, holding up a hand. "We came in peace, we shall leave in peace."

Sarru'kan lunged forward defiantly. McTavish fired the gun over his head. The youngers screamed. Babylonia and the olders shielded them with their bodies. Sarru'kan dropped down again.

His heart rattling inside its cage, Moojie sneaked up on McTavish and threw his body weight fully against him, causing him to drop the rifle. They both toppled to the ground in a fearsome struggle. Moojie laid hold of the rifle. McTavish jumped to his feet and pinned his fingers underfoot.

"AAAH!" Moojie cried out in pain.

McTavish took up the rifle and aimed it at Moojie.

The wind picked up and the light above whirred faster and faster. "What the—?" McTavish said, covering his eyes, and a great whiteness radiated at the center of the spiral.

"Move to the center of the circle!" Ninti shouted over the din. The clan got to their feet and clumped together in the center of the Circle of Trees, wind raking at their hair.

"Oh, no you don't!" McTavish yelled, taking aim at them.

All of a sudden, Auntie Tilda came waddling onto the scene, sucking air as a hippopotamus does after surfacing, brandishing Pappy's shotgun. "Mr. McTavish, drop the weapon and raise your hands, or I'll make haggis of you this very day, I will!"

McTavish looked floored. Weapon down, hands up, he said, "Mighty me, what a woman! Careful, love, so you don't get hurt. I don't want you to get hurt."

Moojie took the shotgun and tossed it into the shrubs. McTavish darted after it, but Moojie tripped him with his cane, and restrained the ruddy huckster face down, arm behind back.

It pained Moojie to watch the clan huddle together below the blazing white light. How would life be now, without Ninti and the twins, without Babylonia? It would certainly be ordinary. No magic. No mystery. He would probably forget to listen to the stars. Babylonia smiled at him. Kinetic energy electrified the wild green morning, and the last thing he saw was her raising her arms above her head, raising them toward the terrifying hole in the sky, the way children do when reaching for a parent, and the light flashing so blindingly white that he had to shield his eyes.

Chapter 10

The rumbling earth, the screeching owl,
and walking in the lilac; with other lessons
for the new era

The sound of the piano in the cabin wakened Moojie.

He lay quietly on his cot, trying to recall the strange dream he'd had. It took place in San Miguel or maybe somewhere far away; at any rate it was dark and the world was breaking apart, and there was a beautiful, terror-striking light in the sky, but before that there was a pretty maiden, a scarred warrior, and a two thousand-year-old baby. *It had to be a dream. It must have been a dream.*

And yet, it seemed more than scientifically possible.

He got up and followed the music into the living room. Through the morning haze, he saw a ghostly figure at the piano. Papa. Moojie went over to him and laid a hand upon his shoulder. His father stopped playing and slumped over, hands to lap.

"Don't stop," Moojie said.

"I'm no good," Papa said. "I need lessons."

"It's nice to hear."

"I, well, I don't—" Papa started to say.

"No, you don't," Auntie Tilda broke in, "you foolish old bellyroot." She lit the kettle.

"Katie tried—" Papa said. He wiped his nose with a handkerchief. "She tried to teach me to look at things differently."

"She should have knocked you over the head with your plumb bob," Auntie Tilda said.

"I-I just …." Papa stuttered.

"It's okay, Papa," Moojie said. "Everything's going to be okay."

Auntie Tilda trotted toward the screen door. "Henry, dear," she said, before heading outside, "they're calling your son a hero." Millie-Mae barked as if to confirm what she'd said, and followed her outside.

Moojie and Papa moved to the window, and Auntie went to McTavish in the yard. He was unrolling a scroll, one of the Light-Eater's fig-paper scrolls, and laying it flat on a makeshift table. How the dickens did he get hold of it? He and Auntie looked it over, holding hands like teenage sweethearts amid a multitude of villagers, some queueing up at the well, some milling about, others huddling under the olive trees. Moojie and his father laughed when Mr. Abu, the green grocer, fired milk from Pearl's teats into some childrens' mouths. Carts, wagons, and buggies lined the driveway, and in the west field, a group of children danced about the headless scarecrow. Beyond them, grownups and older children were clumped together in work groups. They were erecting conical frames that appeared to be made of bamboo culms, dunking mops into buckets of hot wax that hung over fire, and slopping the wax onto sheets of paper attached to the frames. And, gaw, was that Bentley Markham and his mobsters working side by side with Greta and Uma from the park?

"Teepees! They're building teepees!" Papa said.

"I *must* be dreaming," Moojie said. "Bentley helping Greta?"

He put his hand into his pocket and pulled out Ninti's medallion. How could he doubt? How could he doubt anything that had happened—the red moon, the portal, the earthquake, the tidal wave.

The teakettle whistled and Auntie Tilda popped back inside the door, a portly Venus di Milo starfish, jellied cheeks and globular belly, squealing, bracelets clanking. "He's a Scotsman! He couldn't remember his mother's name without a *coup of tay!*"

From the porch, Moojie and Papa heard a group of villagers talking excitedly about the night before. "Lord in heaven," one woman said, "the sky turned pink and green and pink again, like the light of angels!" A man said, "Good God, woman. It was nothing but a meteor storm." Tilly's barkeep piped in, "You're both daft. It's a sign of the end times, I tell you, the end times!" A fisherman spoke of his harrowing ordeal and narrow escape from the advancing seawater, of his fleeing the village in a horse-drawn buggy, and of seeing the captain's wagon and turning—without logic or reason—to follow it. "St. Isidore's, St. Isidore's," he said, "the words just kept whispering to me."

Auntie Tilda backed out the door with two cups of tea, ambled down the porch stairs, past a clutch of women and girls. "Clear the way! I'm the lad's auntie!"

Moojie shuffled out to the yard, and sent the visitors to the apple and pear trees with scuttles, and said, "We can't let our guests go hungry." He turned around and saw Papa pumping well water into a bucket for a little boy. He remembered how the twins saw the world as light, and just then he saw that his father was light and the water was light and the child was light. Light was pumping light into light's bucket, and this made him smile.

"HELP!" a voice rung out.

Everyone scampered down the trail to the creek, where the mayor's houseboat, having come upstream on the tidal wave backlash, had flipped onto its side.

"It's my mother's leg!" cried the mayor, poking her head out of the sky-facing door. Father Grabbe opened a window off to the side and waved the people over, "Here! Over here!" He and Mother Teagardin passed a chair through the window, and then passed Mrs. Latchkey out, her leg a bloody mess. Three men carried her in the chair to the cabin. And while Auntie Tilda cleaned the bloody gash with coal oil and sugar, Moojie sat down in the wing-back chair and silently praised the light of the world. He praised the spirit of life, the Source, the Grace he had come to know, and he called upon the magical, mystical healing light, and gave thanks, and then got very quiet inside. Soon enough the poor Mrs. Latchkey sat up and, grinning like a fool, she drifted outside to the Goat Locker, and took a nap on a fresh bed of straw with the chickens pecking affectionately at her head.

Others began to ask Moojie for help, mostly for emotional disturbances resulting from the pandemonium: a man with a sudden fear of laughing trees; a woman who itched so badly from a rash that she saw green monkeys climbing the walls; a veteran from the Civil War who couldn't sleep because he believed the magnetic poles were pulling his dreams in two directions. Eyes turned toward the heavens, eyes shining, nose flaring, he was flushed with gratitude. So many miracles! He thought about the dragonfly, about what Ninti had said: "You see, my lord, it has all been laid out for him, the momentum, the light, the building of energy—love is ever-crowding him," and he realized that he had never truly been an orphan. Pappy, Ninti, the twins, Auntie Tilda. Hocus Pocus, the bees, the pigeons, there had always been someone, something, looking after him. And he stopped worrying, because there was not a hint of space left for fear in his heart, and he couldn't feel any malice for his father, the man he suddenly realized that he loved, with a big, messy, amorphous love. They were bound to each other for reasons he didn't understand, reasons he couldn't name, reasons that had been stored in the great, Akashic record bank of the universe. And so his story—which began with him abandoned on the chapel porch—could have easily been buried in the underwater graveyard of San Miguel de las Gaviotas; it could be settled, like a sunken ship, on the ocean floor. But there was more that he needed to do with this life, more to discover. What it was, he didn't know, but he was sure of one thing.

He went to his room and took off his leg braces. Up on his feet, he tossed aside the cane. Slowly, carefully, he took one step, then another, checking his balance, and he walked freely for the first time, directly out to the porch. Everyone stopped what they were doing, and turned to look at him go down the stairs, the illogical motion of his legs at last succumbing to grace.

"Say something to them, dear," the misty-eyed Auntie Tilda said.

He calmly looked over the crowd in the yard. *What do I say? I'm a simple kid. No. Not that. It will come. It will come.* He looked into the villagers' faces, and he drew a breath, "Today, under the blue heavens, the sun has shined upon us. Your homes are gone. Your village is gone. It will be hard to start over. But you're here, and you're alive. That's enough for now."

The villagers gathered closer, grownups and children, and even Elsie the cow, Odds and Ends, and Hocus came to the fence to listen.

"Tell us, young man, are you a messenger of God?" Father Grabbe asked.

The question threw Moojie because he wasn't used to being in the limelight.

"Well," he said, "I used to be mad at life, mad at everything. And then, I woke up. It takes a long time to wake up. That's why it doesn't happen to people who are in a hurry. When you're trapped in a prison, and your heart is broken, and you can't move a finger because you don't know what to do, that's when you wake up. And then the prison and the sadness don't matter because you're not afraid anymore. The ones you call Hostiles taught me this. 'Life is making choices,'" he quoted Zagros, "'a million choices, every day. Sometimes they stack up behind each other, like behind a closed door, until the lock can't hold anymore.'"

Everyone nodded approvingly. Papa's chin trembled, tears puddling in his eyes.

"I always knew he was special," Mother Teagardin said.

"I didn't plan to rescue all of you," Moojie said. "At the time, I just did what seemed natural. I can't explain it. It was like something bigger than me, something bigger than this world, brought us all into its own story. I can't say exactly what it was." He smeared away a tear. "Anyway, you are all welcome to stay here. It's a good place to watch the stars and listen to the trees. Stay. Walk in the wild lilac. Stay where you can be still and quiet and safe, and never again fear the changing skies or the rising sea."

Everyone stared at him. And then, they clapped and whistled and cheered.

"He always had a way with words," Papa said to Mother Teagardin.

That night, under a zillion glistering stars, Moojie sat on the porch with Papa, Auntie Tilda, and McTavish, assured that the survivors were sleeping soundly in their teepees, on grass mats and straw beds, well-fed and sheltered from the night. In the morning they would ride to the coast to look for survivors and, if necessary, help bury the dead.

Moojie already missed the clan, but for now, he wouldn't speak of them; he would just feel them in the light breezes, sense them in the riffling leaves. Nothing in Moojie's world would ever be the same, nothing and everything. St. Isidore's would never mean what it had meant to him. It wouldn't be a place of vexing days and restless nights. Is love the measure of a life? Who we love, how we love, and how many? If this were true, Moojie had lived many lifetimes since he came to St. Isidore's. Filled with a holy urgency, he felt the gentle hand of destiny prodding him. He grinned. *Wait till everyone sees my next crop of Ali Babas!* But for now, he would go to bed and sleep soundly, too; for he had found his true family at last.

ACKNOWLEDGEMENTS

The following individuals either provided a nest for hatching this novel or helped it sprout wings and fly:

Jon and Julien, loving husband and son, co-instigators, comedians, and shining lights;

Candice, Deirdre, Jeanne, Joy, Belden, Siri, Addie, Oriana, Leslie, Rod, Lynne, and the Stanford gang: Malena, Mark, Kim, Arlene, Jenn, Catherine, Sulla, Siri, Mary, Suha, Robin, Deepa, Molly, Babita, Joni, Devika, Michele, Seymour, and Harley, inspired readers and writers;

Jay, Caroline, Miss Authoress, Lori, Karen, editing wizards;

Andy Kreche (J. Frederic Ching Planetarium) Hartnell College, for astronomical data;

Edmund Marriage of the Patrick Foundation and Golden Age Project; Christian and Barbara Joy O'Brien, authors of *The Genius of the Few*, for inspiring the clan of the Light-Eaters;

Andrew George of the University of London, for Akkadian translations;

Catrin Welz-Stein for the stunning cover art;

Nancy Cleary, publisher, steward, manager extraordinaire, for breathing life into this book;

And to you, dear Readers, I express heartfelt thanks for taking this mad, mystical journey with me.

Mad Mystical Journey

Hello Dear Readers,

Imagine a world class football stadium that holds 100,000 spectators. Now imagine a book in every seat. Worldometer's official tally for books published on this planet the first quarter of 2015 was 905,000—that's more than two, sold-out, football stadiums per month! You, the reader, have the power to make this indie debut novel stand out in the crush.

Here's how the pros categorize THE IMPROBABLE WONDERS OF MOOJIE LITTLEMAN: **Young Adult (12+), coming of age, literary and/or magical realism.** Description: *It's the story of a disabled boy who is abandoned by parents not only once but twice and seeks to find a family of his own.*

Three easy things you can do to help this book get into more reader's hands:

1) Ask your libraries to carry it.

2) Write reviews on Amazon and Goodreads and in your blogs!

3) Nominate book online for awards (no cost, short online forms):

> ***American Library Assn.***—Alex Award, Printz Award, Best Fiction for Young Adults, and/or Best Books for Young Adults—Ongoing, online nominations. Type in award plus "suggestion form."
>
> ***CYBILS***—annual nominations, Oct. 1-16
> wandsandworlds.com/cybils/nominate.php
>
> ***California Young Readers Award***—annual nominationsdeadline April 1, californiayoungreadermedal.org/recommend-a-title

Discounts are available for schools and book clubs. Contact publisher: rghagemeyer@gmail.com.

Connect with author: Goodreads, facebook.com/RobinGregoryAuthor
Twitter@tweety_robin

Bright blessings to you,
Robin

CPSIA information can be obtained at www.ICGtesting.com
Printed in the USA
LVOW08s0551060116

469341LV00006B/386/P